Fallen Soldiers
The Rise

Niem M. Green

A Green Walk Media Publication

A Green Walk Industries Company

Delaware, USA

Green Walk Media

A Green Walk Industries Company

Delaware, USA

Fallen Soldiers by N. M. Green

Library of Congress Control Number: 2013952442

ISBN 978-0-9889659-1-1

resemblance to actual events or locales or persons, living or dead, is entirely coincidental.

Design: Jiaire D. Adkins

Printed in the United States of America

To the soldiers fallen and standing, their families and loved ones, who fight and have fought for our homes, freedoms, liberties, and loved ones.

Never Forget

Chapters

Chapter : 1

On June 1, 2001, two high school friends are about to graduate from Riverside high school in Philadelphia, PA. Unbeknownst to them, they were preparing to enter a non-sheltered, unforgiving world. At this juncture in their life, there was no sense of the stress, pain, responsibilities, struggles, and let downs that life had to offer. None of this mattered, at least not tonight. For this was a night of celebration, accomplishment, and achievement. For they, like millions of teens in the nation, have reached the first of many milestones. This night was also time to enjoy the company of friends, classmates and even trivial enemies, some for the very last time.

For Jeremy and Tamir, the postgraduate plan was already set in motion. Their years of hard work, drive, and determination had begun to finally pay off. They both had secured jobs at the prestigious World Bank. Jeremy was accepted to the investment banking training program, while Tamir was accepted into the organizational management one. Both programs had exceptional compensation and benefits packages, along with the added bonus of paying their college expenses. The bank would, surely give their highest recommendation for the two boys, and that, along with the help of modest 3.5 GPA's, acceptance to Wilson D. Smith University was a walk in the park.

Therefore, graduation night was full of well-deserved celebrations for the duo, a night to be free and loose, and an inauguration into manhood that they each respectively reached prematurely. Tamir was the man of his house; he had taken the place of his **father** at the tender age of fourteen. He took on the pressures and responsibilities from which his **father** managed. He could not take the pressure of being the provider after their final edition to the family was born, Tamir's little sister Ayana. Tamir, being the oldest, was plagued with clear and vivid memories of all the fights, tears, and pain that his **father** caused. With this, he made a silent yet sacred promise to always take care of his family, for the rest of his life.

With Jeremy though, it was a little different. In his house, it was just Jeremy and his **mother**. However, he as well, was the man of his house. He and his **mother** had a special relationship. She was his best friend as he was hers—a bond that became even stronger after the loss of his **father**. Jeremy's **father** was a fighter; he defended everything he believed in, although he sometimes did so violently. He defended his family, and for this, he was killed. When Jeremy was younger, his family lived in an impoverished section of the city. There were prostitutes on one corner and drug dealers and junkies at the other. Most of the time they would not bother anyone in the family, but this day was a little different. As Jeremy's mom was taking her young son in the house, she was harassed by one of the rift raft from the block. Frantic, she immediately told her husband once she was in the safe confines of their home. She knew he would not stand for this. Her husband already had a strong hate for the area in which they lived, and would, without a doubt, make sure she was never harassed again.

Regardless of the house being situated a block away from hell, inside was heaven. Moreover, he was the guardian, the protector of this safe haven. He did not care what went on outside as long as it did not affect the purity of the angels inside. Therefore, the sex, drug, hate and crime mongers had several city blocks to do what they wanted, as long as they did not touch his fourteen hundred square feet of peace.

So, on this day, he went out to defend his family's honor. However, the harasser was a local drug dealer that controlled this and several other blocks. He was high that day on marijuana, alcohol, and power. Phillip, Jeremy's **father**, a former boxer, approached the harasser. The conversation was a quick one.

Phillip said calmly, "I don't want no problems, but please don't ever bother my family again."

The dealer responded, "Fuck you! This is my block so that means anything or anyone on here belongs to me. You are nothing but a tenant leasing my house, my space, and my..."

With that statement, Phillip did not think. He just reacted and hit the punk with a swift, strong right hook. Like a fury of bullets fired from a semi-automatic rifle, Phillip continued with a barrage of punches. Even after he hit the ground, he did not stop. He was no longer fighting some neighborhood punk; he was fighting all adversity, poverty, and the elements that placed his beautiful family in such an ugly scene.

Finally, his wife and a neighbor pulled him off the victim. A young Jeremy looked on at the commotion trying to process the vision with his eight-year-old logic. Somehow it clicked that this was what the male role in the house consisted of. Like a lion protecting his pride. At all means he was to protect his family and home.

Normally in this area, the police would take an awful long time to respond or appear on a scene, that's if they were even called. Nevertheless, for some reason the siren filled the air. Therefore, under the advice of his wife and the onlookers, Phillip fled. Gone only a few days, when he came back it was in the air that he would not be back for long, and this time when he left, he would not be returning. With this feeling lingering, though never in a verbal sense, Phillip enhanced the bond he had with his son, and tried to spend time teaching him prematurely about being a man. This advanced training was unfortunately justified several months after the fight.

It was a nice spring day, almost unrealistically nice for the area. Jeremy was preparing dinner with his

mother when the air was filled with gunshots. This was common, so they paid it no attention, especially since the fight, the harasser was not seen or heard from. Just a few blocks away, however, he was at war with an undercover narcotics officer. Apparently, he made the narc. The fear of losing the freedom caused him to irrationally kill the officer.

After the fatal shots were fired, he fled on foot. Was it fate that caused Phillip to run into this man at this exact time as he stepped off the bus? The two men saw each other out of the corner of their eyes and proceeded to continue on their journey. Phillip was headed to the sanctity and peace of his home. Wanting to buy his son a pack of his favorite candy and a single rose for his beautiful wife, he stopped at the corner store a few hundred yards up the street from the safety of his steps, a sweet gesture that would prove fatal.

Feeling a sense of having nothing further to lose, the punk ran back around to Phillip's block. Moreover, with perfect timing, he appeared right behind Phillip as he made his way towards his house. Feeling the heat of the pistol being pointed at his back, Phillip quickly reacted with quick reflexes and strength, broke the punk's arm, and took the gun. As he raised it in the air, several police officers pursuing the punk from the scene a few blocks away, saw a man with a gun and fired on him fifty-two times. After all, they were in pursuit of a cop killer. A few minutes prior to the fatal confrontation, Jeremy had asked his mom if they go the door and wait for his **father**. Awaiting that proud look on his daddy's face and the strong affection that he greeted him with each day, as they stepped out the front door the first shot was fired. Jeremy's mom jumped back and thought she had a firm grip of her son but he slipped through. For the second time in his young pure life, he witnessed an extreme act of violence involving his hero, his father.

As Phillip hit the ground, he made eye contact with his son, as if he was talking to him in that split second. The second that felt like an hour, he told him that this was now his pride. He was to protect it with all his soul and might. He told him he was training him for this moment, not to be scared and he loved him. As he hit the ground, the rose and the candy fell beneath him as his blood covered it.

Jeremy's mom sued the city, while this case was dragged out in court. The city did immediately pay all of Phillip's funeral expenses and moved the family to a nicer part of the city on the west side, where Jeremy met his best friend and self-proclaimed brother, Tamir.

So partying and celebrating tonight was validated. Jeremy had a girlfriend and a wealth of friends. Like his best friend, he has had an exceptional academic career to date. It had been an ugly road, but a humbling one and this was just the beginning.

"So what's the plan for the night guys?" Tamir asked his friends as they stood around after the graduation ceremonies.

This was the Riverside elite, academically and socially. They were prepared to venture off into the world ready to become industry or world leaders. You had Jeremy and Tamir who were gearing up to control the Finance and Banking Industry. There was Juwan and Shawn, military buffs, both top of the class of ROTC. Juwan was headed to West Point, the first stop on his road to becoming a great general or Secretary of Defense. Shawn was headed to naval academy, a step closer to becoming a battleship captain. Then there was Michael, aka the brain. Michael was by far the smartest person in the school, including students and teachers. Michael got a full scholarship to MIT. Jeremy's girlfriend, Rasheeda, was headed to Drexel University. Her goal was to become a top engineer. Her best friend Isabella was on her way to the University of Pennsylvania. Even though she could be America's next top model, her goal was to become America's next top lawyer. Amanda was on her way to control the fashion industry; she already had strong creative abilities. Not only did she design everyone's Prom outfits, she had a t-shirt line that she was marketing online. This was paying her way through the Fashion Institute of Technology.

"Yeah...whose party we crashing tonight?" replied Jeremy.

"We all have rental cars and graduation money, so let's head to the shore," responded Juwan.

"Yeah babe let's go away so we can celebrate," Rasheeda agreed as she tickled her boyfriend's ear.

Therefore, it was settled, they would head to the beaches in Wild Wood, New Jersey. By the time the final plans were set, there were about twenty cars headed to the beach. Everyone decided to meet at the gas station by the expressway entrance. Everyone dashed for their cars as they disbursed. They were on their cell phones trying to get reservations at the hotels at the beach.

"Alright, so I'm gonna ride with y'all J," said Tamir.

"Yeah me too," interrupted Isabella.

"Naw Mir, stop being a cheap ass and drive yourself," responded Jeremy.

"Yeah Bella, ride with Mir so y'all can get to know each other better," interrupted Rasheeda.

"Y'all just wanna be nasty," responded Isabella.

"We don't wanna ride with y'all nasty asses anyway, besides, I rented a convertible. Come on Bella, let your hair blow," Tamir said.

Everyone laughed and went on their way to get prepared for the trip that night. At the gas station, Tamir pulled up at the pump behind Jeremy and Rasheeda, with a car behind him. In the car was Rodge. Rodge was smart and a part of the graduating class. However, Rodge had different aspirations; he did not want to become a doctor, lawyer, or banker. He wanted to get money. He was heir to the throne of a drug and crime empire. He grew up with Jeremy and Tamir, too, but his uncle trained him on the street. By the time he graduated, he was already making between five and seven thousand dollars per week. Therefore, he had no desire to waste any more time in school.

"Look who I found," Jeremy exclaimed from his car to Tamir.

"Rodge! What's happening?" asked Tamir.

"Y'all didn't think y'all were going to party without me, did you?" Rodge responded.

Rodge was the black sheep of the bunch, the marijuana smoker, the alcohol drinker, and the thug.

As the extended caravan headed to the beach, they seemed to be focused ahead leaving responsibility, the stress and the fears of tomorrow in the rear view mirror. What was a trip down the highway without a high-speed race among friends? Jeremy was leading the race in his Acura rental. Rodge was right behind him in his Range Rover. Tamir was picking up the rear cruising in his BMW convertible at about a hundred miles per hour.

The caravan was beautifully orchestrated, sort of like the ballet, with every car moving in perfect sync with the next. When the lead slowed down, so did the rear. When the lead shifted lanes, the rest of the caravan followed suit. Approximately two hours later, they were all checking into their hotels. Jeremy and Tamir shared a room, as did Isabella and Rasheeda.

Rodge, being flamboyant and flashy, rented a penthouse suite overlooking the Atlantic Ocean. He slipped the Concierge a hundred dollar bill to stock and open the in-suite bar without checking Rodge's ID. After all, the extra hundred and the thousand dollars per night suite would make anyone look older.

After being settled in, the gang headed to a seafood and grill restaurant on the boardwalk. Everything was on Rodge. The party of fifteen had their own dining room in the back of the restaurant.

"Alright this is my gift to all of you guys, and my way of showing my appreciation of being my friend and classmates. I've cheated off of a couple of you, that's why I was able to graduate," said Rodge.

The whole room laughed and cheered.

"Eat up! After this, we'll party in my suite!" Rodge said.

Rodge was many things but stingy was not one of them. He always made sure everyone in his company had what he had. His biggest thing was making sure everyone had a smile on their face, while in his presence. This soothed him from the stress that he felt in his unattractive line of work. Now if you let him tell you, he would say he loves it, but inside he hates it. He was trapped. He had no way of getting out even if he wanted to. This is who he was, this was how he was made and raised. This was essentially all he knew. As he stared around the room and looked at all of his peers, he gazed into all of their aspirations, goals, dreams, and futures. He had a sense of pride because these were his closest friends and it did not matter to them how much money he had, the drugs he sold to get it, or the guns that he toted. However, at the same time, he felt a little envious and jealous. The pride he felt, though, quickly overpowered it. As they sat around the extended table, they all got quiet and everyone made a toast. With their Sprites, Fruit Punches, Lemonades, and, of course, Rodge's Spiked Iced Tea, it was an emotional scene, almost something out of a movie, like the last supper. Everyone had something to say and was a little choked up. The toast was now on Jeremy.

"I wanna first say, Rodge, my brother, you'll always be my brother. We all know what you do and I just wanna say please stay as safe as possible and try to get out. Oh, and I'm getting the lobster, steak and shrimp, since you paying and all." Everyone laughed.

He continued, "Seriously, I love you homie. Tamir, ever since I moved out the way, you've been my brother. I've played with you, laughed with you, and cried with you. You have helped to fill the void when I lost my **father**. Rasheeda, my angel, my Cherie Amore girl, we been through some things, but we stand together and without you I am lost. Continue to love me and grow with me and I do my damndest to give you all you deserve and more."

Now it was Tamir's turn, "So many faces I see here, so many memories, so many arguments, but most importantly so much love. Rodge, J, y'all are my brothers, always and forever. You people have been that supporting factor that has helped me keep everything in order at the crib. I wanna read to you guys a quote and I hope you hold this dear in your hearts, all of you at this table. We are all venturing out and doing different things. Those who dream by night in the dusty recesses of their minds wake in the day to find that all was vanity; but the dreamers of the day are dangerous men, for they may act out their dreams with open eyes and make it possible. To us, our love, our goals, and our futures cheers." Everyone responded with cheers.

As the group began to eat, they talked about what everyone will be doing this upcoming fall.

"I can't believe you guys are going to the military," said Tamir. "I mean...what if y'all have to go to war?"

"The likelihood of war was slim," Juwan responded.

"Yeah but are you willing to fight and possibly die?" asked Jeremy.

"For the chance of my kids and your kids and their kids to have the freedom and liberties that we have, you're damn right!" said Shawn.

"I can understand that," Jeremy responded.

"But, we as black people have just started getting these freedoms and some of us still have difficult times," interjected Michael.

"Yeah, I get pulled over every other day cause of what I drive and more importantly, for the color of my skin. So, why would I fight for that with the people, and for the people who look down on us?" Rodge interjected.

"But look at what you do Rodge!" said Shawn.

"You are all of eighteen, driving a fifty or sixty thousand dollar car. No disrespect, but look at what you do," he continued.

"Alright cool, but if I let you or Mir or even Michael drive my truck y'all would get harassed. And furthermore, this was the government's plan; take away all opportunities and infiltrate our neighborhoods with drugs," said Rodge.

"That's ridiculous!" Amanda angrily interjected. "I love you Rodge, but that's bull. Look at all of us at this table. We all have opportunities," she added.

"Yeah, but look back thirty or forty years. Our parents and grandparents did not have that. Yeah, civil rights leaders fought to open doors for us but the epidemic already hit and hit hard. Too many of us who did not have that chance was already out here. Look at Big John from up 60th, he had no education, been hustling since he was like twelve, running numbers then eventually moving drugs. Now look, Cadillac after Cadillac, you got a broke hood with people hurting for food, let alone money, and he got it like I got it and more. Do you think people ain't gonna opt to go his route?" Rodge firmly responded.

"OK this is getting depressing! Let's talk about something else," Rasheeda said.

After a filling meal and a good conversation, the group finished up and headed to Rodge's suite. On the way, Jeremy and Rasheeda decide to head to the beach for a moonlight stroll. The night was quiet and warm, but not humid. Couples stroll on the boardwalk as if it was a slow song on at the skating rink. Rasheeda and Jeremy seem to be the only couple actually on the beach. They find a nice spot close enough to hear the waves crash and serenade the couple, but not close enough to get wet. Rasheeda pulled out a blanket from her beach bag. She was prepared, even more prepared than Jeremy knows. She begins to undress removing her DKNY Capri pants, then her matching DKNY blouse revealing her elegant Burberry bikini. Jeremy began to follow suit removing his baby blue Lacoste polo shirt. As he stands in a sensual excitement in a white tank top and Ralph Lauren linen shorts, he stops as if he forgot to turn off the stove or an appliance at home.

"What's wrong babe?" Rasheeda inquired.

"Oh nothing. I need to call **Mom** before I forget," he responded.

"What, you need instructions?" Rasheeda smugly responded.

It is not that Jeremy was a momma's boy or anything like that. It's just that he always makes it a point to assure his **mother** that he was safe, or else she would worry herself sick, an unfortunate side effect after losing her husband.

"Hey Mom…yeah we're cool, how are you? You OK?… Alright, well make sure you eat something and get some rest; I'll call you tomorrow. Ok, yes **Mom** I will get you some saltwater taffy. I love you too," said Jeremy.

"Aww…aren't you the cutest thing," Rasheeda said as she smiles.

If she were not already madly in love with Jeremy, this showing of sensitivity would have surely sealed the deal. Meanwhile this proves to seal another deal. Rasheeda pulls her man closer and begins to passionately kiss him. She kicks off her Prada sandals, he kicks off his white Nike Air Force ones and they lower themselves to the blanket.

She then stopped and said, "Wait a minute I forgot something."

She reached into her bag and pulls out a bottle of wine and two crystal wine glasses, courtesy of Rodge.

"Damn you really are prepared, huh babe?" asked Jeremy.

"Damn right! You think you've been waiting a long time for this. I have made love to you a million times in my head and I want this to be right. Tonight is our night, boo," she responded.

Under the moonlight, they sensually and playfully drink from their bottle of Moet and Chandon. As the waves grow, so does their passion. Now neither Jeremy nor Rasheeda are very experienced in what they are commencing. Of course, you would not think this was true from watching them or the maturity of their relationship. But, tonight they seem to both be sensual aficionados. Pure love seems to be their guide on the romantic carpet ride. Jeremy lays Rasheeda down slowly and softly as if he was laying a newborn child into a bassinet. He begins to tenderly caress and kiss her soft body in an exploring manner, sending his hands and lips on an expedition to find her soft sweet love spot. Over the hills of her breast to the valley between her legs, in perfect rhythm of the ocean as he licks her below, Rasheeda moans and groans in sync with the crashing of the waves on the lonely shore. Her toes begin to curl as she loses control of her body's movement. Such ecstasy and bliss beautifully orchestrated between two young lovers.

Rasheeda arises to her knees, lays Jeremy down, and slowly begins to kiss and rub him from head to toe. She poured what was left of the Moet like a gentle waterfall from his rock hard chest creating rapids over his washboard stomach and begins to sensually sip from the pool collected in his navel. She removes his shorts and sits atop his waist as he removes her bikini. He fumbles a little with untying her top. It is ok he was after all an amateur. In fact, he only made this amateurish mistake all evening. She leans down, passionately kisses his neck, and bites his ear as they begin to make love. Back and forth, in perfect timing with the waves, he rolls her over and relaxes comfortably in between her legs. He opens his eyes and locks with hers and tells her he loves her. She responds telling him she loves him more. They seem to be making love to the rhythm of, "Moments in Love," by the Art of Noise. Truly, the noise that they made was artistic, subtle and sweet like the introduction to the song. They both orgasm in perfect harmony, but just then Jeremy had a flashback. His mind escaped back to when his **father** died for some unknown reason. He suddenly sees his **father** falling to the ground locking eyes with him. He feels the conversation that they had between their eyes. After the flashback, he had a warming and proud smile.

Back at the suite, the celebration was in top gear, as the three-bedroom penthouse suite was nearly full. Not only with the classmates and friends, but they invited everyone who would come. There were locals, hotel employees, and even the night manager was there. They had games of tonk going for money, and Spades games for fun. The air was full of smoke and the scene was that of a casino similar to the Trump several miles up the coast. Whatever your vice was, it was found in suite 1803.

Rodge again was very smart, between the money he collected spanking the room in tonk and the proceeds from his marijuana sales that night, he more than doubled the money he spent on the trip in the first night. Tamir watched this in supreme astonishment. Everyone was so high on life amongst everything else to be high on in the room. The vibes of the evening itself was euphoric. After a few drinks, everyone became the opposite of who they were in reality.

Isabella pulled at Tamir and asked to dance with him. This broke his focus and calculation of how much Rodge was raking in.

"Come on sexy, dance with me," Isabella said as her body gyrated to the beat of Jay-z's. "I just wanna love you."

For a drunk room, everyone seemed to be completely on key as they sung along with the song especially the line, "Both in the club, high, singing off key, and I wish I never met her at all."

Just then, Jeremy and Rasheeda walk in. Although they were not in the room, they were both high from something else, the look on their faces said it all. Well if that did not, Rasheeda's messed up hair full of sand sure did. After a few minutes of mingling, they decided to head to Tamir and Jeremy's room. Clearly, the lovebirds did not have enough; it seems that they started an addiction. As soon as they hit the door, in a passionate frenzy they began undressing, kissing, and headed for the shower.

Back at the party, Tamir loosened up thanks to Isabella. Hot from the lack of air conditioning and the saturation of intoxicated bodies in the room, the two headed outside on the balcony. They talked and conversed about everything from school and future plans, to their favorite colors and foods. They found that they had a lot in common, including the fondness that they had for each other. The whole two hour ride down to the beach they did not talk this much. It is amazing what a little alcohol and the acknowledgement of adulthood could do.

"Wow this is crazy! I would have never thought that we'd have so much in common," Isabella said excitedly.

"I know," concurred Tamir.

"Why didn't you ever say anything to me?" Tamir asked.

"What! I'm the lady in this situation! You should've approached me. Damn, I guess chivalry really is dead," she responded.

They both laugh.

"Naw Bella...it ain't like that. I just didn't think I would be someone you'd dig," he said.

"Well you'd never know unless you try," she said.

"You right...you got that one," he replied.

As the party started to wind down to the original classmates, friends, and a few new lady friends that Rodge made, some people, like Michael, found a corner to pass out in. The others decide they are not going to sleep. The immature games had begun. They did everything from playing doorbell-dixie, which consisted of running through the hotel, knocking on doors and running, to sneaking to the pool and throwing each other in at about 2:00 AM. Now, it was not a perfect world, and not everyone understood there was a group of recent graduates just having a good time. Nevertheless, Rodge insured every bet that the night manager would make the complaints disappear. It was now about 3:30 AM, Mr. Sand man's evil brother, Mr. Drunkardness, had collected his victims. He got Shawn, Juwan and a couple of girls by the pool, so that was where they laid and made their bed. He got Amanda, as she snored from the ground floor to the penthouse floor and back down again. Finally, he had his sights on Isabella and Tamir, they did not want to leave each other's company after the wonderful night they had. Unbeknownst to them both, they would be together sooner than they planned.

Tamir walked Isabella to her room and said his good nights.

"Alright, well, this was fun. We'll definitely get together tomorrow, right?" he asked.

"Yeah, I want you to go to the amusement pier with me. We'll probably all go," she responded.

"Well, go ahead in and make sure everything is cool and let me know. I just wanna make sure you get to bed safely," said Tamir.

"Aww...aren't you Prince Charming," she replied.

She walked into her room and came back to inform Tamir that Rasheeda was not there. They then headed up to his room. Which proved to be a bad idea upon arriving at the room.

Tamir walked in, "Hello???"

He called into the darkness.

Jeremy responded, "Oh what up homie, um look can you uh...."

"Is that Sheeda?" Isabella interrupted.

"Yeah, it's me. Hey girl, did you have fun?" Rasheeda responded.

"Now, you know you wrong girl! We gonna have to talk tomorrow," Isabella responded.

"Anyway, like I was saying, right...can you go stay up Rodge's?" Jeremy interrupted.

"Naw...I'm not staying up there, you know what he up to, plus he met him a couple freaks," Tamir responded angrily.

"Look you can just stay with me, but don't think anything crazy because we got two beds," Isabella said.

"Yeah we can push them together," joked Tamir.

"Keep it up and you'll be sleeping in the hallway tonight!" responded Isabella.

"Ok, so sleeping arrangements are set. We'll meet in the morning for breakfast, now get out!" said Jeremy as he rushed Isabella and Tamir out.

Tamir and Isabella head back to her room. They both take separate showers and wind up falling asleep in the same bed holding each other.

The next morning, everyone met in the hotel restaurant for breakfast. Everyone was filling Rasheeda and Jeremy in on what they missed, when Amanda stormed in.

"What up Manda?" Rodge asked.

"Oh don't what up me!" she responded angrily.

"Girl, what's wrong?" asked Rasheeda.

"Oh nothing, I just found myself being awaken by the elevator door closing on my head at 7:00 AM this morning," she replied.

The room got quiet shortly then the whole table burst out laughing.

"That's right, laugh it up but all y'all gonna get it watch!" she said with authority.

"So I see everyone had a good time and even some couples came about," inquired Rodge. "Let's see. Juwan and Shawn have new friends, I got a new friend or two, I caught Tamir creeping outta Isabella's room early this morning, and Michael well...wait, where the hell is Michael?" he questioned.

"That's a good question. And by the way, I wasn't creeping out of Isabella's room I was just..." said Tamir. "It was a ground breaking night of excitement to say the least."

"Aww...save it homie, look at how close y'all sitting and I saw you making her plate at the buffet. You ain't fooling anyone," interrupted Rodge.

Chapter : 2

The group planned their day. They decided to go to the beach, hit the amusement pier, and then shop at the outlets.

Everyone hung close together that day enjoying each other's company. They were not only classmates they were family. Rasheeda, Jeremy, Tamir, and Isabella, stayed coupled up in the middle of it all as if they were on a series of double dates. At the water slide on the amusement pier, they decided to incite a competition. Tamir and Isabella challenged Jeremy and Rasheeda in a race to see who could get to the bottom first. The guys sat in the parallel tubes first and the ladies sat atop them. Off they went, they shot down to the bottom it close but apparently, they had some turbulence. Jeremy came out on top of Rasheeda, and Tamir and Isabella came out backwards. Tamir and Isabella won this competition. Later the girls that Juwan, Shawn, and Rodge met told everyone about an under twenty-one nightclub that was in the area. Plans had been set for the night. In a consensus, everyone agreed to go shopping for outfits for tonight's outing. They were headed to a local shopping mall. Everyone split up and agreed to meet in the parking lot in two hours. The split was not what one would typically expect. There were six boys and six girls, typically meant that the boys went with boys and girls went with girls. Not this group, still having the competition spirit from earlier, Rasheeda instigated a new challenge.

She said, "I bet me and my babe have the best matching outfits."

Isabella not backing down said, "Yeah right you're on!"

Rodge jumped in and said, "Y'all crazy I've always been the flyest. I got five hundred dollars for the best dressed couple."

Everyone grabbed their partners and headed to the stores, this leaving Amanda and Michael by default. Due to Amanda's fashion expertise, Michael calculated a guaranteed victory. It was shopping for the prom all over again. The couples went from store to store trying to coordinate everything from colors to accessories, from shoes to jewelry.

After two hours of shopping pandemonium, the couples met in the parking lot. Juwan so impressed by what his date put together, reached into his bag and started to pull out his outfit when Tamir stopped him.

"No, no...I don't wanna see that now, how bout we all go get dressed and meet in the hotel lobby? Then, we'll ask a stranger who look the best," he explained.

"Yeah that'll work, we'll get the night manager to judge," Rodge replied.

"Yeah and we all stupid too, huh Rodge?" Shawn sarcastically asked.

"What you talking about?" Rodge responded with a sly grin on his face.

"You think we don't know you have that night manager in your pocket?" Shawn responded.

"Ok...so like I was saying, why don't we stop a total stranger and ask them?" Tamir firmly said.

With the agreement being set, the group raced back to the hotel. Upon arrival, they headed immediately up to their rooms. Of course, Rasheeda and Jeremy got dressed in his room after a quick love making session. The two seemed to be caught up in the beauty of each other's bodies as if they were seeing them for the first time. Isabella and Tamir got dressed in her room. Juwan got dressed at his friend's house. Shawn and his friend got dressed in his room, Rodge and his date in his suite, and Amanda and Michael in her room. This trip was a magical one to say the least; it seemed to cause awareness in people and situations. Tamir found the underlying beauty in Isabella, mesmerized by the radiance of her freshly moisturized Colombian skin, courtesy of Nivea. She too was into him as she noticed for the first time his physique, as he stood shirtless in his boxer briefs.

"What you looking at?" she asked standing in a towel covering her breast and pink lace Gucci panties.

"Nothing," he replied smiling.

"Oh, so I'm nothing now, huh?" she asked with a smirk.

Stuttering, Tamir responded, "No...No...it's not that I just umm...."

"It's ok boy, I'm just messing with you," she teased.

"Come here, I need you to do something for me," she asked.

"Wipe that smile off your face boy! I don't mean that! Come and rub that lotion on my back for me," she continued.

He agreed and proceeded to slowly massage and moisturize her back as she laid on her stomach.

"Um that's nice, ay papacito," she softly exclaimed.

"You know Isabella...I'm having a really nice time with you," he said.

"Me too, Tamir," she replied.

He began to make his move, as he slowly moved her long flowing silky hair from covering her neck. He started to kiss her gently on the back of her neck to her shoulders.

She stopped him, turned over with a smile and said, "What do you think you're doing, buddy?"

"Oh nothing...I thought that..." he replied.

"Shhh," she said as she puts her finger over his mouth and follows with her lips.

After a few moments of kissing, she said, "Not right now, we gotta get ready. Besides, it'll be better if we wait.   The two continue to get dressed and head down to the lobby to meet the others. As they got down to the lobby, they realized that they are the first couple to arrive.

"See baby, we could've...ya mean. We all early," Tamir said in disappointment.

"Hush boo hush. Oh...now I'm baby, huh?" she responded.

"Yeah, if you want to be. Can you be my b-a-b-y?" he sang.

"I don't know we'll have to see about that, won't we?" she responded.

"Look, here they come now," she continued as she pointed to the elevator.

Juwan leads out of the elevator with his date, followed by Rasheeda and Jeremy greets Tamir.

"What's up y'all? I see you playboy," said Tamir.

The second set of elevator doors open revealing Rodge, his date, Michael, and Amanda.

"Wow look at everybody!" exclaimed Amanda.

"Where's Shawn? I wanna collect my five hundred dollars," said Michael.

"Uh, hmm...our five hundred dollars?" Amanda said as she poked Michael.

The night manager walked over to Rodge and said, "All the arrangements have been made Mr. Sampson."

"Thank you," replied Rodge.

"What's he talking about Rodge?" asked Jeremy.

"Nothing, I got a little surprise for us after the club," Rodge replied.

"Damn! You just full of surprises this weekend huh, big money?" Amanda questioned jokingly.

After a few moments of idle chat and compliments, Shawn and his date arrive in the lobby.

"Damn! it's about time slow poke," said Juwan sarcastically.

As the group lined up, the look and feel was of the prom. It was clear that this challenge was not taken lightly. Rodge and his date matched from head to toe. He wore a classic burgundy Philadelphia Phillies jersey with matching fitted hat, black Roca Wear shorts, and a pair of wheat colored field boots. His date matched wearing the exact same color and year jersey dress with a pair of ladies field boots. In her hair was a Phillies headband. Juwan wore a soft pink linen Dolce and Gabbana shirt with matching soft pink Prada loafers and pair of cream linen pants. His date wore a matching pink Escada halter-top cocktail dress. She wore matching pink open toe Escada stiletto shoes with three-inch heels. She was toting a matching Jimmy Choo clutch purse. Shawn wore a black satin Armani shirt with matching black Armani slacks. He also wore black Armani shoes to match. His date wore a black silk Dolce and Gabbana spaghetti strap cocktail dress with a matching black Dolce and Gabbana clutch handbag, and a pair of Dolce and Gabbana stiletto shoes. Isabella wore a linen strapless Dolce and Gabbana sundress with matching Stilettos. She wore an elegant satin shawl around her shoulders. Tamir wore an Armani white linen shirt with matching white linen pants and brown Prada sandals. Jeremy wore a red silk shirt with matching red pants and red ostrich skin shoes. Rasheeda wore a red strapless cocktail dress with match red stilettos and a red clutch purse. Michael wore a money green patterned silk Versace shirt with matching green pants and green alligator shoes. Amanda wore a matching green halter-top evening gown, with matching green shoes and purse.

"Damn, I'm all underdressed and we look like a box of crayons," said Rodge.

"Yeah, we could be Crayola spokes people," agreed Juwan.

"Now we just need a judge and we can be on our way," said Jeremy.

As the couples waited in the lobby, Rodge and Jeremy stopped a couple of people walking through.

"Excuse me sir, ma'am, could you help us out?" Jeremy asked.

"Yeah, would you guys like to earn a couple of dollars?" inquired Rodge.

"Sure, how can we help?" the couple asked.

"Well, we are having a contest to see which couple is actually dressed the best," responded Jeremy.

"And, we would like you to tell us who you feel is the best dressed couple," said Rodge.

The couple agreed and began to look at each couple closely from head to toe. They had each couple step forward one at a time and had them turn slowly, as if they were professional judges. After they looked at each couple, they took a few moments to talk amongst each other to make a decision.

"Ok, we have made our decision, let us first say it was a very hard decision. While the Phillies are my favorite team," he said pointing to Rodge.

"And, red is my favorite color," he said pointing to Jeremy.

"Ladies, I love all of your shoes and purses, you all are so well coordinated," said the man's girlfriend.

"We decided to pick you guys in the pink," they said as they pointed to Juwan and his date.

"Well, thank you guys, and here you go for your time," Rodge said as he handed the couple a fifty dollar bill and shook their hand.

"Now...let's go tear up the town!" said Rodge's date excitedly.

As they arrived at the club, they realized that everyone besides Rodge and his date was extremely overdressed for the club. They did not let that bother them. They knew they looked good and besides that, they felt good. The club was packed full of young adults mostly in the same boat as the group from Riverside, a club full of recent graduates. Almost immediately after finding a seat for the group, Rodge and his date started working the club. With Rodge, it was always business first although it was hard to tell, he calculated that he could pull about ten thousand dollars from this club. It was a good thing the secret storage space in his Range Rover was filled with pounds of marijuana. The other couples hit the floor hard, with exception to Michael and Amanda. Michael was not a dancer, so he sat and watched while eating his fries. Amanda decided to get up and join the rest of her friends dancing to every song. She even danced with several of the locals. Around 1:45 AM, the last song came on; it was Xscape's, "Softest Place on Earth." The glamorously dressed couples headed out for a hot last dance. The lights seemed to get a little lower. Everyone grabbed his or her dates a little tighter. Amanda grabbed Michael and made him dance with her.

"Come on boy! You gonna at least give me this one!" she said firmly.

He agreed.

Jeremy grabbed Rasheeda by her waist as she rested her head on his shoulder.

"You having a good time babe?" he asked.

"Of course boo, this whole weekend is like a dream," she replied.

Meanwhile, Tamir and Isabella stared into each other's eyes and smiled at each other.

"Hey you," Tamir said playfully.

"Hey you," Isabella replied.

"Thank you for spending this weekend with me," he said.

"No, thank you!" she replied.

Just then they began to kiss. As the song went off and the light came on, the two were still kissing.

"Uh hmm," Rodge said as the other couples stood on and watched in amazement.

"Come on y'all, I still have a surprise for us waiting," he continued.

"Ok, ok," replied Tamir.

"This better be good," Isabella said.

"Oh, it will be and you'll have plenty of time for that," Rodge replied.

The caravan of cars followed Rodge's Range Rover back to the hotel.

As they arrived out front, Rodge jumped out and said, "Leave your cars out here, run up and get something to sleep in, your swimsuits, and something to wear for tomorrow."

Confused, everyone did as told and ran to their rooms and grabbed their things.

As they got back to the waiting cars, Rodge stopped them and said, "I want to show you some place that we see every day but from a different view."

"Um ok," replied Tamir.

"Just follow me, you'll see," Rodge responded.

The group again followed Rodge about twenty minutes down the coast way to a local marina where they found awaiting a huge lit up yacht with a crew of three. No one really paid this any attention. They just parked their cars.

"Aight Rodge, you got us all the way out here in the middle of the boonies it's like three something in the morning. What the hell?" said Juwan.

Rodge walked without responding, heading down the pier and finally stopped at the well-lit one hundred ten-foot, Horizon Motor yacht.

"Alright guys; surprise!" Rodge exclaimed.

Everyone was in total shock, not saying a word. They just stared completely amazed, trying to process what they were seeing.

"Damn Rodge! We thought you were done when you left prom in a helicopter!" an astounded Jeremy said.

"But how did you...? How could you...?" uttered Shawn.

"Don't worry about it, a little something from my uncle and I," Rodge said.

"I'm going to show you all Philadelphia from the water," he continued.

"Rodge, we're all the way in Jersey on the Atlantic though," Tamir said.

"I know. That's the fun part. We're going to party and cruise all night and get to Philly later on in the morning," Rodge said.

"We'll end at Penn's Landing, right Captain?" Rodge asked the Captain of the ship.

"That's correct sir! Now, if everyone could follow us aboard. We will give you all a quick tour and get this voyage underway," said the Captain.

"Aye Captain!" Shawn saluted.

"Navy man huh?" the Captain responded.

"That's correct, Sir! I'll be attending Annapolis in the fall, Sir!" Shawn responded.

"Sir what is the name of this beautiful vessel?" he continued.

"The Lady Destiny. Welcome aboard!" the captain responded.

After everyone boarded the huge luxury ship, they started picking staterooms. Once everyone was settled, they headed to the sundeck to watch as the mega yacht disembarked. At Rodge's request, the crew put on the best of The Isley Brothers. The mood was set perfectly, the music was right, the night was clear, and the moon was full. As the coastline slowly disappeared, Rodge and his date cuddled up on the sun deck draped in a blanket and sipping wine coolers. While Jeremy and Rasheeda, Tamir and Isabella joined them. Isabella and Rasheeda sat in between the young men's legs covered with blankets. Shawn and his date sat in the cockpit with the captain while he piloted the ship into the Atlantic Ocean. Juwan, his date, Amanda, and Michael sat in the lounge and watched TV.

After watching TV, Juwan's date whispered in his ear, "Are you ready?"

Juwan smiled and replied, "You damn right!"

The two newly acquainted friends quickly headed to their stateroom, leaving Michael and Amanda alone in the lounge.

"I'm hungry, I wonder if the S.S. Minnow has anything to snack on," Amanda said.

"Let's see," Michael replied as he pressed the call button on the intercom.

A voice responded, "How may we service you?"

"We're hungry, is there any way we could get something to eat?" Michael asked.

The crewmember joked, "We'll be sure to pull in at the next McDonald's drive thru. I'm just kidding, Sir. Meet me in the Galley and I'll prepare something for you."

The two headed down the hall to the Galley. Back up top, the three couples conversed.

"Rodge, good looking on this weekend," said Jeremy.

"Yeah we appreciate this," Tamir agreed.

"Aww man, look it's nothing really, y'all my people and besides I'm enjoying this right along with y'all," he replied.

"I'm just curious Rodge, how much does this little excursion cost?" Tamir asked.

"Don't be rude!" Isabella interrupted.

"No, it's cool, you know I tell y'all everything. It's like this, Unc gave me a hell of a graduation gift. He gave me a couple hundred grand, but it is just money. Like, I wanted to do something different, feel me. So on the way down here I noticed all the ships and was like it would be cool if we could go out on one," he explained.

"Yeah, that's hot!" Jeremy replied.

"Yeah, so you know how if you go down Penn's landing there's always Yachts and boats out there?" he asked.

"Yeah, like on the fourth of July or when they have those festivals and concerts," Jeremy said.

"Yeah, so I was like, it would be cool if we could take a yacht from Wild Wood all the way back around to Philly. Therefore, I asked the night manager if he could hook that up for me. So here we are!" Rodge explained.

"But how much does it cost?" Tamir asked.

"About seventeen grand," Rodge responded.

"DAMN!" Jeremy and Tamir exclaimed.

"Yeah, so y'all better enjoy yourselves," Rodge said.

"I got to go to the bathroom," Rasheeda said as she winks at Isabella.

The three women excuse themselves as they head to the bathroom for some good old fashion women talk.

"Girl...I ain't talk to you it seems like all weekend," Rasheeda said.

"Yeah that's cause Jeremy has had all of your attention. Aight, so what happened I want details," Isabella responded.

"Well Friday night after dinner, girl...we did it. We made love right there on the beach," Rasheeda said.

"Aww...that's sooo sweet, y'all first time on the beach," Isabella responded.

"Girl it felt sooo good! Like, it felt like hours and hours," Rasheeda said.

"Well, you must've liked it cause that's all y'all been doing all weekend since then," Isabella responded.

The girls laughed then Rasheeda replied, "You should talk how many times you and Tamir do it?"

"None!" Isabella responded.

Not believing her, Rasheeda asked, "None?"

"Yeah girl...what's going on is a lot different than with other guys," Isabella replied.

"How so?" Inquired Rasheeda.

"We actually connect, like we have so much in common. He is so sweet, and we have genuine conversations, like we can talk and laugh for hours," Isabella said.

Just then, Rodge's date interrupted, "Yeah I know what you mean girl, it's like that with Rodge."

Isabella and Rasheeda look at each other and try to hold back from laughing.

"Well that's nice girl," Isabella said. "Anyway, I think I'm going to give in tonight, but the good thing is, he hasn't been pressuring me or anything," she continued.

"That's good, that's how Jeremy was, no pressure, he just went with it," Rasheeda replied.

Back upstairs the guys are talking.

"So...I see you all wifed up now Mir," Rodge said smugly.

"Yeah, what's up with you and Isabella?" asked Jeremy.

With a giant smile on his face, Tamir responded, "Nothing much, we just chilling man, having a good time." "Yeah whatever man, your mouth says that but your eyes and smile say something different," Rodge said.

"It's us, your brothers, you can tell us anything," said Jeremy

Reluctantly, Tamir opened up and said, "Man...it's different with her, from just looking at her I thought she was one of those stuck up girls, you know? One of those girls you could not approach unless you had money like Rodge or was buff like Shawn or Juwan. However, she different, like she was no airhead, she was down to earth, and smart. Like, someone you can really settle down with, build and grow with," he explained.

Just then, as he was talking the girls slowly walk up behind them. Isabella heard all of the things that Tamir said about her and a tear came to her eyes. She had fallen in love with him just in that instant.

She walked up behind him, wrapped her arms around his waist, completes his sentence, and said, "Someone you could take home to mom, huh?"

"Oh hey you, how long you been standing there?" he asked.

"Long enough to hear what I needed to hear," she responded.

"Yeah, I was telling the guys about this girl I met this weekend," he said jokingly.

"Oh yea? I guess you'll be sharing a room with her on this ship! I hope she's on here!" Everyone laughed.

With the fresh love in the air, everyone made their way down to their staterooms. They passed Michael and Amanda who are knocked out in the saloon in front of the TV. Shawn's date was asleep in the cockpit while an excited Shawn was at the helm of the ship. A preview of what he hopes to become. Back in Jeremy and Rasheeda's room, the two took a shower together and took turns massaging lotion onto each other. When they were finished, they decided to take it easy that night, just held each other, and went to sleep. In Tamir and Isabella's room, however, it was a different scenario. They lay in their elegant stateroom with the ceiling full of recessed lights, and the room was outfitted with exquisite gloss finished cherry wood and solid gold fixtures. The bed where they lay was lined with satin sheets and mink pillows. Isabella lay loosely across the bed topless in a red Prada thong. Tamir lay opposing her with his head at her feet. He played with her beautiful tiny toes and massaged her feet.

"Having fun down there?" She asked as she giggled.

"Of course I am. Are you relaxed?" he asked.

"So, did you mean everything you said?" she inquired.

"Yes, if I didn't mean it, I wouldn't have said it," he replied.

"True, you were with your homies and you didn't know I was standing there," she replied.

"It's crazy because I was telling Sheeda the same thing about you. Now, if we do go a little further, I don't want you to think this was some kind of weekend fling," she continued.

"Hold on miss, let me stop you there. I do not think that this was some kind of fling. Like, I do not do the fling thing, I feel somewhat connected to you. I...." Tamir said.

Just then, she stops him, "Shhh...I know boo boo, come here."

She gets up and meets him in the middle of the bed. They begin to kiss and Tamir lays her back gently on the bed. He gets up and turns the lights off. As the ship makes its way down to the lower tip of New Jersey, the two make love. A little later, Rodge, being the jokester that he was, makes his way up to the cockpit.

"Captain, is there an intercom system that I can use that can be heard in all rooms?" he asked.

"Sure, here you are," the Captain responded as he handed Rodge the unit.

"Attention passengers, this is Captain Rodge. I would like to give everyone an update. That is not a storm you hear, that is Juwan snoring. That is not the waves you feel, that is Michael in the bathroom, and on a positive note, Tamir is finally going all the way. That is all, good night." Everyone in the cockpit laughs.

It was now about 9:00 AM in the morning, the ship was making its way up the Delaware River along the coast with Delaware to the left and New Jersey to the right. A crewmember on the ship was in the galley preparing breakfast. He was making several different kinds of pancakes, chocolate chip, walnut, blueberry, and of course regular. He had prepared bacon, sausage, and ham. There are home fries and an assortment of fresh fruit. He also was making omelets to order. The aroma was a mix of a five star restaurant a southern kitchen on a Sunday.

The Captain made an announcement over the intercom system, "Good Morning, guests of the Lady Destiny, breakfast is being served in the dining room in five minutes. We are cruising the Delaware River at approximately fifteen knots. We will be arriving in Philadelphia in about one hour and thirty minutes. We are now passing under the Delaware Memorial Bridge. Thank you again for joining us on the Lady Destiny and Congratulations Class of 2001."

"Baby, you ready to get this day started?" Isabella asked Tamir.

"As long as I'm starting it with you," Tamir replied.

"My baby is so sweet!" she responded.

"So, are you confirming that I am your baby and you are mines?" he asked.

"Yes I am!" she confirmed.

"Ok, so it's settled. Let's say this is our day," he said.

"What do you mean our day?" she questioned.

"Like next year on June 3rd, 2002, it will be our anniversary," he said.

"Ok, so this is the day we officially become a couple?" she asked.

"Yes baby, it is," he replied.

They smiled, hugged, and then kissed to confirm their new union. At the dining room table, everyone was eating and watching TV.

"I'm sorry. I hate to ask this but is there any way we can stop the ship?" Amanda asked the crewmember.

"Stop the ship? Manda, you tripping," Michael said.

"That breakfast and the waves aren't mixing," she responded.

"It's cool," Rodge said as he called the captain on the intercom.

"Hey Capt, can we stop and anchor? You come on down and have breakfast with us," Rodge continued.

"Certainly, I smelled that good food and I was wondering if you all were going to invite the ol' Captain down. I'm on my way," said the Captain.

After a world class breakfast, the ship made its way back up the Delaware to their destination, Penn's Landing, Philadelphia. It was now about noon and there seems to be a lot going on at the historic port. The ship docks and everyone sat atop the sun deck, in their bathing suits. The passersby looked on as if they were celebrities. Of course with a multimillion-dollar yacht anyone would look like a celebrity.

As the day began to wind down, the ship set a sail back down the Delaware River headed back to the shore. Though it was just the port in Pennsylvania, it felt more like an exotic port of call. Well, the whole trip was exotic to the group, as they had never been on such a trip, nor have they ever, as Rodge said, seen Philadelphia from such a view. Therefore, they partied that night as if they were celebrities on some exotic vacation. Being that this was such a rare occasion and no one was driving, they drank. Luckily, the wine case in the galley was filled with bottles of Dom Perignon, the drink of the night. The crew of the ship also made virgin mixed drinks for the under-age guests.

Chapter : 3

The ship arrived back at the marina just in time for the group to go back to the hotel and check out. The weekend had finally caught up with everyone. They all hid their eyes behind expensive sunglasses and walked at a slovenly pace. This weekend was a success in every way, new experiences, new memories, new friends, and new relationships. Everything had settled from the graduations and the vacations afterwards. Amanda was interning in New York City preparing for her upcoming first semester at the Fashion Institute of Technology. Michael moved out to Massachusetts to get things settled at MIT. Shawn got a job on the Lady Destiny. He was assisting the crew as the Captain in the Caribbean until he was due at Annapolis. Juwan moved in with his new friend that he met in Wildwood, it seems that they hit it off much like Tamir and Isabella. Jeremy and Tamir worked at World Financial, both in Investor Services. Isabella got a job downtown, assisting a paralegal at a prestigious law firm. Rasheeda received an internship at a Mechanical engineering consultant firm down town, and Rodge of course was on the block doing what he does best "getting money." It was a little after five one Friday evening and Tamir and Jeremy are about to get off of work.

"What up homie?" asked Jeremy.

"Ain't too much, what we getting into this weekend?" Tamir responded.

Just then Jeremy gets a text on his cell phone that read, "We need to talk over dinner tonight?"

"Yo Sheeda just hit me up. She wants to do dinner," Jeremy said.

"She probably means just you and her. Call her back and I'll call Bella to see if she wants to do the dinner thing," Tamir responded.

Tamir called Isabella and said, "Hey babe, how was work? Cool, what we doing tonight? I was thinking the same thing. Let's do dinner. You wanna double with Jeremy and Sheeda? Aight, well call her, I'm with Jeremy right now. OK baby, I love you too."

Rasheeda and Isabella rented a townhouse in the Overbrook section of West Philadelphia. They decided that they were going to have dinner that night at the girls' house. Rasheeda had a surprise for Jeremy. She had strong indications that she might be pregnant. The only person she told was Isabella, tonight she had bought several pregnancy tests to preliminarily confirm what she felt was true. It was important to her that Jeremy was a part of it all. The guys arrived at the girl's house at approximately 7:30 PM, with grocery bags in hand.

"Hey baby," Jeremy greeted.

"Hey boo," Rasheeda responded.

"Hey boo boo," Isabella greeted.

"Hey imperial queen of my desires," Tamir responded.

"Damn all that though?" joked Jeremy.

"So what's in the bags? Y'all cooking tonight?" asked Rasheeda.

"No y'all the women we just brought home the bacon, right Mir?" said Jeremy.

"Yeah, Fred Flintstone? Notice Fred and Wilma slept in separate beds, keep it up and you'll see what that's like!" joked Isabella.

"Baby you know we just playing, although I did want some of your Colombian cooking. We going to make steaks and potatoes, and even a cake for dessert," replied Tamir.

"Ok...before we get started, I wanted to tell you something," said Rasheeda

"What's up baby, what's on your mind?" replied Jeremy.

"Ok baby...don't get upset but I think I'm pregnant," Rasheeda responded.

Shocked, Jeremy took a moment to collect himself and said, "You? What?...Argh!"

"Baby I'm sorry, please don't be mad," responded Rasheeda.

"I'm just messing with you girl, oh my god, this is beautiful. Are you sure?" asked Jeremy.

"Pretty sure, but that's why I wanted you all here, my baby and my closest friends, while I take these tests to confirm," she replied.

"Ok, so great...tonight is pregnancy test night, huh girl? Where's my test?" joked Tamir.

Everyone laughed.

"Baby, you are such a fool," said Isabella.

As the guys began preparing dinner, the girls headed to the bathroom to take the first test.

"Girl, I'm nervous," said Rasheeda.

"Why? You basically already know and your man is with it," inquired Isabella.

"I don't know girl, this is going to change my whole life, our whole life," Rasheeda replied.

"You just nervous, here I'll take it with you," said Isabella.

"What's that gonna do, you know you ain't pregnant," said Rasheeda.

"Well still, I'll do it to show you I'm here with you," responded Isabella.

"Aww, that's just why you my sister and I love you," said Rasheeda.

The girls take their tests one at a time.

Meanwhile, the guys are in the kitchen cooking up a storm.

"Damn man, so you gonna be a **father**?" asked Tamir.

"I know, it's crazy," replied Jeremy.

"So how do you feel?" Tamir asked.

"I don't know. I'm happy but at the same time I already knew what it was," Jeremy said.

"How did you know?" Tamir asked.

"Well you gonna think I'm crazy but it's like this, a long time ago when my **father** died, I saw it and as he was dying, we kind of connected," Jeremy explained.

"I'm lost, what does that have to do with this?" Tamir asked.

"Well it was like he was training me all my life up until that point and it was like, at that moment, he confirmed it. So, the first night Sheeda and I did our thing. It was like I saw that moment again and it was like, he was telling me I'm about to be a **father**," Jeremy explained.

"Yo that's deep J, for what it's worth man you a good dude and I feel you'll make a great **father**. And you my brother so that makes me an uncle," Tamir replied.

"Yeah, but I also want you to be the godfather," Jeremy said.

"That's what's up!" Tamir exclaimed.

In a bad Marlon Brando impression, Tamir said, "I only have one request as the godfather, and that's naming the baby after me if it's a boy."

Laughing, Jeremy replied, "I don't think so godfather but we'll see."

The girls walk into the kitchen as the guys are laughing.

"What's so funny?" Rasheeda asked.

"Nothing, just Tamir in here doing really bad godfather impersonations," Jeremy responded.

"Babe, I took one too," Isabella told Tamir.

"Took one of what?" Tamir asked frantically.

"A pregnancy test," she replied.

"Why babe? You think you pregnant?" he asked.

"No, I just wanted to be supportive for my girl," she explained.

"Besides, there's no way I can be pregnant," she continued.

Moments later, Tamir takes the steaks out of the oven, while Jeremy mixes up the cake mix.

"OK girl, I think it's time to check the test," Rasheeda said as she sighed.

"Oh girl, look…I'll go get them, stop worrying," Isabella responded.

As the three patiently waited in the kitchen, Rasheeda clutched Jeremy's hand in nervousness. Tamir, being the clown that he was, made faces at the two in attempts to lighten the mood. Suddenly, Isabella screamed,

"Babe what's wrong?" Tamir yelled as he ran for the bathroom.

As everyone congregates in the bathroom, Isabella was a frantic wreck, crying and shaking.

"What is it babe? What's wrong?" Tamir asked as he made a step towards her.

"Don't move! Stay right there!" she exclaimed.

"Girl, what is going on? I'm pregnant, right?" Rasheeda asked.

"Not only are you pregnant, so am I!" she replied.

Tamir instantly hits the floor. He fainted. Jeremy carried Tamir out to the couch and laid him down. Isabella sat by him and rested his head in her lap as she rubbed his forehead.

"Babe? Babe? Wake up," she whispered as she kissed him softly upon his brow.

Groggy, Tamir asked, "What? What happened?"

"That's what I'm trying to figure out," Jeremy said with a smile on his face.

"Girl, we are both pregnant!" Rasheeda exclaimed with a nervous smile on her face.

"Wow godfather, you don't believe in protection huh?" Jeremy jokingly asked.

"First off, we were on the Atlantic Ocean. Where were we gonna stop and get it from? Secondly, don't throw stones from a glass nursery," Tamir jokingly replied.

Jeremy stood up and said, "Well now it looks as if this dinner is now a celebration."

"Sheeda, we have to make doctor appointments to confirm this on Monday," said Isabella.

"Yeah girl definitely," Rasheeda agreed.

That night, the couples ate dinner, talked, and even watched a medley of pregnancy movies such as, "She's Having a Baby," and, "Fools Rush in." They talked about names and having the best for their children. Everything from schools to vacations, clothes to toys. They decided that the next day they were going to window shop for baby stuff.

Tuesday morning, the girls headed to their doctor's to get official pregnancy tests. The guys took off from work early that day to surprise the girls with their support. They walked into the doctor's office and approached the receptionist.

"Hello gentlemen how can I help you today?" greeted the receptionist.

"Yes, I'm looking for my girlfriend she had a 12:15 appointment today," Tamir said nervously.

"Yeah me too," Jeremy interrupted.

"Wait...same girl?" the receptionist asked as she giggled.

"No, of course not," Tamir responded.

"My girlfriend is Isabella Rodriguez," Tamir said.

"And mines is Rasheeda Jackson," Jeremy said.

"Oh ok, they are both back with the doctor now, you guys will have to wait here. Do you want me to let them know you guys are here?" she asked.

"No, that's ok we'll surprise them," Jeremy replied.

Meanwhile, back in the exam room the girls are waiting for their results.

"Girl, I am so psyched!" Rasheeda said.

"I know girl, I keep thinking about that cute little Polo dress that we saw," Isabella replied.

"So you want a girl?" Rasheeda asked.

"It really wouldn't matter as long as it's healthy," she responded.

"I know, ain't that the truth," Rasheeda responded.

"But, a girl would be nice," Isabella responded.

The girls laughed as the doctor walked in.

"Ok, so I have your results ladies. I must say...I seen a lot of things but I've never seen something quite like this," the doctor said.

"What's that doctor?" Isabella asked.

"Well, it seems that you ladies are both pregnant and you have been for the almost same amount to time. It was almost to the date, as a matter of fact, Ms. Jackson, your due date is approximately March 8th. Ms. Rodriguez, your due date is approximately March 11th," explained the doctor. "I want you ladies to come back in a month, make sure you make an appointment with the receptionist on your way out. Have healthy pregnancies ladies. I'll see you next month," added the doctor.

The ladies gathered their purses and walked out to the receptionist. As they stood at the front desk and made their appointments, the guys watched and tried to hide behind magazines.

"Shorty, what's good?" Jeremy called at Rasheeda from behind the magazine.

"That is sick! How you going to try to holla at somebody at an OB/ GYN?" Rasheeda said with a frustrated tone to Isabella.

"What are they even doing here?" Isabella asked.

Knowing that it was the girl's boyfriends, the receptionist said, "Between you and me, they are here to support their girlfriends."

"Um that's sad, I'm going to say something," Isabella said.

"Excuse me, but we have men and as a matter of fact we just found out we are carrying their babies, so I think you should maybe support your own girls instead of trying to kick tired game, Isabella continued.

Tamir stood up and said, "For your information, we are here to support our girls, sexy."

"Boy you are so crazy! What are y'all doing here?" she asked, pleasantly surprised.

"We decided to surprise you ladies, so what's the verdict?" Tamir asked.

"OK boo, well...we are both six weeks pregnant," Isabella said.

"OK well lets go get something to eat," Jeremy insisted.

The couples headed off to lunch after receiving the seemingly good news.

The remainder of July seemed pretty good the couples and future parents had everything planned out. With the salaries that the guys made at the World Bank, they would be able to comfortably cover the ladies expenses while they attended school and maintained healthy pregnancies.

It was now around the middle of August, Tamir and Jeremy were hanging out with Rodge at one of his and his Uncle's fronts.

"So you guys made me an uncle huh?" Rodge asked in excitement.

"Yeah!" Jeremy confirmed.

"You know babies are expensive, if y'all need anything holla at me, but you can also come get down if you need to get that change," Rodge explained.

"Naw, we good," Tamir replied.

"Yeah Rodge, the bank is treating us well, so we'll be good," Jeremy explained.

"Well, the offer will always be on the table even if the bank's isn't," Rodge said.

Just then, Rodge's uncle, Charles, walked in. Charles was Kingpin of the city; he took over after his brother was locked up. He had looked over not only Rodge but also knew the operation as if it were his own.

"What's happening boys? How are the markets doing?" Charles asked.

"Nothing much Charles, just maintaining," the guys replied.

"Rodge I need to talk to you for a few, boys can you excuse us?" Charles asked.

"No problem, we gonna get out of here anyway," Jeremy Replied.

"We'll holla at you later Rodge," Tamir said.

The guys headed out.

"What up Unc?" Rodge asked.

"Well, your **father** wrote me, He want to know why you have not been writing or visiting him," Charles explained.

"Man, what he want? I don't fool with dude like that, he probably want me to put something on his books," Rodge replied.

"Yeah, well…that is your **father**, so you have to pay respect and homage. Besides, this is his operation," Charles said.

"Correction, was his operation, if it wasn't for us he wouldn't have an operation. If it wasn't for you, he would have pissed it away like he did me, so with all due respect…Fuck him!" Rodge replied angrily.

"But still he built it, you have to respect that Rodge," Charles said.

"Man Unc, we out here taking all the risk while he sits in the security of prison," Rodge exclaimed.

"Wow, security?" Charles asked.

"That's right security! He gets his meals, he has a roof over his head, and we make sure he has money on his books. To top it off when he do get out he'll be set up to have everything he needs," Rodge explained.

"Well Rodge, I do understand that, but still go see him at least, he is your **father**," Charles demanded.

"OK Unc, off the strength of you, I will, but not for his sake," Rodge said.

"OK, well thank you, I appreciate it," Charles said.

A few weeks later, Rodge went down to Grater ford prison to visit his **father**. The room was full of women and children visiting their boyfriends, husband, brothers, and **fathers**. As Rodge sat and waited, he watched everything that went on around him. To be in such a dark place, he could not help to notice that the room was filled with love, although it was situated in a place filled with hate, anger, and rage. Finally, after twenty minutes of waiting his **father** walked out in an orange jumpsuit looking like a spitting image of an older him. This scared him on the inside; for once he saw one of the consequences of his actions and career.

"My boy, my boy, what's happening, my boy?" Derrick asked.

"Shit!" Rodge replied.

"Wow son, don't seem so happy to see me," Derrick sarcastically replied.

"Yeah whatever, anyway you will have money on your books next week," Rodge firmly replied with a straight face.

"Is that what this is about? First off, that is not all I wanted, secondly, how you going to bitch about a couple measly hundred dollars. I know how much you getting out there. Don't think the streets don't talk and the jails don't listen!" Derrick angrily replied.

"See...even now you're stuck and you think you know everything. No, that's not what it's about I know what I make, what I don't know is you, and you constantly take that for granted," Rodge explained.

"What you don't get is I been in here all your life, I been in here for twelve years," Derrick replied.

"Is that supposed to be some excuse? Do the math, I'm eighteen now! That means you got knocked when I was six. Understand, I have no memories of you and don't give me that I was too young to understand bullshit, cause I remember **Mom** crying over you every night and her going crazy and MIA because of you! I remember Uncle Charles taking me in and filling both voids that you left. Plus, my best friends, both of them lost their **father**s at the same age and they remember them!" Rodge explained full of rage.

"Look, look, this is going in the wrong direction. I can't make up for the past. I can only create the future," Derrick replied.

"Create a future where? In here? With who? Me? I don't know you! I'm a grown ass man! I don't even know if I wanna know you!" Rodge replied.

"Look, just give it time, you'll see. I come home next year. I'll leave it up to you," Derrick explained.

"Yeah ok, I'll keep holding my breath. Anyway, I gotta get out of here," Rodge replied.

"OK, well I lo..." Derrick said.

"Save it!" Rodge interrupted as he walked away.

Out of all the prisoners getting visits, Derrick was the only one sitting there, left by his visitor. As he sat and watched his son walk away, he put his head down. A few moments later, he headed back to his cell.

It was now September. Just as celebratory and exciting the summer came in, it was about to leave. In West Philly the best way to this was a block party. City blocks all throughout the city were closed due to the parties popping up. The one in particular was the one on Aldan Street. Every other house on the block had a grill burning. This had set up to be another great gathering. Everyone had come back from the graduating class of 2001. Michael flew back in from Massachusetts. Amanda drove down from New York. Shawn flew up from Florida, Juwan and his girlfriend picked him up from the airport on their way into town. Everyone was excited about Isabella and Rasheeda's pregnancies. Almost everybody, Tamir and Jeremy's **mothers** had their reservations. Besides them, everybody else kept rubbing their stomachs and calling them **Mom**.

This was the last hoorah and good bye before the class of 2001 started their professional lives.

Everyone from the class gathered on Rodge's porch at the end of the block.

"So this is so great, like you guys got pregnancy buddies," Amanda said excitedly. "Now being the god**mother** and aunt of two, you know I'm gonna make sure these babies are so chic," she added.

Everyone laughed.

"I know girl; this is so cool, like we both go through the same stuff with each other at the same time," Rasheeda said.

"Have you guys thought about getting a place for the six of you?" Michael asked.

"Naw, we haven't," Jeremy replied.

"Forget them, we have," Isabella exclaimed.

"You have, huh?" Tamir asked.

"Yeah we have," Rasheeda replied.

"When was y'all going to tell us?" Tamir asked.

"I don't know, but now seems like a good time," Isabella replied.

"Uh oh trouble on the front," Juwan joked.

"Naw it's cool, I think it's a hot idea," Jeremy replied.

"Yeah me too, we always over there anyway. Why not?" said Tamir.

"So it's agreed then?" Rasheeda asked.

"Yup," Tamir replied.

"Good cause we already found a couple of four bedroom rentals to look at. I'll make appointments tomorrow," Isabella said excitedly.

"How did I know this was already set up?" Jeremy joked.

Everyone laughed.

As the party went on, everyone had a good time. There were girls playing Double Dutch, boys playing basketball, old folks dancing and singing. There was a DJ set up at the top of the block. The air was filled with good music and the smell of great bar-b-que, courtesy of Mr. Jenkins, the block captain. A lot of grills were cooking but he makes sure just like every other party that his burns the best. No one contends this because this was the pride of his life, that and the cleanliness and quietness of the block, ever since he lost his wife. As the party wound down, the DJ spun one last song as an ode to the season that was passing by, a simple good bye in true West Philadelphia tradition, "Summer Time," by DJ Jazzy Jeff and The Fresh Prince. With the end of the song came the end of the road for some, but goodbyes for all. It was truly an emotional scene, tears, smiles, hugs and kisses said it all.

"Juwan, Shawn, make us proud and remember your family here in Philly," said Jeremy in an emotionally charged tone.

"Yeah, thanks to you and Tamir we have additions to our family. Take care of those beautiful babies and women and send as many pictures as possible," Shawn responded.

"If you get sent to war or anything like that Juwan, it's ok to run, like that time in fifth grade when we ran from Jamal and them. Oh and Shawn, in your case swim, swim fast, swim far, just swim," Rodge joked.

Everyone laughed.

"Ms. Young, fly, and flashy, Amanda, what can I say girl? I'm proud, my sister you ready to tear the fashion world up," Rasheeda said tearfully as she hugged her.

"Girl stop, you gonna make my MAC makeup run. I'm gonna miss you, but I'm only an hour and a half away," Amanda replied.

"Professor Michael, don't hurt them out there, go ahead and start the next Microsoft, just don't forget about us and make us stock holders," Tamir said to Michael as he firmly shook his hand.

"I won't. I can never forget you all. Y'all are a part of me and I'll be back every chance I get. You know if you guys have a boy, Mike is a good name," he replied.

As everyone parted and headed their separate ways, Tamir, Jeremy, and Rodge held each other's shoulders and started singing the chorus of, Boys II Men's, "End of The Road".

Chapter : 4

Later that week, the couples found a beautiful four-bedroom house in the, "Old City", section of Philadelphia. It was not too far away from the girl's jobs and schools so they decided to take it. Everything was good, well almost neither Tamir nor Jeremy told their **mother** the plan to move out. This was not good because the property owner said they could move in next week. That Friday the couples decided to split up and go talk to their **mothers**. Jeremy and Rasheeda went to his house and Tamir and Isabella went to his house. Ironically, they lived right across the street from each other.

"OK, we'll meet you guys at the car when we're done," Jeremy yelled as he and Rasheeda headed up to his porch.

The boys tightly held their girlfriends' hands, for they knew this would not be an easy task they were embarking on. Tamir's **mother** had grown a fond dependence on her son after his **father** left and he stepped up, and he knew this, but he also knew that it was time for him to leave the nest and start his own family. It was similar for Jeremy. He was the emotional stability in his home after his **father** died. He was more like his **mother**'s husband than a son. Nevertheless, he too had to move on.

"Hey son," Jeremy's **mother** excitedly greeted as he walked in the door.

"Hi Mrs. Davis," Rasheeda greeted.

"What's up **Mom**? Listen, let's sit down we need to talk," Jeremy said.

"Oh boy what now, you already told me that she's pregnant, what you wanna tell me now? Y'all getting married?" she joked.

"Well not exactly, we um..." Jeremy said

"Spit it out boy!" she interrupted.

"OK...well, we decided that we are getting a place together. Me, Sheeda, Jeremy, and Isabella," he responded.

"Now with all due respect, I think you need to think about that son, you may not be ready for that just yet. Damn it boy your only eighteen!" she said firmly.

"Mom I know but I have responsibilities, I have a baby on the way and this job and I'm going to school. Besides, we're moving next week," he said.

"Next week, and you come and tell me the Friday before. I like your nerve!" she yelled.

"What about your responsibility here? What about me?" she asked as her eyes began to tear up.

"Mom, I know…I'll check on you virtually every day, and if you need me just call," he said as he attempted to console her.

"Look, you're practically grown now so you do what you feel is best," she said.

"Well when are you moving?" she asked.

"Well, we took off next week so we can get all settled in, plus I have some orientations for school. Mom I just want you to be proud of me," he said.

"I am proud of you, one question, did Tamir tell his **Mom** yet?" she asked.

"No, actually he's over there right now," he responded.

"Oh boy we better head over there, she ain't gonna hear that," she said.

The three hit the door and rushed over to Tamir's house. It may have been a little too late as his mom's yelling could be heard up and down the block.

"Just cause you getting a little education, got a little job and some little girlfriend, don't mean you grown!" Tamir's **mother**, Gladys yelled.

"I know **Mom**, I just have to take care of my responsibilities. Please try to understand," Tamir pleaded with his **mother**.

"I knew this girl was going to be trouble! And furthermore, what about your brother and sister?" she asked angrily.

"What about them?" Tamir replied.

"Oh no, you see...your little mouth getting too big already. They are your responsibility, did you forget about them?" she asked.

"No, but they are my brother and sister, not my kids, I have my own family now. I can't abandon my responsibilities like..." Tamir responded

"Like who? Your **father**?" she interrupted.

"See...but you're leaving me like him," she continued.

"But **Mom**, I have to start my life. What if I was going away to college?" he asked.

"But that's different, that's school," she said.

"It's the same thing, only difference is I'll be in the city still," he replied.

"You know what? You come in here and tell me you have a baby on the way, and then you come in here and tell me you're moving out next week. You know what? Fine, get the hell out! But, I'll tell you this, don't think for one second in that cartoon like brain of yours, that you can come waltzing back in here once you leave. I ain't let your punk ass **father** do it and I'm damn sure not letting you! Bye!" she yelled erratically.

"Mom, it don't have to be this way. Nick and Ayana can come visit whenever, you know it'll give you a break," Tamir said in an attempt to justify his decision.

"Whatever!" she responded nonchalantly.

"OK, well, listen next week I have to go to New York for orientation with the banks investment banking trainer, so Jeremy, Rasheeda, and Isabella will be here to get some of my stuff," he said.

"Whatever!" she responded rolling her eyes.

With that conversation going horribly, Isabella and Tamir go outside and meet an awaiting, Jeremy, Rasheeda, and Christine, Jeremy's **mother**. They heard the yelling clearly, they attempted to console Tamir.

"It's OK baby, she just don't want you to move, and it was so unexpected, she'll get over it," Christine said.

"No she won't. She meant what she said. What she needs to realize is I'm not my **father**! I didn't hurt her! I only tried to help, but I have a life too!" Tamir replied angrily.

"I just want to get out of here. Let's just go please," Tamir continued, fighting back the tears thinking of the things his **mother** said.

With that being said the four went out to the mall to clear their heads and go shopping for the new house.

At 5:00 AM, on Tuesday morning, September 11, 2001, Isabella got ready to take Tamir to the train station. He was taking the train to New York City, where he was headed for his first day at the World Bank investment banking training course. This was to be the first of many trips into the city that he would take. This course was a part of his curriculum established by the bank and the university. They both were excited. Isabella bought him a new suit to wear the weekend prior, solely for this occasion. He stood at the door with a blue pin-stripe suit with a light blue, French collared shirt and burgundy tie, with matching burgundy cap toe shoes and an attaché case in his hand. He had a proud smile, he felt as though he was already an investment banker ready to start a day at the office. Surprisingly, Jeremy and Rasheeda walked out in their sleep wear and robes. They were riding with Isabella to show their support. Once they arrived at the train station, they said their goodbyes.

"Ok babe, don't be nervous, make me proud. I'll be waiting for you when you get back. I'll cook some of your favorite rice and beans when you come home," Isabella said with a proud look on her face.

"OK baby, thank you, you hear me? I love you," Tamir said seriously.

"Look homie, don't hurt them but go make our money boy, you look like a million bucks," Jeremy said with a proud smile on his face.

"I'm so proud of you rock head," Rasheeda said proudly.

"I love you guys. I'll see y'all tonight and be careful with my stuff when y'all go pick it up," Tamir said.

With that statement, the announcement was made over the PA system, "Now Boarding 6:05 train to Penn Station, New York."

"Well, let me go. I'll call y'all on my first break," Tamir said as he was off on his first stop to conquering the investment world.

Jeremy, Isabella, Tamir, nor Rasheeda knew that certain events would take place that day that would change their lives forever. At about 8:15 AM, Tamir arrived at the World Trade Center, Tower 2. He and about ten other future investment bankers waited in the lobby of the 31st floor.

"Wow I can't believe I'm in the World Trade Center," Tamir exclaimed.

"Me either, this is unreal, by the way I'm Dan," Dan replied.

"Nice to meet you Dan, I'm Tamir."

Dan and Tamir conversed for about fifteen minutes while they awaited their trainer. They talked about where they were from, and where they were hoping to go. Dan was from Newark, New Jersey and went to NYU. He recently moved to the city for this opportunity. Like Tamir and Jeremy, he too worked for the bank.

At about 8:40 AM, their trainer, Joseph Smith, walked out to greet the class. Joseph introduced himself and asked everyone to put on a nametag and introduce themselves and tell where they were from. At about 8:48 AM, there was a loud explosion and strong vibrations felt in the room.

"Wow, what was that?" Dan asked.

Shaking and nervous, Tamir replied, "I don't know but that didn't sound good at all."

"Ok everyone, calm down we'll find out what's going on," Joseph said.

Meanwhile back in Philly, Jeremy, Rasheeda, and Isabella just arrived at Jeremy's house. Jeremy's mom had boxes ready and had started moving his stuff from his room. About twenty minutes into the move, Tamir's **mother** came running into the house.

"Oh my god, where is he?" she cried.

"Who? What are you talking about Gladys?" Christine asked.

"My son, oh my god!" she replied.

"He's in New York, Ms. Jones. Why?" Isabella replied.

"Where in New York?" she asked.

"Gladys, grab a hold of yourself. What's going on?" Christine said.

"The World Trade Center!" Isabella replied.

"Oh dear god no! Turn on the news, a plane crashed in the one of the tower!" Gladys responded

"What!" the room cried.

Christine fumbled for the remote control and turned on the news. A plane did in fact crash into Tower 1 of the World Trade Center.

Isabella immediately grabbed her cell phone and called Tamir, "Hello? Babe are you ok?" she asked.

"Yeah boo, I'm fine. Why, what's wrong?" he asked.

"A plane hit the World Trade Center!" she replied.

"What? Hit what? I'm there now, we felt an explosion but we're fine. They told us to stay put," he said.

"Ok babe, where are you?" she asked.

"The 31st floor of Tower 2," he replied.

"Baby, I'm fine. Don't worry. I'll keep you posted. Hey? You hear me?"

"Yes boo, I hear you," she responded.

"I love you baby. Stop worrying, I don't want you to upset yourself or the baby," he said.

"Ok baby, I love you too," she said as the phone cuts out.

Just then, as she watched the news a huge plane hit tower 2.

"Oh my god, he just said he was fine and he's in tower 2. Now look!" Isabella cried.

The whole room begins screaming and crying as they attempt to call him back but to no avail.

"Oh god my baby is in there, I just said all those horrible things to him," Gladys cried.

"It's ok Gladys, he knows you didn't mean it, he's going to be just fine," Christine assured her.

A tearful Isabella approaches Gladys and said, "Ms. Jones, I know you have your reservations about me but I want you to know that I love your son so much and I'm here for you. I never wanted to take anything from you, just give you an addition, me and your beautiful grand baby that's on the way."

This seemed to comfort Gladys, she responded, "Aww thank you so much Isabella and I'm sorry if I came off harsh, it's just that, that my, my...."

Just then, she broke down and cried, "My baby."

Isabella gave Gladys a strong hug and consoled her.

The mood in the room was extremely depressing, it started to affect everyone. Jeremy was starting to breakdown.

"Yo, I can't take this. I gotta go get our brother Rodge," he said.

Jeremy kissed the women in the room and ran down the street to Rodge's house.

Back in Manhattan, everyone in the office was terrified.

"OK everyone, calm down. Apparently both towers have been hit by airplanes. We're going to evacuate; everyone, if you could follow me out of the building down the fire escape," instructed Joseph.

Tamir frantically tried to call home and Isabella, but his phone was not getting in any reception. He dashed for the phone on the front desk and called Isabella.

"Hey babe, you ok?" he asked.

"Me, we're sitting here worrying about you but the phones aren't working," she replied in a nervous excitement.

"Where are you?" he asked.

"We're all over Jeremy's; your mom is here too. Jeremy went to get Rodge. Baby, I love you. Please come home," she said.

"Ok baby, don't worry, I have a beautiful woman carrying my child. I will get to you. I love you more than anything. Thank you for being in my life," he said as he began to cry.

"Oh my god baby I need you. But here, talk to your **Mom,** she's a mess," she replied.

"Hello son, I am so sorry. I love you and I love your family, just come home now. Please!" Gladys said.

"Mom, I love you too. I always will. I'm coming to you and Nick and Ayana," he replied.

A security guards yelled, "Sir, you have to get out of here we're evacuating!"

"Ok sir, here I come," he responded.

"Baby it's me, Mom handed me the phone," Isabella said.

"OK baby, I'm coming. I'll be there soon," he replied.

"Ok baby, I love you I'm waiting for you," she said.

They hang up the phone and Tamir quickly ran to catch up.

Back in Philadelphia, Tamir, Rodge, and his friend, Saul, came running in the house.

"Anything change yet?" Jeremy asked.

"Yeah they talked to Tamir again. He was ok, they were evacuating the building," Rasheeda responded.

As they watched the horror unfolding on television, Rodge said, "I can't believe that my brother is in there."

"I know, like we just were with him this morning. It seems like we just dropped him off down 30th street," Jeremy said.

Isabella began to break down, Rasheeda quickly ran to console her.

"Girl, it's going to be ok, you said he was cool and leaving the building, right?" she asked.

"Yeah, it's just...I know it ain't been long but it's special between us, you know? He is my everything," she cried.

"It was meant to be, that's why y'all came together. So god is going to make sure y'all are back together," Rasheeda said as she comforted Isabella.

As everyone sits around in anxiousness and fear, their phones began to ring. Michael called Jeremy, Juwan and Shawn were on a three-way call with Rodge, and Rasheeda tried to call Amanda.

Saul seemed to be the only one watching TV, just then he cried, "DAMN!"

"What? What is it?" Rodge asked in fear.

"Tower 2 just fell. Ain't no way that nigga made it out of that," he exclaimed.

Gladys, Christine, and Isabella broke down.

"Watch your damn mouth homie!" Jeremy said in rage.

"What? I can say what I want. I'm just being real," Saul responds.

"That's my brother in there!" Jeremy said as he hauled off and punched Saul in his mouth.

Rodge quickly broke up the fight and sent Saul on his way. Gladys fainted. Christine and Rasheeda tried to bring her to. Juwan, Shawn, and Michael said they were going to try to get out to Philadelphia as soon as they could to be with the family.

Several hours later, lower Manhattan was covered with dust and debris. The dust had yet to settle from the collapsing of both towers. Emergency personnel are all over trying to flee the dust and debris and trying to recover any survivors. Several blocks north of Ground Zero, Jeremy awakens. He was laying half way under a parked car and half way on the sidewalk. Coughing and covered with dust, he had no sense of where he was but he knew where he needed to be, back home in Philly with his family. He tried to stand and walk, but as soon as he got to his feet, he feels a sharp and bruising pain in his leg.

As another victim comes limping up the street, he asks, "Hey excuse me, where are we?"

"Hell!" the man responded.

He continued to walk seemingly aimless north from the disaster sight. Back at Jeremy's house, everyone from the block was sitting around praying and attempting to console the family.

Gladys became enraged from the fear and the praying and yelled, "Stop, just stop it all of you. You're all praying and mourning as if my son is dead."

She began to cry and said, "My son never lied to me and he said he's coming home, right Isabella?"

"That's right **Mom**," Isabella tearfully agreed.

The good thing so far in this tragedy, was the common bond built on the love of Tamir that was found between Gladys and Isabella. Jeremy's mom even opened up and showed stronger signs of acceptance toward Rasheeda and Jeremy's new family.

"You know, you guys can stay here, we have more than enough room and I can help out with the baby," Christine offered to Jeremy and Rasheeda.

"I know **Mom** but that's ok," Jeremy replied.

"Yeah **Mom**, if I may call you that, we couldn't impose," Rasheeda agreed.

"You can always come over and stay with us and spend time with the baby, and we'll even drop him or her off to spend time with you," Jeremy said.

Somewhat disappointed, Christine replied, "Well ok, you know what, bring those babies over here. I'll watch them while you're at work or school or whatever," she offered.

"Ok **Mom**, you gotta deal," Jeremy said as he smiled and hugged his **mother**.

Hanging over the city that never sleeps, quietness, shock, and apprehensive uncertainty of damage and vulnerability. For once it actually was sleeping, besides the emergency workers and families of the victims, trying desperately to find survivors and loved ones. It was now night time and there was an awkward surreal feeling. Tamir limped up the street in his ragged suit that was brand new only several hours before. A member of the EMS team stopped him.

"Sir, Sir," the medic called out to Tamir trying to get his attention.

Tamir stopped and continued to look forward. He stood looking like a zombie, in the sense of the walking dead. What had been fueling up to this point had been his adrenaline, and drive to get home. However, after hours of walking and constant flashes of the horror that he saw, the feeling of despair was wearing him down. He collapsed as the medic rushed over to him pulling out the stretcher and breathing devices. When Tamir awakened, he was being lifted out of the back of an ambulance.

Startled, he tried to fight and talk with virtually no energy, "Where am I? What are you doing? I have to get home to my family and my baby," said Tamir.

"Sir calm down, you're in New York, you're wounded Sir. It's ok you're in a hospital. We'll take care of you," a nurse responded.

They finally got him settled; the hospital was packed with victims. There were no more available rooms with people lined up in the hallways in wheel chairs, stretchers and even makeshift beds. The nurses check his vital signs and treat his wounds. As he lay in the stretcher, they give him pain killers to stop the pain and lightly sedate him.

Back at Jeremy's house, the scene was still the same, one full of despair and anxiety. Rasheeda, Rodge, and Jeremy are trying to get Isabella to eat.

"Come on girl, you gotta eat, if not for you at least for the baby," Rasheeda said.

"But what about Tamir? I bet he's not eating, what if he's trapped and no one can find him," she replied.

Jeremy and Rodge go out to the front porch to talk.

"You know this is messed up, why would these terrorist do this?" Jeremy asked.

"I don't know man," Rodge responded.

"Man this ain't our fight! We ain't do anything to them! What the hell did Tamir do? Huh? He was just trying to reach his goal and now look, we don't know if he's dead or alive!" Jeremy exclaimed in anger.

"Look at his girl man, she's worried half to death, about to have a baby by him and he is lost. They tried to take him away from her. We gotta do something," he continued.

"Homie, I know, but what can we do but be here for her and his mom and Nick, and Ayana," Rodge replied.

"I know man that's what he would want. I just keep hoping he's gonna run down the street smiling at us. What I would give just to see him or at least be there with him. That's our brother, I should have been there with him," Jeremy said as he began to break down.

"Come here man, I need you to be strong, it's going to be ok," Rodge said as he hugged Jeremy.

A few hours later, a little after midnight, Tamir wakes up and calls for the nurse. Not only had he awakened physically but also mentally, his drive began to awaken as he saw pictures of his girlfriend smiling and then crying waiting for him. He kept hearing her voice in his head.

He called for the nurse, "Nurse, excuse me?"

"Yes, how can I help you sir?" the nurse responded.

"Thank you for everything. I need to go now," he replied.

"Go where sir?" she asked.

"Go home, to Philly, my family is waiting," he answered.

"No sir, you can't leave yet, besides the city is closed off. It's no way in or out," she replied.

She laid him back down and covers him up. Determined to get home, he waited until the coast was clear and made a break for it. Tamir now outside of the hospital still a little groggy headed down the street. With no sense of direction, being driven only by his destination, he walks into the night.

It was now well after midnight and Isabella lays awake in Jeremy's bed. Jeremy and Rasheeda covered her in his blankets. They figured by covering Isabella up with his things, his smell would comfort her and help her sleep. He and Rasheeda tucked her in. She finally fell asleep with his pillow clinched in her arms. She slept as if she were holding him.

Meanwhile, in New York, Tamir was still walking through the night trying to find his way across the Hudson, a milestone that would be the first in his journey home. Several hours later, he found himself at the entrance to the Lincoln Tunnel. He stared up at the sky and focused on one star in the clear sky. He thought back to a night when he and Isabella laid out at the plateau in Philadelphia's Fairmount Park, and watched the stars. He smiled as he remembered their conversation.

"Baby, you see that?" he asked.

"What am I looking at babe?" she replied.

"That star right there," he said as he took her arm and pointed at the sky as she lay in between his legs.

"Yes I see it," she said.

"That's our star; I'm claiming that as ours," he said with a huge smile.

"That's our star, the energy that powers the stars billions of miles away, so that we can see it signifies our love," he explained.

"Aww...you are so sweet," she exclaimed as she began to cry.

"No matter where we are in this world, that star will always be there, much like our love. So if ever we're apart and you want to know if I'm thinking of you, look to the sky and see if you can see the star, that will secure your answer," he further explained.

He softly began to sing to her, "Come bring me your softness comfort me through all this madness, woman don't you know with you I'm born again."

She responded in song, "Come give me your sweetness, now there's you, there is no weakness, lying safe within your arms, I'm born again."

At virtually the same time that he had this thought, Isabella awakened and ran for the window. She stared up at the sky as she noticed their star twinkling. She had the same memory that Tamir had at the same time. At the same time, Tamir focused back in on reality, he's stared at the star as it twinkled. He suddenly felt this closeness with Isabella.

He begins to softly sing to himself, "I was half not whole, and stand with none."

Isabella sang, "Reaching through this world in need of one."

Amazingly in perfect harmony as if they were together, they sang, "Come show me your kindness, in your arms I'll find this, woman don't you know with you I'm born again, lying safe with you I'm born again."

With that last note, they both began to tear and smile.

Jeremy walked past his room to check on Isabella, and notices her crying at the window and said, "It'll be ok, I'm sure he's fine," he said.

"I know he is, go get him," she replied.

"What?" he asked confused.

"Go get my baby, I know he's alive, go get him please," she replied.

Jeremy ran down stairs and woke up Rodge.

"Yo, let's go!" Jeremy demanded.

"Go where?" Rodge replied in a groggy tone.

"To get Tamir, let's go look for him," Jeremy said.

"Man, it's like three in the morning, how we gonna find him?" he questioned.

"I don't know, but it's early so it'll be no traffic. We gotta go look at least. That's our brother up there he needs us," Jeremy answered.

"Alright, let's go, I'm with it, three the hard way for life homie," Rodge agreed.

As the boys snuck out the front hoping not to wake anyone, Isabella looked on from the top of the steps and whispered, "Thanks, y'all, bring my baby back."

Back at the Lincoln tunnel, there were national guards everywhere. Tamir made an attempt to walk through, but a guardsman stopped him.

"Whoa, whoa...Where are you going sir? The tunnel is closed," the guardsmen said.

"I have to get home," an emotional Tamir replied.

"Where's home?" the guardsman asked.

"West Philadelphia," Tamir answered.

"Wow, that's a long way to go on foot, Sir," he replied.

"It doesn't matter how I get there or how long it takes me, I just have to get to my girl and baby," Tamir replied.

"I can understand that, my wife and I just had a little baby girl. Well, look, you can't walk through the tunnel sir, it's closed," the guardsman explained.

"Well, Sir, you have two options. Either you let me through or kill me but I have to get home or die trying," Tamir responded angrily.

"Calm down son, you didn't let me finish. Look, I have to go pick up some engineers in Jersey, so I can give you a lift to the first rest stop on the turnpike, but that's as far as I can go," the guardsman offered.

"Thank you, Sir," Tamir replied.

"Yeah, no problem, I better get you off this road before you get yourself shot," said the guardsman.

Tamir hopped in the guardsman's Jeep and headed through the tunnel.

Meanwhile, Rodge and Jeremy drive into the early morning up the New Jersey Turnpike.

With sheer determination to find their friend, "Do you think we'll find him?" Jeremy asked.

"I honestly can't answer that, but we'll damn sure try," Rodge responded.

Back at a rest stop at between Exit 11 and 12, the guardsman dropped Tamir off.

"Thank you again, officer!" Tamir yelled.

"No problem, be safe and get to that family of yours," he replied.

As he walked towards the entrance to the turnpike, he noticed a group of firefighters and EMTs. They seem to be upset. Apparently, they were turned away from the city when they attempted to enter and help. They were from Delaware.

"Man I can't believe they wouldn't let us help," said a paramedic.

"I know, it's not like we're amateurs, we're professionals," replied a firefighter.

"We drove one hundred thirty miles to help and were turned away, in a time where we need to unite as one," exclaimed the medic.

Tamir approached and said, "I overheard what you all were talking about. I was in Tower 2, I'm from Philadelphia, just trying to get to my family, so if you still feel the desire to help, could I trouble you all for a ride?" Tamir desperately asked.

"Wow, a survivor. It would be our pleasure and an honor to help you," the medic replied excitedly.

As Tamir walked to the ambulance, the medic noticed Tamir's wound on his leg and said, "Wow son, that looks bad, let me get you in the back and see if we can't patch you up."

With the help of the medics, Tamir was situated in the back of the ambulance. As Tamir relaxes, the pain from his wound sets in, he lets out a slight scream.

"Ok, son, take it easy we have something for that," the medic said as he gave Tamir some painkillers.

The drug quickly took affect and knocked Tamir out.

Across the Turnpike at the rest stop, opposite the one that Tamir was pulling away from, Jeremy and Rodge are pulling in. It was now about 5:30 AM, the sun was rising, as Jeremy buys some candy from the shop his phone rings. It was Isabella.

She inquired, "Are you guys there yet?"

"No not yet, we're at a rest stop getting gas and using the bathroom," he replied.

"Well, please find my baby," she pleaded.

"We will Bella, take it easy and I'll keep you posted," he replied as they hang up.

The cashier listening in asked, "Looking for someone in the city?"

"Yeah, why?" Jeremy answered.

"Well you won't be able to get in; they locked the city down, they're turning anybody and everybody away. I recommend you head back at least until they unlock the city," the cashier explained.

"Damn, thanks," Jeremy responds disappointedly.

He met Rodge back at the car with a disgusted look on his face and said, "Well we gotta turn around!"

"Why?" Rodge asked.

"The city is closed down; they're not letting anyone in or out," Jeremy replied.

"Damn!" Rodge responded.

As they headed back onto the turnpike, Jeremy called Isabella back, "Sis, don't be upset."

"What's wrong?" she nervously asked.

"The city is closed down; they're not letting anyone in or out," he explained.

"We're on our way back now. I'm sorry sis," he continued.

As they hang up the phone, Isabella began to breakdown and Rasheeda was at the door of the room and noticed.

"Hey girl, what's wrong? Where are Rodge and Jeremy?" she asked.

"They went to find him," Isabella replied.

"The city is closed; they won't let anyone in or out. We'll never find him now," she continued as she cried.

"Come here, don't think like that. We'll find him," Rasheeda said as she consoled her friend.

A couple hours later, the ambulance carrying Tamir makes its way in to Philadelphia. The medics try to wake Tamir up. He awakened but was not coherent. Not knowing where he lives, they decide to take him to a local hospital in Philadelphia. In the triage area of the hospital, the medic explains Tamir's story to the admitting nurse.

"Ok, we'll get his ID and find his family members and number to contact someone," the nurse explained.

"Take care of him, that's a soldier there. He was going to walk down the NJ turnpike to get here," the medic said as he left.

After a few moment of searching the hospital's records, the nurse finds a number to Tamir's mother, Gladys. She calls but no one answers. Back at Tamir's house, Tamir's younger brother, Nick, wakes up from the ringing phone and runs across the street to get his Mom. Gladys is sleeping on the couch in Jeremy's living room, when Nick runs in.

"Mom, Mom, wake up!" Nick cries as he nudged at his **mother**.

"What is it baby?" she said as she began to wake up.

"The phone just rung at home," he said.

"This early?" she asked.

Rasheeda and Isabella heard the commotion and raced downstairs to see what was going on.

"What's happening Mom? What's going on?" Isabella asked.

"Nick said someone called this morning," she replied.

"Let's go see who it was," Rasheeda said.

The four of them race across the street to see who called.

Gladys looks at the caller ID on the phone and said, "It was Hanneman Hospital."

She tried to call back, but the number was a general number. After a few moments of dialing through the automated maze, she gets to a live person.

"Yes someone called here this morning but I missed the call," Gladys said.

"OK ma'am what were the last four digits of the number that called?" a woman answered.

"4302," she answered.

"Ok, that's our triage unit, hold on I'll put you through," the woman replied.

"Triage, this is Deena, how can I help you?" a woman answered.

"Yes, I received a call this morning from this number," Gladys replied.

"OK what is your name Ma'am?" Deena asked.

"Gladys Davis," she answered.

"Oh yes, we did call. It seems we have your son," Deena explained.

"Oh my god, you do! Is he alive?" Gladys asked.

"Yes ma'am, he's alive, he just has some minor wounds but he's been medicated and treated. Someone can pick him up," Deena replied.

After they hung up the phone, the whole room celebrated after Gladys shared the great news.

Rasheeda called Jeremy, "Babe!"

"Hey baby, good morning," Jeremy replied.

"Tamir is fine, he's here in Philly at Hanne man," she explained.

"How the hell did he get there?" he asked confused.

"I don't know, but babe please go get him," Rasheeda said.

After Jeremy got off the phone with Rasheeda, he told Rodge the news. Rodge excitedly sped up and headed back to Philly.

At the hospital, Tamir came to and decided he needed to go home, not knowing the nurse talked to his family and arranged for him to be picked up, he left. As Tamir walked out of the entrance to the hospital, he noticed he was back in Philly. He reached into the pockets of his worn out suit and pulled out five, one-dollar bills and a ten. He headed to the bus stop. This was going to be one of the longest commutes he'd ever taken on public transportation.

Later that morning, Rodge and Jeremy rushed into the hospital. They asked the nurse in the triage unit where they could find him.

She replied, "Oh, our WTC survivor? He's right this way," as she led them to the room she left him in.

On the number ten trolley the other passengers looked at Tamir curiously for about ten minutes, finally one asked, "Hey buddy, where you coming from?"

Tired and beat down, Tamir gasped deeply and replied, "Hell."

Back at the hospital, the nurse and the guys go into a room where Tamir was supposed to be. He was not there, the nurse nervously said, "I don't understand. I just left him in here a little while ago."

In a sense of panic, Jeremy called Rasheeda, "Baby there's a problem."

"Oh my, what now?" she asked.

"He's not here," Jeremy said.

"What the hell do you mean, he's not there?" Rasheeda exclaimed.

After a few questions, Rasheeda hung up and looked at Gladys and Isabella. They over heard the phone call.

"You know what...forget this, let's go Isabella," Gladys said as she grabbed Isabella's hand and headed out the front door.

Rasheeda ran outside and asked, "Where are y'all going?"

"To find her man and my son," Gladys replied.

As the women made their way up the street, a worn down figure appeared at the top of the street. It was Tamir; Isabella locked eyes with him as tears rolled down her cheek. He limped towards her.

She ran towards him and cried, "Baby, you're back!"

"Here I am baby," he whimpered.

They met in the middle of the street, Isabella embraced Tamir with warm love and affection.

Tamir still full of dust said, "I'm sorry I messed up my new suit."

Isabella laughed and responded, "Oh baby, I'm not worried about that thing, we'll get you another."

Gladys interrupted their reunion. Tamir noticed her standing by the car and crying.

He limped over to her and said, "Mom, I'm here do not cry."

"I know, I'm just so happy to see you," she said as she grabbed her son and hugged him.

At this point, everyone from Tamir and Jeremy's houses ran out to join in the reunion. Isabella rushed into Tamir's house and drew a warm bath for her boyfriend. As Tamir relaxed in the warm bath, Isabella washed his back and shoulders.

"Babe, you can't believe what happened up there," Tamir said.

"I know boo, we watched down here on TV," she replied.

"I mean there were so many people in that building. We got out just in time. The last thing I remember was looking up at the fires in the tower once we made it down. We tried to run back in to see if we could help others inside. The fire fighters would not let us, as they led us up the street, I heard someone scream, 'It is coming down run.' As I ran up the street, there was darkness behind me and things were flying in the air. The noise was horrible, it sounded like the earth was opening up and trying to swallow its self with explosions. Next thing I knew, I was waking up under a car," he explained.

"Damn babe, I'm just glad your back. I was so worried that I would never see you again," she sighed.

About an hour later, Rodge and Jeremy arrived at Tamir's house.

"Brother, where are you?" Jeremy yelled.

"Shhh...he's upstairs sleeping," Gladys responded.

Jeremy and Rodge went upstairs and looked in on him as he slept in bed with Isabella. They looked over to his dresser where his dirty suit laid. This suit explained everything; it gave a view into the horror their best friend had endured.

"That man was getting back to his woman; I don't blame him I would've been the same way," Jeremy said.

Chapter : 5

Afew weeks later things were working their way back to normal. Jeremy had gone back to work and school. The couples had finally moved into their new home and Gladys and Christine were a lot more supportive of their decisions. They even went on several shopping trips with the girls to get everything from maternity clothes to baby furniture and bottles. Gladys and Christine were the proudest grandparents in Philadelphia. Every chance they could, they spoke of their future grandkids. They even called Rasheeda and Isabella on three-way every night to check on them.

One Wednesday afternoon in the beginning of October, World Bank called a mandatory staff meeting. As they walked to the conference hall with no sense of worry, Jeremy and Tamir talked.

"I wonder what this is about," Tamir asked.

"I don't know. They probably decided to release a new retail banking product," Jeremy replied.

Jeremy and Tamir found seats and sat down unaware that they were about to hear news that was going to ultimately change their lives.

"Good afternoon fellow team members," the director of the site greeted the room.

"I know you all are wondering what we're doing here so I'm going to jump right into it. Last month this company as well as the nation suffered a horrible loss. As a matter of fact our very own Tamir Davis was in Tower 2 and managed to get out and survive before the tower fell," the director explained.

This stunned Tamir, he did not expect that they would mention anything about his ordeal.

"What, is he gonna give me an award or something?" Tamir whispered to Jeremy.

"Tamir, if you could stand up please. I think a round of applause is appropriate for his braveness and survival. Tamir, we're glad you made it out of that tragedy and continue to be a part of our team," he continued.

"Tamir was the only person from this particular World Bank site. Now...to the ugly news," the director continued.

The room was completely confused about what was going on and a slight mumble came over the audience follow by a strong silence.

"Unfortunately, since the tragedies of 9/11, we are projected to take a huge loss, per our analyst. What this means for us is unfortunately cut backs. All incentive programs are hereby suspended until further notice. We will have to lay-off a large number of people. Now I will open up the floor for all questions in a moment but I will say this before it is asked. The exact number of employees has yet to be determined, and they are looking at judging who will be cut by seniority. Now, with that being said, are there any questions?" the director asked.

Jeremy jumped up and said, "Sir, when you say incentives, does this affect the tuition reimbursement or scholarship programs, or the college co-ops?"

"At this point sir, no, that has not been addressed," the director replied.

"Do you know if this will be affected?" Jeremy further asked.

"I have to say honestly I don't know, but in my opinion, I would say that would not be affected," the director answered.

Another team member stood up and asked, "When will the lay-offs take place?"

"We estimate that come January, we will start. The people who have been selected to be laid off will get notice from the end of this month through January," the director answered.

After the meeting, the feeling in the office was gloomy. Everyone had a feeling of the unknown and worry. Tamir and Jeremy felt it but they were so confident in their abilities this did not bother them. They felt that they were to be the next leaders. After all, they were putting them through school and had them in training programs.

By the end of November, over two hundred people received notice for the Philadelphia site alone. Tamir and Jeremy were oblivious to any further ramifications and still carried the feeling that they were the chosen ones, the golden kids. It's now December time for cheer and holiday spirit. Rasheeda and Isabella were definitely showing. Tamir and Jeremy met every night around the same time to head to the store as the girls' cravings set in. They were completely opposite in taste. Rasheeda would want something sweet while Isabella would want something sour.

Around the fifteenth of the month, the women had their six-month checkups. This visit was special; this would be the first time they would get ultrasounds. At the doctor's office, they got a peek at the lives that were inside of them, their little bundles of love that had been sending their bodies and emotions through all types of changes.

Once they finished their visits, they met in the reception area, Rasheeda exclaimed with excitement, "Girl...I'm having a baby girl!"

"I'm having a boy, a little Tamir, he's gonna be so psyched," Isabella replied.

"I have an Idea," Rasheeda said.

"What's that?" Isabella inquired.

"We'll give the guys special gifts; let's not tell them about the visit today or the sexes of the babies. We'll go to the store and get baby clothes and wrap them up with the ultrasound pictures," Rasheeda responded.

"Yeah that's a great Idea," Isabella agreed.

Off to the mall they headed, Isabella called Gladys and Rasheeda called Christine, they agreed to meet them at the King of Prussia mall. At the mall, the women told the future grandmothers the good news.

"Oh my, I'm having a little granddaughter?" Christine asked.

"And I'm having a Grandson?" Gladys exclaimed.

This incited a shopping rally through the mall. The Grandmothers and mothers-to-be shopped all that day working their way through the holiday frenzy of shoppers.

Meanwhile, Jeremy and Tamir had their own ideas of surprises. This by far was the most Jeremy and Tamir ever shopped in their lives. They bought everything from clothes to movies and cd's. It was not that they wanted to buy the girls everything but they had no Idea what to get them, so by default they bought everything they thought the girls would like. Finally, on their way out of the Gallery, they walked past a Jeweler. In the window sat a one-carat diamond engagement ring. Tamir noticed this because it shined like the star that twinkled in the sky that represented their love.

He stopped Jeremy and said, "This it right here."

"Whoa buddy, slow down, engagement rings?" Jeremy asked.

"Yeah, why not? Man, look, I'd rather have a wife then a baby momma any day," Tamir explained.

"Dawg, we're young though," Jeremy responded.

"And what does that mean? Like, you been with Sheeda forever, anyway, and she bout to have your baby, you love her to death, might as well seal the deal. Forget what you doing. I'm doing it, worst she can say is no," Tamir said.

"Alright Chuck Woolery, I'm in," responded Jeremy.

The guys entered the store and bought the engagement rings.

It was Christmas Eve, Christine, Gladys, Nick, and Ayana are spending Christmas at the couples' house. Everyone's busy doing last minute things. Tamir and Jeremy were putting the tree up. Rodge was playing PlayStation with Nick. The women are cooking a feast in the kitchen. They have a full menu planned for Christmas dinner. They planned to have ham, turkey, baked macaroni and cheese. They also plan on having Isabella's Colombian rice and beans, penil and yucca, platano maduro, candied sweet potatoes, and collard greens. The dessert menu consisted of sweet potato pie, pineapple upside down cake, apple pie, pecan pie, and cookies.

Tamir yelled into the kitchen, "Mom...Mom...make sure you make the cookies!"

"Boy, be quiet and get that tree up!" Gladys yelled as she laughed.

"Gladys, don't make me come in there!" Tamir joked.

Gladys grabbed a spatula and ran after her son.

Isabella stopped her and said, "No **Mom**, I got you on this one."

She took the spatula and ran after Tamir and yelled, "Come here boy!"

Tamir stopped and grabbed Isabella and said, "What you gonna do sexy, huh?"

He playfully began to tickle and kiss her. This was the mood of the house; everyone was happy and playful. Nick was blowing out Rodge in John Madden football. This proved to be profitable for little Nick. Every game that he won Rodge gave him twenty dollars. By the end of the night, Rodge had paid Nick two hundred dollars. The smells of a Christmas ham and ginger cookies filled the air along with the sounds of the Motown Christmas collection that was blaring from the stereo.

At around 9:00 PM, the doorbell rang. Standing at the front door was Amanda and Michael, armed with presents. Everyone sat around and talked, as the ovens are baking. Tamir told everyone about his experiences on 9/11. Amanda made everyone sweaters that she handed out while they gathered in front of the television and watched, "A Christmas Story." There was a wealth of presents under the tree. Not surprising, the most presents seem to be for the unborn children. About 11:30 PM, Nick and Ayana are sent to bed, and Michael and Amanda head to their families. Christine and Gladys are still cooking away in the kitchen.

"Mom, go ahead to bed. I'll be up for a while. I'll take over, you too Ms. Christine," Tamir offered.

"OK, but you better not mess up our work." Gladys replied.

"Mom, you taught me to cook remember?" said Tamir.

"I'll be up, I'll supervise Mom, don't worry," Isabella offered.

Christine and Gladys headed to bed, Tamir dims the lights. Rodge was knocked out in the chair and ottoman. The couples sit and continue to watch TV.

"So it's almost midnight, you guys wanna open one present each?" Tamir asked.

"Sure, why not," they all agreed.

The girls grabbed two identical presents and handed them to the guys. The guys grabbed two identical presents and handed them to the girls.

"OK so who goes first?" Isabella asked.

Excited, Rasheeda said, "Let them go first."

The guys open their presents and look at each other with confused smiles. In Jeremy's box was a little pink Polo shirt with a matching skirt. In Tamir's box was a little blue Polo shirt with matching pants.

"This is so cute but um...I'm confused," Tamir said.

"Yeah me too," Jeremy agreed.

"Just keep looking silly," Isabella said.

As the guys continued to look in the boxes, they found the ultrasound pictures.

"There you go baby, that's your daughter," Rasheeda said.

"There's your son," Isabella said.

Jeremy's face lit up as he reached over and hugged Rasheeda and said, "You mean I have a beautiful baby girl coming?"

"Yes baby," Rasheeda said as she smiled.

"Oh my god, I got a son coming?" Tamir asked.

"Yes boo boo," Isabella said as she leaned over and kissed Tamir.

Tamir looked over to Jeremy and said, "You see now what I was talking about?"

"Yeah, we picked the perfect gifts," Jeremy replied.

What are y'all talking about?" Rasheeda asked.

"Did y'all know already?" Isabella asked.

"No, babe, just open your presents," Tamir said.

As the girls began to open their gifts, the guys got down on one knee in front of them. They opened the boxes, the guys took their girlfriends hands and said, "Will you?"

"Of course I will," Isabella, answered.

"I don't know, you do have a kind of big head," Rasheeda joked.

"Yeah, but you love this big head though," Jeremy replied.

"You know I will," Rasheeda said.

As the couples hugged and celebrated, their **mother**s watched from the top of the stairs.

"Girl, our babies ain't babies no more," Gladys said.

"I know but at least we got a wedding to plan," Christine responded as she hi-fived Gladys.

Early Christmas morning, Nick and Ayana rushed down the stairs to open their presents. Christine and Gladys followed down the stairs and headed to the kitchen to start breakfast. The aroma of the Christmas ham and cookies changed to that of the seasonings of the home fries and the crisp bacon. In the partnership that Gladys and Christine formed in the kitchen, they realized another partnership they had. They had each other for support, so somehow the loss of their sons to two beautiful young women didn't seem so bad. Ever since the 9/11 incident, they became more like sisters. The smell of the breakfast had awakened Rodge first. His yawning and the kids opening their presents woke the ladies up.

"Oh hey, good morning Rodge, Merry Christmas," Rasheeda said as she yawned and stretched.

"Merry Christmas Rodge," Isabella exclaimed.

"Good morning and Merry Christmas ladies," Rodge replied.

The women put their ring hands together and reached for the sky and said, "Look Rodge!"

"What are you girls thunder cats or something?" Rodge joked.

"No rock head, we're getting married," Rasheeda exclaimed.

"I know congratulations girls, or should I say sisters," Rodge said as he kissed them on their cheek.

"Get your hands off my woman," Jeremy said as he grabbed his leg from the floor.

"Damn, ain't been engaged twenty-four hours and someone pushing up on my woman already," Jeremy joked.

They laughed and woke Tamir by stepping on him.

Christmas had officially started, as the couples enter the kitchen, Christine and Gladys started humming, "Here comes the bride."

"You guys know already? We were just about to tell you," Isabella said surprised.

"Honey, as you will soon learn, a power you get as a **mother** is the know all," Christine said.

"You ain't never lie child!" Gladys exclaimed.

"Wow **Mom**, what do we get as **fathers**?" Jeremy asked.

"Lazy," Christine and Gladys said as they laugh.

A beautiful Christmas indeed, everyone got mainly what they wanted. Rodge being himself, didn't buy gifts, he just gave everyone hundred dollar bills with the exceptions of Christine, Gladys, and the unborn babies. He bought Christine and Gladys expensive cookware sets. He bought the babies five pairs of sneakers each. Later that day they played all kinds of games. The biggest hit however was Karaoke. They played in teams, there was Ayana and Nick, Christine and Gladys, Tamir, Jeremy, and Rodge, and Isabella and Rasheeda. Tamir's group sung Jodeci's, "Forever My Lady," Nick and Ayana sung Michael Jackson's, "Rock with You," Rasheeda and Isabella sung Xscape's, "Who Can I Run to," and Christine and Gladys sung Rene and Angela's, "Your Smile." Isabella and Tamir did a surprise performance of Frederick's, "Gentle".

That night, Michael, Amanda, and Isabella and Rasheeda's family had dinner at the house with the family. Isabella and Rasheeda's parents were pretty easy going. They were generally happy with the girl's decisions. They valued their daughter's judgment and intelligence. As long as they were happy the parents were happy. Christine, Gladys, Janice, Rasheeda's mom, Abigail and Juan, Isabella's parents, sat around after dinner and talked. This was the first time, the couple's parents formally met and conversed. They talked about everything from their ideal wedding plans to their initial reactions when they received the pregnancy news.

"I first was shocked at first when Rasheeda told me she was pregnant. But she told me her plans and how she and Jeremy had set fail safe plans to ensure that she could continue school," Janice said.

"Girl, I was like it could have been worse you know? But I knew that Jeremy and Rasheeda have been pretty responsible and are basically good kids," Christine replied.

"Juan was a little upset as we all probably were, but realizing that Tamir was a standup guy and seeing the love Isabella had for him it soothed the pain," Abigail said.

"I'm just glad Tamir did the right thing and stood up as a man should and took on his responsibilities and is marrying my princess. I have to give it to you Gladys you raised a hell of a man," Juan said.

"Yeah girl, you too Christine, your sons are truly upstanding individuals and our going to make good husbands and great **father**s," Janice agreed.

"It could have been worse," Janice said jokingly as she looked at Rodge.

The parents laughed and Gladys said, "Rodge is a sweetheart, that's a true lemon to lemonade story. He doesn't bring that nonsense around us, that's our other son."

As the parents talked and talked, they were having a good time and enjoyed each other's company. The couples walked in and joined the conversation. The mood was very peaceful and loving the family atmosphere was prevalent.   Tamir was a little intimidated by Isabella's **father** Juan. Juan would stare at Jeremy with an ambiguous grin. Tamir did not know if he was proud of him or he was thinking of ways to kill him without anyone knowing.

After a few moments Tamir asked Juan, "Can I talk to you for a minute?"

"Sure," Juan replied.

As the two walked out to the back porch, Isabella said, "Papa, be nice."

Juan replied in Spanish, "I'll leave him with use of his legs," and laughed.

"Mama, tell him to stop," Isabella said.

"You know your **father** is just playing," Abigail responded.

"What? What'd I miss?" Tamir asked in confusion.

"Nothing son," Juan replied as he grabbed Tamir by the back of the neck and led him out back.

Out back Tamir said, "Mr. Rodriguez, I love your daughter. She is amazing and the best thing that ever happened to me."

"Yeah well that is my princess, and I trust that you will take care of her and my grandson," Juan replied.

"Listen Tamir, let's be real for a minute, am I upset that my little girl is pregnant at such a young age? Damn right! I can say though I have watched how you have carried yourself and I'm aware of your academic accolades, besides that, I talked to your mother. I am aware of how your **father** was; I am assured though that by seeing that and you stepping up at a young age. You learned from his mistakes and I am secure that you will do what is right. So with that said, welcome to the family son," Juan explained.

"Thanks pop," Tamir replied.

"I'm sure by now you know that life is not easy and it's just starting for you all. There will be many challenges and disagreements. You're not expected to know everything, but I want you to know that you have a huge family that you can ask if you need help," Juan further explained.

"Thank you", Tamir replied with a sense of relief written on his face.

The two shook hand and walked back inside. The rest of the night was beautiful and fun for all. They talked all night about the babies, the weddings, and just life in general. This was the family, a huge family thanks to the couples unions. Christine, Janice, Abigail, and Gladys, seemed to form a new alliance, sort of like the Grandmothers club. They exchanged numbers and even made plans to go out and shop together. They even exchanged recipes.

The holiday had passed and it was back to life as normal, only difference was now there were four grandparents calling the girls as opposed to two.

That Friday, Jeremy and Tamir were back at work, still oblivious to the possibility of either one of them getting laid off. It was the last day before the holiday weekend, what was left of the team members are scrambling to finish last minute projects and assignments. Some clearing their personal belongings due to the notifications of the layoff, Jeremy was called down to HR, in his heart he knew that this was it but his mind wasn't processing it. As he walked in to the reception area of the HR department, he noticed Tamir sitting and waiting.

"They called you down too?" Jeremy asked.

"Yeah, me too," Tamir responded in a disappointed tone.

"Tamir come on in," the HR generalist called.

As he walked into the generalist's office, Tamir locked eyes with Jeremy and shook his hand.

In the office the Generalist started, "Listen Tamir, I hate to say this but unfortunately we have to let you go."

"What, I mean I can't say that I didn't expect this when you guys called me down but up to that point I didn't because we're at the cutoff point," Tamir replied with disgust.

"We were trying to keep you Tamir, you must know that but when it came down to dollars and sense, we couldn't do it," the generalist said.

"But what about my tuition and school?" Tamir asked.

"Well unfortunately we have to cut that as well," the generalist replied.

"Are you kidding me? I mean what am I supposed to do? It is one thing that I lose my job but my education too. I can't afford that on my own," Tamir said.

"Tamir no one could have predicted the tragedy that we all have suffered from 9/11. Do you think I like to be the one who has to give the bad news to half the staff here?" the generalist argued.

"Yeah well you still have your job and as far as 9/11 is concerned I was there. Did you forget I almost lost my life for this company in the tower? So don't give me that cop out!" Tamir angrily replied as he began to walk out.

"Tamir, listen I'm sorry, this could be a temporary thing. You will be at the top of our list in the event of rehires. You should receive a severance check in about four weeks," the Generalist said.

"Yeah I'll be sure to let my fiancé and my unborn son know that you guys care so much," Tamir responded sarcastically.

Tamir walked out the office heading back to his office to get the rest of his things. As he walked out Jeremy was called in. The conversation between Jeremy and the generalist was pretty much the same. The difference was Jeremy used a lot of profanity and actually made the generalist cry. When he headed back to his office, security escorted him.

Back at the house, Jeremy and Tamir sat with looks of despair on their faces. Angry, Jeremy blamed this misfortune on the terrorists.

"Man what the hell, first they try to take my brother away from me, now they wanna take my family's income and livelihood away," he said.

All Tamir could think about was the words, dollars and sense, of which the generalist mentioned.

"Dollars and Sense, if it doesn't make dollars it don't make sense," he uttered as he stared off with a calculating look on his face.

Just then, Rodge came walking in the door. "What's happening brothers?" Rodge greeted.

"Ain't too much man, we just lost our jobs," Tamir responded.

"What? Both of you? Y'all were the banks prodigies," Rodge responded.

"Yeah man the 9/11 thing, it cost the company to lose so much money that they had to cut most of our building back," Jeremy explained.

"What about school? They still paying for that?" Rodge asked.

"Hell no!" Tamir firmly answered.

"Well look, I'll cover the expenses of the house for y'all until y'all find something else," Rodge offered.

"Good looking brother, we gonna need that," Tamir accepted.

"Do the girls know yet?" Rodge asked.

"No not yet, they out shopping as usual," Tamir responded.

"Well look let's forget about this bad news for now, it's New Year's Weekend, let's celebrate and party now and worry and stress in the new year," Rodge said.

On that note, Rodge pulled out his phone made a couple of calls and said, "Ok here's the plan, run upstairs, pack your bags and pack something for the ladies, our plane leaves at 10:30 PM. I'll be back at 8:30 PM to pick y'all up."

"Damn, Rodge, where the hell are we going?" Jeremy asked.

With a giant smile on his face, Rodge replied, "Miami."

The three laughed and cheered as if they had not any bad news at all. The girls walked in during the celebration.

"What's going on?" Rasheeda asked

"Yeah, why are we so happy?" Isabella asked.

"Babe we're headed to Miami tonight for the weekend courtesy of Rodge," Tamir answered.

"What?" the girls cried in disbelief.

"Yeah now stop asking questions and go get packed. I gotta go run a couple errands and get ready. 8:30 y'all, I'm serious, we can't be late," Rodge said.

The couples frantically ran through the house packing and turning things off. The girls were back and forth doing each other's hair. Finally, it was 8:30 PM.

Rodge was outside sounding his horn and yelling, "What did I say? 8:30 let's go!"

Chapter : 6

Philadelphia International Airport, their first stop before the sun and sands of Miami Beach, Florida. On the plane the girls slept, Rodge was busy flirting with the flight attendants; meanwhile Jeremy stared out the window in a daze. Tamir watched Rodge and thought, *"If it don't make dollars, it don't make sense. Rodge was making more sense than a dictionary."* He gazed at his fiancé and turned to Jeremy. "You good man?" he asked.

"Yeah just wondering what those people went through on those planes on 9/11," Jeremy responded.

"Yeah well I would hope they didn't see it coming and it was quick and painless," Tamir said.

"Yeah well it still wasn't right, somebody gotta do something." But yo, how we gonna tell the ladies about the jobs?" Jeremy asked.

"I don't know man, I don't want to scare them or feel like we headed for disaster," Tamir replied.

"I know like I wanna say something, but part of me is like don't say nothing," Jeremy said.

"I never lied to her and I don't wanna start now," Tamir said.

The next day in Miami, the friends shopped all day up and down the concourse in South Beach. The girls being six months pregnant waddled up and down the street not wanting to miss one beat. Jeremy and Tamir though were on vacation at the courtesy of Rodge, began to feel guilty.

Tamir walked up beside Isabella and said, "Babe, you like being able to shop like this?"

"It's cool, why? What kind of question is that?" Isabella responded.

"I don't know just asking, you seem happy when you shop," Tamir said.

Isabella stopped and looked at Tamir and asked, "Hey, what's that look for? What's going on?"

"Nothing babe, I'm cool, just thinking is all," he said.

"Thinking about what?" she asked.

"I don't know stuff, like the baby is on the way and things are going to change, what if you can't shop like this anymore? How would you feel? Would you lea..." he asked as Isabella interrupted.

"Hey, stop that, first of all money don't make us, secondly I know we won't be able to shop like this when the baby come that's why I'm doing all this shopping now. Lastly you have a great career and I will have one as well so we'll be fine, stop thinking negatively," Isabella waddled over to Tamir and embraced him.

Tamir finally smiled as they continued their day.

The rest of the weekend was full of fun and relaxation. The girls continued to have weird craving late at night and sent the guys on mission through the hotel and out on the town to satisfy them. Rodge was being himself, becoming the light of the town. On New Year's Eve, the friends decided to hang out on the beach and watch the fireworks. Rodge was drunk on Dom Perignon, Mai Tai's, money, and life.

As everyone on the beach began to countdown, the friends joined in, between every number Isabella and Tamir said "I love you."

Jeremy and Rasheeda kissed in between every number, and Rodge took a sip from his champagne bottle between every number.

Finally down to one "Happy New Year!" the whole beach cheered.

Rodge began to start a drunken rant, "2002 is our year, fuck all the haters, Fuck the World Bank, they lost two of the best people they ever had," just before he passed out.

"What?" Isabella said as she looked at Tamir.

"What the hell is he talking about?" Rasheeda questioned as she giggled and quickly turned to a serious tone and demeanor.

"Oh boy," Jeremy exclaimed.

"No OH Boy, we need some explanations!" Isabella said.

"Look baby I was going to tell you," Tamir began to explain,

"When Tamir? When we were out on the street?" Isabella asked.

"Jeremy when did this happen?" Rasheeda asked.

"Friday, I told you about the company cut backs that were coming, well they decided to let us go on Friday," Jeremy explained.

"Well, why the hell are we in Miami living it up as if everything is cool?" Rasheeda asked.

"Yeah and why did y'all not find it necessary to tell your life partners about a life altering event?" Isabella asked.

"Look we were going to tell y'all it's just now wasn't a good time," Tamir explained

"Ant...wrong, bad excuse!" Rasheeda said.

The girls walked away in anger as Jeremy and Tamir stood and looked on. Rodge laid peacefully on the beach passed out from the alcohol. The girls decided to stay together in Rasheeda and Jeremy's room, while the guys just wandered the beach all night trying to plan their next move and how to get their women to talk to them again.

"We gotta make this right Mir," Jeremy sighed

"Yeah I know, I was gonna say something to you sooner, I been watching Rodge, he gets money all day," Tamir replied.

"Yeah what does that have to do with us though?" Jeremy asked curiously.

"Well you think he has to worry about company cut backs or not having money?" Tamir said firmly.

"Yeah, but it ain't like he can enjoy it, always watching over his shoulder," Jeremy replied.

"Look at him!" Tamir said as he pointed at Rodge sleeping on the beach in a thousand dollar Armani linen outfit.

"Do you think he has a care in the world? When things get stressful, what does he do? Vacates," Tamir said with excitement.

"So I ask you is that not a career?" Tamir continued.

"But I can't help but to think it's wrong though," Jeremy said

"So what the bank did to us was right? What the terrorist did was right? It is not right but it happens and is a part of life. When that HR clown let me go, do you know what he said to me?" Tamir responded

"No what?" Jeremy asked.

"He said, they tried to keep me but it basically didn't make dollars or sense, which leads me to believe that's the theory of life, if it don't make dollars, it don't make sense," Tamir replied.

Jeremy and Tamir continued to talk about their lives and the potential change they were going to make in both meanings of the word. Then by the early part of the morning the plan had been set about the conversation and proposal they were going to have for Rodge.

Early that morning, the three guys were awakened in Rodge's room by the silent angry stares, and deep sighs of Rasheeda and Isabella.

Finally as Jeremy came to, Rasheeda asked, "Is there anything else you wanna tell me?"

In a groggy voice, Jeremy responded, "No baby."

"Well get up we need to talk both of you," exclaimed Isabella.

"Yeah y'all go talk about this, and let me sleep," Rodge said beginning to awaken.

"Aww, this is your fault so you need to get up too," Tamir said as he hit Rodge with a pillow.

"Don't blame him, you should have told me, I shouldn't of found out through Rodge's drunken rant," Isabella said with an attitude.

"Aww damn it, I'm up now! Let's go get some breakfast or brunch or whatever. Not that I'm going to take fault in any of the proceedings, but y'all my people so I guess I'll mediate the situation," Rodge said with a guilty tone.

They all looked at him, hit him with pillows and said, "Shut up Rodge!"

Later that day the group had lunch at a little cafe on the beach in Miami. The mood was tense, all except for Rodge with his normal carefree demeanor and his platinum framed Cartier sunglasses blocking his eyes and the evidence of the drunken binge he came of the night before. This was unchartered territory for the couples, never a real argument or even any anger. However, just as certain as the seasons change and the sunsets, this day had to come. No one could have predicted that it would have come like this or for this reason.

"Look!" Rasheeda said as she started the conversation.

"We're not mad that you lost your jobs, these things happen," she continued.

"Right the problem is you didn't tell us," Isabella interjected.

"How the hell am I supposed to say, baby I was everything yesterday but I'm nothing today, I lost my job and my tuition for school," Tamir said remorsefully.

"First off, you're not my everything because of a job or career potential, your my everything because of what we build together and the way you make me feel," Isabella replied.

"Wait a minute you guys lost your tuition too?" Rasheeda asked.

"Yup," Jeremy said as he lowered his head.

"Aww baby, I'm sorry, I can see how that would be hard to tell me or even deal with," she said in an attempt to comfort Jeremy.

"Well ok, we've dealt with the anger, let's address the issue and the realities of the potential problems," Isabella said.

"We collectively have about five thousand dollars in expenses each month without the babies. We have no income and more importantly no health insurance," Rasheeda said.

"Well we don't want y'all to worry about it, we will handle it, just go to school and focus on the pregnancies," Tamir offered.

"Well, how are we not supposed to worry? And we are not about to be in the dark again," Isabella asked with concern.

"Well I got a plan," Tamir said.

"No Mir," Jeremy interrupted.

"Here we go again, no Mir what?" Isabella and Rasheeda said angrily.

I figured, we'll get down with Rodge for a minute until things come back around for us and the economy picks back up," Tamir said confidently.

Rodge catching the tail end of Jeremy's statement almost chokes and spits out his cherry Moet Mimosa.

"Get down with who?" Rodge asked.

"You," Tamir responded.

"What? Have y'all completely lost your minds?" Isabella asked.

"Yeah Mir, what the hell? I said I would cover your expenses. I didn't say you gotta pay me back or work with me," Rodge said.

"Well, what am I supposed to do? Have my family live off of you?" Tamir questioned.

"Naw, but you my brother and if the role was reversed, you'd do the same for me. Besides you ain't built for this," said Rodge.

"So what am I built for? Built like my **father**, run when shit gets hard?" Tamir said almost tearful as he got up abruptly and walked off.

Isabella tried to stop him and Rodge and Rasheeda called him. He continued to storm down the beach.

"Just let him cool off, this is a touchy subject for him. You know this is rather why his **dad** left. And being that we're here in the wake of a crisis partying in Miami, makes him feel bad," Jeremy explained.

"Damn he could have at least talked to me before making this decision though," Rodge said.

"Rodge what you don't know, I guess what no one knows is that he's been watching how you move and comparing it to what he's been trying to do, not like envious but just comparing. I believe he thought about this the instant they let us go," Jeremy explained.

On the plane on the way back to Philly, Isabella attempted to talk to a quiet Tamir, who hadn't spoken since the cafe.

"Babe, Babe, please talk to me," Isabella pleaded in a low concerned voice.

Tamir looked Isabella directly in her eye and rubbed her pregnant stomach and said, "I won't let y'all down."

He seemed to have a fire burning in his pupils with a strong calculating look on his face. Isabella tried to engage in more conversation, but he just turned and looked out the window. This worried Isabella, she got up and went up a couple rows to Rodge and asked him to attempt to talk to Tamir.

Rodge sat down and had a straight face, which was rarity for Rodge.

He opened with, "Mir, everything that glitters ain't gold. This is not all what it seems; it's not just fast money, cars, and women."

Tamir looked at Rodge emotionless without saying a word.

"I know it's a tough situation you in now, but that's one of the dues you have to pay. I would rather have your situation than mine. Have a beautiful woman waiting for me at home with a beautiful child on the way. The truth is I envy you guys, that's why I'm always over the house and hang with y'all all the time," he continued.

"Yeah...well you have no worries, like, how is your family going to eat, or is your beautiful wife to be going to get fed up with your lack of finances, and seek better, or more," Tamir finally said.

"Yeah, well in life's card game you can only play with the hand that you're dealt to the best of your ability," Rodge said.

"Yeah well, what part of the game is this? It just started and I'm forced to fold my hand already?" Tamir replied.

"Well who said you have to fold? That's the beauty of the struggle of life, finding creative ways to get out of situations," Rodge explained.

"Well look Mr. Metaphor, I gotta feed and take care of my family. I'm asking you as my brother and best friend, are you going to let me in or what?" Tamir firmly asked.

"Well you're a grown man, so you're entitled to make your own decisions. So I'll put you on, but you promise me this, if at any time you wanna stop or you feel you can't handle it, you let me know. This game can chew you up and spit you out. Me knowing this and that, this is not really you. I am taking the responsibility for you. This is temporary, you hear me? Temporary!" Rodge said as the two shook hands in agreement and hugged.

"Now put a smile on your face and embrace your wifey, she's worried sick about you," Rodge said as he went back to his seat.

Isabella walked back over to her man and greeted his smile with her smile.

The two have developed a way of communicating without speaking.

Holding hands as Isabella rested her head on Tamir's shoulder, he whispered in her ear, "I love you," and rested his hand on her stomach.

Back at Jeremy and Rasheeda's seats, Jeremy had been focusing his attention on a marine in uniform a few rows up. For some reason he could not break his focus of the soldier as if he were glowing. He thought to himself, *"He's a fighter, I'm a fighter."*

Rasheeda looked at her fiancé as if she were reading his mind, and said, "Baby I don't think so."

Jeremy was oblivious to her comment, as he fantasized about fighting in a war for his country, more importantly for his family and loved ones. He began to hear the words of his good friends Shawn and Juwan, about fight for the freedoms and liberties of the country. Contrary to the plans Tamir had set, Jeremy had in that instance planted the seeds of his own plans.

The next day Tamir and Jeremy wasted no time getting their plans underway. Jeremy kissed his fiancé and excitedly rushed out the door, with his cell phone dialing Juwan as he exited. Tamir followed behind him in a different direction, headed to Rodge's Range Rover parked up the street. Today was going to be his first lesson in the industry that was the gift and the curse of thousands of neighborhoods around the country. The industry that rewarded many but plagued more, the plague was not on Tamir's mind nor was conscience, all he saw a way to capture means to provide for his family. Meanwhile, Jeremy was on the prowl for information to justify and validate the decision he made within his self. He was going to be a marine. He called Juwan on his way to a local recruitment office. Between the call to his friend and salesmanship of the recruiter, the justification was found. He was told about all the benefits he and his family would receive and the income he would receive. This was it, the answer. He could be a fighter for a seemingly good cause and provide for his family. Two things stood in the way of his final commitment, the ASVAB test and more importantly the acceptance of his wife to be.

On the other side of town there was a different lesson being learned. As The Notorious B.I.G.'s, "Ten Crack Commandments," blared from the Range Rover Speakers, Rodge asked, "Do you know why we listening to this over and over?"

"Yeah cause biggie the truth!" Tamir responded as he nodded his head to the beat.

"No, what he's said is the truth," Rodge said as he paused the track.

"Listen Mr. Brain, just like any banking or investment business there are rules and regulations, i.e., ten crack commandments, now listen again," Rodge explained as he resumed the track.

"#1, don't let anyone know how much you holding or worth; #2, never let anyone one know what you're thinking or what you about to do; #3, never trust anyone, well other than me, remember the business you in, at the end of the day we all criminals; #4, never get high on your own supply, matter fact you should never get high, keep your head clear, let me catch you getting high, I'm going to fuck you up myself; #5, never bring your work home, money, dope, whatever; #6, I couldn't say it better than biggie myself, no credit, if you think a crack head paying you back forget it; #7, keep family and business apart; #8, never keep no work on you, it's an easy loss for you and come up for stick up kids; #9, If you ain't getting arrested stay away from cops, streets is always watching and if they start talk about you talking to the law, it's over; #10, consignment, it may look cool and seem to make sense like dude hit you with a key and tell you to bring whatever back and you keep the rest, but if you ain't got the clientele and can't move it, they still want they money, this ain't like a bank where they'll foreclose on your house or repossess your car. They taking your life straight like that. So that's the basics, you got it?" Rodge questioned.

"I think so," Tamir responded.

Later that day, back across town, Jeremy was rehearsing to himself how he was going to break the news to Rasheeda about his decision. As he pulled up, Tamir and Rodge are pulling up as well. As they exited their vehicles, Isabella and Rasheeda's parents are leaving the house. As everyone waited, they got comfortable and stared at each other in silence with something to say.

Rasheeda opens up and said, "Baby, how was your day?"

Before Jeremy got to respond, Isabella and Rasheeda said with excitement, "We got good news!"

Isabella continued, "Our parents came over and we told them the situation."

Rodge interrupted, "Oh boy I see where this going. I'm out."

With that statement, Rodge kissed the ladies on their cheeks shook, Tamir and Jeremy's hands and told Tamir to get with him later, and left.

"Anyway!" Rasheeda exclaimed with an attitude.

"Hold up!" Tamir responded in anger.

"Why would you tell them? Now, they're going to have their opinions, not to mention they probably already on the phone with our moms," Tamir continued.

Isabella interjected, "Calm down, it's not like that, let us tell you the good news, damn!"

"Ok babe your right, but I think the plan was to let everybody know at once if they had to know at all," Tamir responded.

"We ain't gonna throw stones about when to tell people important shit alright!" Rasheeda said angrily.

"Ok so look my **dad** said he can get y'all down at the plant where he works," Isabella said with excitement.

"Look babe, I appreciate that but you know what I wanted to do and plus I'm not a laborer," Tamir explained.

"What the hell does that mean?" Isabella asked.

"You know what, it don't even matter. Y'all need to realize we have two extra mouths to feed in less than three months so get off that pride shit," she continued.

"Hold up! Y'all went ahead and started thinking for us, talking for us, and making moves for us! We men, we doing what we gotta do! I got a plan and I know my brother got a plan too!" Tamir yelled.

Now this was a different type of situation for both couples the first for both couples. While they have been in the real world for a short period of time and they have had their share of problems. None had brought them to the crossroads they seemed to be at now. The room was tense and clearly divided. The only person who was not active in the ongoing argument was Jeremy, who was in his own world. While he stared on as if he was paying attention and involved, he zoned out. It was clear to him for some reason that now was the time to let everyone know what his plan was.

"I'm going to be a marine!" Jeremy exclaimed.

Just then in the midst of arguing and yelling, the room instantly got quiet and all eyes focused on Jeremy.

"You're going to what?" they all asked.

Jeremy looked at Rasheeda, took her hand and said softly, "Baby, this is it, this is my plan, this is what I have to do."

Rasheeda snatched her hand away and said, "No, No, this is not what you have to do, this is what your pride is pushing you to do."

Tamir jumped in with disgust and said, "Yo, man what is this? You tripping, a Marine though? What happened to the plan?"

"This is my plan. I'm not you or Rodge, I can't do the drug thing," Jeremy responded.

Isabella grabbed Tamir's arm and said, "What? Drug thing? Rodge, oh no, isn't this the day of surprises."

"Y'all are seriously tripping, I know things are scary right now and they look desperate but y'all are not thinking clearly," she continued.

"I don't know about him but I'm definitely thinking clearly. I think this is the clearest I've ever thought," Jeremy replied in a calm deliberate way.

"Think about it, we'll have a home, benefits, and financial security," Jeremy explained.

"But at what cost? This risk of losing you? I'd rather struggle and be broke with you than be rich without you," Rasheeda explained.

The couples went to their corresponding rooms, each pleading their cases. By the end of the night, the house was quiet but no one slept, Tamir and Isabella lay in bed and stared at each other, without saying a word. After a whole night of arguing, crying, and explanations, the two had nothing further to say. Down the hall, Rasheeda and Jeremy lay still staring at the ceiling. Jeremy rubbed Rasheeda's stomach as the baby began to move.

After about a week, things began to get back to normal, the girls seem to accept the paths that guys have decided to take. Feeling that there was no way the change their minds, the love they had for their men, forced them to go along with their plans. Tuesday morning, January 29, 2002, Jeremy stood by the front door with a packed bag holding Rasheeda's hand as she told him how sad she was that he was leaving.

He tried to console her and said, "Baby it's only eight weeks, it'll go by like that and I'll write you and call when I can."

"Yeah but it's not the same, we need to see you when we awaken and before we go to bed," Rasheeda pleaded as she rubbed her stomach.

Upstairs Isabella and Tamir were having a similar conversation. While Tamir returned each night, Isabella felt his risk of not returning was far greater.

Two soldiers preparing for training that would inevitably train them for two different wars, one for the country one against the country. Nonetheless, they were doing this for their families. The sounds of two horns stopped the farewells, Rodge's and the recruiter who pulled up right behind him. As the two stepped out the house they stopped and looked at each other.

"I hope you know what you doing, brother," Jeremy said.

"Likewise," Tamir replied as he hugged his brother.

"Don't get out there and get killed, we need you here," Tamir continued.

"Yeah I can definitely say the same for you. I know that fast money, cars, and women, impress you but remember that ain't you, Money, you're smarter than everyone out there, don't get caught up," Jeremy said.

"I respect that good brother. I'm always here, you better know that," Tamir responded.

With that masculine yet emotional goodbye, the two headed to their corresponding rides and went their separate ways.

Rodge yelled out the window, "Be safe homie!"

Jeremy smiled and waved his fist in response.

Two weeks have passed since Jeremy's departure. It was 5:00 AM in a dusty military barrack lined with twenty men who for their own reason have decided to serve their country. The day was beginning; the men are suiting up ready to start another day of intense training.

As Jeremy laced his boots up, he kissed a picture of Rasheeda, as he does every day, he sighed, "I hope you understand, Shit, I hope it's worth it."

Seven hundred miles away, back home in Philadelphia; Tamir was just getting in the house, ending his day.

Isabella, sleeping rolled over in a groggy voice and said, "I hope it's worth it baby."

Tamir sat down on the bed, leaned over and kissed his bride to be and said, "It will be baby, shhh...go back to sleep."

Just down the hall, Rasheeda, laid awake in her and Jeremy's bed. It had been almost a week since her last phone conversation with him and a day since she received his letter. Being completely in-touch with her future husband, she sensed he was changing already. It was not anything major just minor changes in his words and his overall tone. He was becoming tougher, angrier, and anxious to battle, he was becoming a marine. She blamed these changes on his new surroundings, and the company he kept. Jeremy was not easily influenced by any means; this change was not really a change at all. His fighter spirit that had been encased in him for so long had finally had a chance to come out, it was in good company, and it was encouraged. The subtleties of his **mother** were becoming more distant in his heart and mind; he became less understanding of his **father**'s death, or of his best friend almost being taken away by terrorist. The thought of the same terrorist threatening his and his family's livelihood seem to cause rage to accompany the fighter's spirit and its entrance.

Chapter : 7

Later that day, Jeremy, sat with his fellow marines and ate lunch in the mess hall. The other privates took an instant liking to Jeremy; this was due to his personality and ability to get along with everyone. They sat around much as they did every day, talking about everything from where they were from to the sexiest celebrities. The most time was spent talking about their impatience, willingness, and desire to fight and kill. Jeremy was no stranger to diversity being as though he was a white boy growing up in West Philadelphia. This was the most diversity he had never seen, there were people of all races together in one room, for one reason, one cause, and dressed completely the same. He stared and thought for a moment about how it was when he and his **mother** moved to West Philadelphia from South Philadelphia. It was like the taking of grain of salt and dropping it in a peppershaker.

Summer of 1992, an eight year old Jeremy watching his **mother** and uncle's move their belongings into their new home. He noticed the whole neighborhood watching them as they moved in. The attention was mainly coming from a house across the street. A young Tamir stared curiously at this sight that he never seen before, a white family was moving to his predominately-black neighborhood. Jeremy and his mother were the only white people on Aldan St. They were the only white family in a twenty-block radius.

Jeremy being social, shot across the street and approached Tamir.

"Hey," he said.

"Hey," Tamir responded.

"What are y'all doing here?" Tamir asked.

"I don't know," Jeremy replied as he shrugged his shoulders.

"I mean your, white," said Tamir.

"So, your black," replied Jeremy

"White people are rich, they don't live around here," Tamir replied.

Jeremy's mom overheard that comment and said, "Aren't you cute, who told you that?"

"Everyone knows that, that's how it is on TV," Tamir said.

"Well, that's why they call it an idiot box," Christine replied with a chuckle.

Just then, Tamir's mom came flying out of the house in a robe and slippers yelling, "Boy I been calling you for twenty minutes, what are you doing out here?"

She grabbed Tamir by his arm and asked, "I'm sorry, is he bothering you?"

"No just enlightening us with the ways of the world," Christine replied.

"I'm going to enlighten his behind if he don't get in there and clean that room," Tamir's mom responded.

Christine laughed and said, "I know the feeling, and by the way I'm Christine, as you can see, I'm getting settled as your new neighbor."

"I see...I'm Gladys. Girl, if you need anything feel free," Tamir's **mother** replied.

From that day on, two strong bonds were formed, Jeremy and Tamir, of which Jeremy was often introduced as, "The white friend who was not rich, like us."

In addition, Gladys and Christine, who spent time over each other's house every day sharing everything from parental and cooking advice to the occasional beer. They became second **mothers** to each other's child.

Back on Parris Island, Jeremy's commanding officer called him into an office with a Lieutenant.

"Private, we are impressed to say the least with your performance these past couple of weeks," the Sergeant said.

"Yes Private, your accuracy on the range is incredible and your focus and shooting is incredible," the Lieutenant agreed.

"With that Private, we have decided to train you in a program a little different than the rest," the Lieutenant continued.

Jeremy had a confused look on his face as the Lieutenant placed a camouflaged case on the desk.

"Go ahead open it," the Lieutenant commanded.

Jeremy opened the case to find a rifle. The rifle was not like the rifles the unit trained. This was a sniper rifle; without hesitation, Jeremy quickly assembled the sniper rifle part by part. The CO and Lieutenant smiled, nodded and whispered to each other in agreement with the moment. Jeremy seemed to do exactly what they expected. After he assembled the weapon, Jeremy stood at attention and asked permission to speak freely. The Lieutenant agreed.

"Why sir, that is why me, why this?" Jeremy asked.

"I'll take this one," the CO said.

"Well it's like this private. We have noticed certain qualities in you that none of your other unit possess, with that we decided that we have special missions that the Marines can benefit from your abilities," the CO continued.

The Lieutenant interjected, "You should be honored private, this is a damn privilege."

"I am Sir, I just wondered why I was chosen, as I'm no different than any of the other privates," Jeremy said.

"That's where you're wrong; you possess a silent killer aspect about you. You are timid and calm on the outside but we know on the inside lies an assassin awaiting the proper opportunity to come out," the CO explained.

In Philadelphia, Tamir was posted on the corner in Rodge's Range Rover. He watched the underworld commerce and traffic commence with his calculating mind and eyes. Watching the traffic going in and out of the bar, the crap games on the corner, the whoremongers posted by the strip bar, and his drug traffic up and down the street, his take from this action was about three to four grand per week. This was more than enough to support his family, but something was changing rather evolving in his mind. Maybe it was the influence of Rodge or the comfort and luxury of the Range Rover seats that hoisted him while he watched the emerging illegal empire. It could have been his queen at home that was going to give birth to his prince. The feeling that he wanted to give them the world without fret; whatever it was it was growing inside of him. In mid-thought Rodge popped in and handed Tamir a, .45 caliber handgun.

"What's this?" Tamir asked in a nervous tone.

"Aww homie, stop bitching and take it. This is your next lesson. If you think everyone is just gonna sit out here and let you stack up, you tripping. Now, I'm not saying get out here and wild cowboy it, but you need to be able to protect yourself," Rodge explained

With that statement, Tamir took his new tool and admired it. He thought about the power he now held in his hand, the power to stop a life and protect his and his family's livelihood.

The two drove off, Tamir asked, "Where are we going now?"

"Well my niece and nephew are due in a few weeks and I need to go get baby shower gifts," Rodge replied.

"Oh cool what did you have in mind?" Tamir asked.

"Nothing major, I was thinking car seats and strollers," Rodge said with a smirk.

They finally pulled up at an old factory.

"Rodge, you gotta hook up on baby gifts? Tamir asked.

How cheap can you be Uncle Rodge?" Tamir continued with playful disgust.

Rodge did not say anything; he just continued to smile and sounded his horn. At the sound of the horn, the two huge doors opened. Rodge continued inside. Parked side by side were two brand new 2002 Mercedes-Benz E430s. One was Blue the other was red. In the back of the cars we Mercedes-Benz car seats, they jumped out of the Range Rover, Rodge gave his keys to the worker as another worker rushed over and handed him the Mercedes keys.

"What Mir, why so quiet?" Rodge asked.

"Hold up one second," Rodge said as he turned to the worker that was already in his truck and smiling.

"Turn that damn music down, drive like you got some sense, and make sure you fill up my tank and you better not use that 89 shit again I need 93. And my truck better be out my spot in an hour no hit stops," Rodge continued.

"Don't you mean pit stops?" Tamir asked.

"Naw, hit stops is when this clown uses my car to try to get some ass," Rodge explained.

They all laughed.

"So which one you want Red or Blue?" Rodge asked.

Amazed, Tamir quickly responded, "Blue is our favorite color."

The two drove off headed back into the city to Tamir's house, which was already programed in the Navigation systems as, "The love nest."

A few weeks later on an unseasonably warm Saturday morning; Rasheeda was walking around frantic and full of stress. Her frenzy did not go unnoticed. Isabella was in the kitchen cooking and yelling,

"Girl, will you calm down? Today is just like any other day," Isabella said.

Isabella was wrong. Today was a different day, for today was the ladies' baby shower. Everyone was coming over but there was one special guest, Jeremy. He was on his way home after graduating boot camp. Tamir and Rodge were sleeping in the living room with controllers in their hand. They had a long night and a dispute. Whenever they have a dispute, they settle it in a series of Madden football games. In addition, when they have a long night Rodge normally sleeps over.

"Wake the hell up damn, do something, clean or something!" Rasheeda yelled as she kicked the guys.

"What girl, damn," Tamir responded with a groggy tone.

"Don't what me! Everyone is coming over and your brother is coming home. There's so much to be done and y'all lazy asses just laying around."

"Ok, ok," Rodge replied as he began to get up.

Isabella waddled into the living room with two plates and said, "Good Morning Papi, don't worry about her. I been dealing with her neurotic self all morning."

"It's ok, I would expect you to be that way too if you hadn't seen me in eight weeks," Tamir replied as he gave Isabella a kiss.

"Y'all are missing the point it's not her missing him, it's something bigger," Rodge said with a serious face and tone.

"Do y'all realize she has not had sex in over eight weeks?" Rodge said as he laughed.

"I heard that Rodge, that's why you need to take your water head home somewhere," Rasheeda said.

Everyone laughed as their **mother**s rushed in the front door like a platoon of storm troopers, armed with gifts and pots full of food.

"Damn, what they got keys now?" Tamir asked.

"Shut up boy and get outside and get the rest of the stuff!" Tamir's mom said.

Tamir and Rodge rushed over and greeted the mothers. Tamir's mother and Jeremy's mother rode together and Isabella and Rasheeda's mother rode with Amanda. Jeremy's mother quickly put her things down and ran to Rasheeda and said, "Hey Mama, today is the big day our baby comes home."

"I know Mom, I'm so nervous," Rasheeda replied.

"Nervous for what?" Rasheeda's mother asked.

"Look at how big I am," Rasheeda replied.

"Oh girl hush, as much as that boy loves and misses you," Isabella's mother said.

"Not to mention as horny as he probably is," Rodge joked.

"Shut up Rodge!" the whole room said and began to laugh.

"I don't have to take this, I'm shutting up," Rodge said.

"We should probably head to the airport to go get him now anyway. His plane lands in a half hour," Tamir said.

With that the guys kissed the room full of moms and moms-to-be and headed on their way. They decided to pick up Jeremy in the car that Rodge gave him and Rasheeda a few weeks ago. As they pulled up at the airport arrivals door, Jeremy stood with his bags in a marines' uniform and hat. Rodge and Tamir barely recognized their best friend. His posture was firm, and his physique was noticeably toned. He looks like a walking recruiting advertisement.

"At ease soldier!" Tamir called out of the window.

Tamir and Rodge jumped out of the car to greet their friend of which they have not seen in weeks that felt like years.

"I'm back!" Jeremy said in excitement.

"I missed y'all man seriously," he continued.

"We missed you too Sgt. Rock head," Rodge replied.

Jeremy began to admire the shiny red Mercedes the two had pulled up in and said, "Rodge, you shouldn't have."

"I didn't," Rodge replied.

"Aww man stop playing give me the keys," Jeremy said.

"Give you the key to what?" Rodge asked.

"My car!" Jeremy said.

"Your car? What makes you think this is your car?" Rodge asked.

"Aside from the car seat in the back, my baby wrote me and told me and sent me a picture," Jeremy explained.

"Damn that woman got a big mouth," Rodge laughed and said.

"Here you go punk," Rodge said as he handed Jeremy the keys.

"This is nice, thank you so much," Jeremy said as he pulled off.

The three pulled up to their house that was covered in a collage of decoration that were a mix of "It's A Boy," "It's A Girl," and, "Welcome Home." Rasheeda and Jeremy's **mother**, Christine, were already outside waiting for Jeremy. As he stepped out of the car, they took a second to take in the sight of the new Jeremy. Christine was impressed at how handsome her son looked and Rasheeda was amazed with how sexy her fiancé looked.

"There they are, my two favorite ladies in the whole world," Jeremy said with a large smile on his face.

He grabbed Rasheeda and kissed her passionately and deeply for almost a minute.

"Ah... hmm...," Christine said.

"Oh sorry **Mom**," Jeremy said.

"What I tell you? Horny!" Rodge said as he and Tamir gathered Jeremy's belongings out of the car.

Tamir and Rodge laughed.

As they all walked into the house full of women, Isabella stopped them, kissed Tamir and gave Jeremy a hug.

"OK brother, it's good to see you, I'm happy your home. Now, y'all have to go," she said.

"What do you mean go? We just got here," Tamir said.

"It's a baby shower babe, it's all women here," Isabella said.

"Yeah, but I thought it was a welcome home party too," Tamir replied.

"That's tonight, now leave!" Isabella's mom called from the dining room.

"You know what? We don't have to take this, we're leaving." Tamir said.

Later that day at Rodge's Penthouse, in Center City, the guys sat at Rodge's bar and talked over a few drinks.

"So what is it like? I mean boot camp, being a marine," Tamir asked.

"It feels great, well the training wasn't but you get used to it," Jeremy replied.

"Yeah, I guess but I still feel you should've stayed here and got money with us," Rodge said.

"You don't understand it's not about money. I mean the money is great and I appreciate all you guys help, but it's more of a satisfying feeling of doing something to feel purposeful," Jeremy explained.

"I guess I dig that," Rodge said.

"I mean there were so many people there all united for the same cause, to fight for this country. They trained me to be a sniper," Jeremy said.

"A sniper for what?" Tamir asked.

"They will give me special assignments to take out key opposing figures in battle," Jeremy explained.

"So, you are like a hit man for the marines?" Rodge said.

"Yeah I guess you could say that," Jeremy replied.

"That's crazy, but cool at the same time," Rodge said.

That night they had dinner with all of their family and friends. Everyone was amazed at the change in Jeremy. He was the same person full of love and humor, but he had a noticeable aura of a soldier.

Later that night Jeremy and Rasheeda made love as if it was their first time, and as if she weren't pregnant. Rasheeda fell asleep in Jeremy's muscular arms. She felt extra secure with him tonight. Not because of his strength, training, or muscles, but because he was there with her. They had passed a test of time, she felt secure in that her man loved her no matter how big or small she was. No matter how strong or sexy he was, he was truly hers, well hers and their baby's that was due in a couple of weeks.

Early on a March morning at about 3:00 AM, as Tamir and Isabella lay peacefully in their bed, he felt something warm and wet in the bed. He thought maybe he wet himself. He checked his pants, he was dry. He turned to Isabella as she was crying.

"Oh baby its ok, accidents happen," he said as he reached to console her.

"It's not that Pa, my water broke," she said.

"It's time?" Tamir asked in nervous excitement.

"Yes baby, it's time," Isabella answered with teary eyes and a smile.

Tamir softly wiped her tears away and gently grabbed her face and said, "I love you so much baby, let's do this."

He kissed her, hopped out of bed and rushed for the packed Louis Vuitton bags.

He then opened the door and screamed down the hallway, "It's time let's go. I'm about to be a **father!**"

After a few moments, Rasheeda and Jeremy rushed down the hall realizing what Tamir yelled. Rasheeda came prepared with her matching Louis Vuitton luggage filled with her belongings in case she was to go into labor. She rushed to her best friend's side and began to do her hair. She quickly wrapped it and covered it with a Gucci scarf.

"Girl this will have to do for now, I'll braid it when we get in your room," Rasheeda said.

The four piled into Tamir and Isabella's car. Everyone was on the phone, Tamir with the doctor, Rasheeda with the **mothers**, and Amanda, and Jeremy with Rodge. Tamir rushed through the empty Philadelphia streets in the German luxury car; although he was driving it like an Italian sports car.

As the cityscape passed through the rear-view mirrors, his life flashed before him like a silent movie, he saw his mom and her raising him and his siblings and Jeremy's **mother**. He saw his **father** leaving and Jeremy's **father** being killed. He saw his whole relationship with Isabella. He saw her smile, her tears, and her peacefully sleeping. A tear slowly rolled down his cheek.

Isabella, as if she was in Tamir's head, turned and wiped the tear from his face and rubbed his neck and said, "Its ok baby, I know you'll be a great **father** and I love you. We're going to do this together."

He smiled and said, "Ok baby I know," as he rubbed her leg.

Finally, after the thirty-minute roller coaster car ride, they arrived at Children's Hospital of Philadelphia. The sun had still yet to rise over Philadelphia, yet inside the hospital the doctor's nurses and patients were buzzing like bees in a beehive. The couples while not completely dressed still managed to look like they stepped out of a magazine. Both couples were draped in luxurious nightwear. The women accessorized with Prada and Gucci clutch purses while their men lugged their overnight Louis Vuitton bags. At one point, one of the assisting orderlies asked his colleague what celebrity they may have been. A few hours later the commotion had settled much as Isabella had settled in her room with Jeremy, Tamir, and Rasheeda at her side. Jeremy and Tamir played cards while Rasheeda braided Isabella's hair. Rodge accompanied by one of his workers armed with baby outfits and boxes of sneakers. Rodge sat the gifts down and dismissed his worker.

"Hey Mama, finally ready to have my nephew?" Rodge asked as his kissed Isabella on the cheek.

Everything was calm in room 938 at 11:00 AM. Isabella was relaxed. Rasheeda alternated rubbing her pregnant stomach and her best friend's stomach.

There was a slight commotion down the hall. The Grandmother squad had arrived. All the parents were making their way down the hall with gifts in tow. The nurses attempted to stop them as they were clearly over the number of allowed visitors.

"What the hell do you mean wait in the waiting area? That's my grandbaby being born!" Isabella's mother, Abigail argued.

Gladys, Tamir's mother, also argued, "That's my grandson too and grandparents as chic as us don't wait in a waiting room."

"Ma'am please calm down this is the hospital's policy," the nurse responded.

"Babe you might want to handle our parents before we get thrown out," Isabella said to Tamir.

Jeremy, Tamir, and Rodge rushed to the hall to greet the angry mothers, they decided to wait in the waiting room to allow the parents to have time with Isabella. Isabella's father spent a few moments with his daughter and returned to the waiting room. The guys attempted to engage Isabella's father in dialogue. To no avail, he sat quietly and gazed disappointedly almost angrily at Tamir.

Finally, Tamir broke the tense silence and asked, "Is there something bothering you, Mr. Rodriguez?"

Tamir asked but he knew what was wrong. It was the lifestyle Tamir lived with Isabella, the way Tamir opted to provide for Juan's daughter.

"I trusted you!" Juan, Isabella's **father** said angrily.

"It's bad enough you took my daughter from me, you made her pregnant and have the gall to sit in front of me and ask is there something bothering me. You are bothering me, you petty drug dealer!" Juan further explained.

"Wait a minute Mr. Rodriguez!" Tamir firmly interjected.

Juan got up and approached Tamir.

"Am I beneath you? Is the way I provide for my family, beneath you?" he asked.

"No sir," Tamir replied.

"You were in a bad situation, yet my faith, respect, and belief in you assured me that you would do right by my family and daughter. I even pulled some strings to get you down at the plant with me, and you, you turn your nose up to me, you and your punk ass friends," Juan said as he pointed at Jeremy and his friends.

Tamir became upset, rose from his chair and said, "With all due respect Juan, I am a grown ass man responsible for my family and the choices I decide to make. I do not frown upon you. In fact, I have the upmost respect for you. But you cannot judge me for you are not me and Isabella is grown and now my responsibility."

Juan stood silent as if he were taking in what Tamir said. He then quickly lunged at Tamir. Jeremy and Rodge jumped in between the two. Jeremy took Juan to the ground and restrained him. Everyone rushed from Isabella's side and ran to the hallway. Gladys took Tamir outside. Abigail helped her husband from the floor and walked him into Isabella's room. Jeremy and Rodge sat in the waiting room talking about what had just happened, with Rasheeda sitting on Jeremy's lap.

Outside, Tamir and his **mother** talked. Tamir still upset explained, "That man don't know me **Mom**. He doesn't know what I do."

Gladys interrupted, "But he does son, we all do. What do you think, we're stupid? Son, you kids have more now, than you did when you were working."

"Why didn't you say anything **Mom**?" a puzzled Tamir asked.

"Well son, I know you, I raised you and I know more importantly what's in your heart. You are beautiful and pure. You are doing what you feel you have to do to provide for your family. I cannot stand in the way of that; while it may be a bad way to do it, you are doing it, which is more than I could say for your **father**. You see he is a piece of shit; he is ugly inside, a bad person. He ran from my side when responsibility appeared," Gladys explained.

"I'm sorry **Mom**," Tamir said.

"Don't be sorry son, be smart. I know you're going to find your way but know what your risking and the consequences of your wrongdoings, and son, go back to school. My son is going to become an investment banker," replied Gladys.

With these caring words, Tamir hugged and kissed his **mother** and they walked back inside.

Meanwhile, back in Isabella's room, Isabella and her parents discussed the altercation.

"Papa, why here, why now?" Isabella asked.

"Because it needed to be said. I did not raise you to be like this. You are independent and strong, to be a powerful lawyer. Everyone else ignores this nonsense. Everything that glitters isn't gold, I cannot sit back and watch someone ruin your life or the values I instilled in you," Juan explained.

"Regardless Juan this is a day of joy, your daughter is giving birth today. She does not need this drama and aggravation," Abigail said.

"He's wrong Abi, and you know it. This is our baby girl. He spits on me and my job, the job that provided for you Isabella and got you into school!" Juan replied.

"Pa, he does not spit on you. He's a little lost but we will be fine," Isabella said.

In the waiting room, another commotion was brewing as Rasheeda's water broke.

"I can't believe my water broke in front of all of you," Rasheeda said.

"Well babe actually on me," Jeremy said jokingly.

The nurses quickly registered and admitted Rasheeda. They were able to put Rasheeda in the same room as Isabella. A little after midnight after a busy day of labor, family quarrels, laughter and bonding, Rasheeda's contractions were close and she was 9.5 centimeters dilated. It was time; the love that was growing inside her stomach was ready to make an appearance in the world. Jeremy looked on and held Rasheeda's hand.

They both had tears, Jeremy whispered, "You ready baby?"

"As ready as I'm going to be," Rasheeda responded with a nervous smile.

"Well I'm here," Jeremy assured as he gently squeezed her hand.

"So am I," Rasheeda's **mother**, Janice said as she held her other hand.

The doctor interrupted, "That's it ten centimeters, we're ready this baby is ready to come out."

The nurses wheeled Rasheeda down to the delivery room, pass a waiting room of anxious parents and grandparents-to-be, Isabella laid smiling and staring at her friend being wheeled away.

The doctor came in and said jokingly, "You still in labor? Let's have a look and listen."

He examined Isabella and looked at the monitor.

"Hmm this doesn't seem right," the doctor said.

"What is it?" Tamir asked.

"Just a minute," the doctor replied.

The baby monitor starts to sound. The baby's heart rate began to drop.

Isabella began to panic and asked, "What is happening? Oh my god, what is going on?"

Tamir rushed to the waiting room to get Gladys and Isabella's parents. Abigail rushed to her daughter's side and began to cry.

"Clear this room, we have to get to an OR stat!" the doctor demanded.

Confused, Tamir ran behind the stretcher carrying his fiancé and unborn child. As the stretcher entered the operating room the nurses stopped Tamir, Rodge caught his best friend as he began to fall to the floor.

"That's my life in there and they can't even tell me what is happening," Tamir said.

"Look at me, Look at me!" Rodge demanded.

"It's going to be OK, I promise we're strong, Isabella, you and that baby," he continued.

As they walked back to the waiting room, the alarms blared from the operating room.

The PA system blared, "All available maternity residents and nurses to Operating room 515."

Isabella was in this room. Tamir pushed Rodge off and ran past the nurses into the operating room.

He cried and yelled, "Baby I'm here!"

The orderlies and security wrestled Tamir back out of the operating room.

"I just want to know what is going on, my babies need me, get off of me!" Tamir yelled while he cried.

To his side, Rodge and Juan ran and attempted to fight off the guards.

"Look it's going to be ok, just wait here. We will be back in a few minutes and you can come in then," the chief nurse explained.

As Juan and Rodge carried Tamir away, he watched the OR door swing closed. He saw Isabella lay unconscious surrounded by blood. He broke down and cried. His whole world seemed to teeter in an uncertain balance. Abigail, Gladys and Christine waited to comfort him. They were all in tears.

Abigail reached in and said, "It's going to be fine I promise."

Abigail uncertain and in an anxious pain used all the strength inside of her to secure her son to be. She was also assuring herself. Tamir thanked everyone, gave Abigail a hug, kiss on the cheek, and walked to the window to be alone. He stared out the window at the city that made him. Juan watched Tamir and finally got up and walked over to him, everyone tried to stop him. He ignored them, walked over to Tamir, and firmly grabbed his shoulder. Tamir turned to Juan and look him directly in his eyes with anger.

Juan said, "It's ok," as he shook Tamir's hand.

"I'm sorry, Tamir and thank you," he continued.

He pulled Tamir in with the handshake and hugged him. Tamir tried to stand tall and fight his emotions but the tears streamed. Juan saw how protective Tamir was and how much he cared for his daughter. The pride he initially had for Tamir had returned.

An hour past and Tamir still sat silently looking out the window. Jeremy came back into the room happy and smiling. He had yet noticed the mood of the room.

"Why the long faces?" Jeremy asked as he walked toward his best friend.

Tamir turned and revealed his teary eyes, he tried to smile but it was as if the muscles in his face were strained.

"What up man? Is Isabella alright? Where is she? Where's the baby?" Jeremy asked frantically.

As Tamir reached out to his friend, the nurse burst through the door.

"They're ok, the baby and the **mother**," the nurse happily advised.

"Can we see them?" Tamir asked.

"Sure, in just a few moments, we are getting them settled into the room," the nurse replied.

Relief settled over the room; the tension had finally broken.

The next day the new **mother**s and children lay in their room, seemingly exhausted from the labor that took place the day prior. Armed with gifts and clothes the proud **father**s emerged with Rodge.

"Hey Mama, how are you?" Tamir asked.

"I'm ok Papi," Isabella replied in a tired tone.

"You know how scared I was yesterday, I can't stop thinking about it," Tamir said.

"Well stop thinking about it, please," Isabella asked.

In the other bed, Jeremy showed Rasheeda all the clothes he bought his new daughter.

"See baby, this one is runway all day," Jeremy said as he held up a pink and green dress.

"I don't know what kind of fashion show you talking about, but that is horrible. Where is your mom and why didn't she help you? Oh god let me get out of this place before my baby becomes the spokes model for Crayola," Rasheeda joked.

"It's not that bad Sheeda," Rodge said.

"He worked hard all morning putting stuff together," Tamir added.

"Oh yeah well, let me see what kind of Monet painting you gonna have my son wearing," Isabella said.

Over the next few days it was pretty much the same. The guys brought gifts and outfits for the babies, as the girls rejected them. Life had finally started to settle in for the new families. The girls took the summer off from work and school to take care of their children. Jeremy was back and forth between home and the base in New Jersey. Most of the change was with Tamir, the streets were absorbing him, but he was making more and more money. He was applying all the fundamentals that he learned in school and at the World Bank to his and Rodge's criminal operation. This definitely did not go without notice. Rodge's Uncle was the first to notice. It seemed all the money coming in on the fronts could not keep up with the accelerated cash flow. It was time to expand and the key person to head that expansion was Tamir.

Chapter : 8

On an early June evening, Tamir was playing with his son and goddaughter. Tamir decided to give the girls a day off. He treated Rasheeda, Isabella, their mothers, along with his and Jeremy's mother to a day at the spa. As he finally got Tamira, Jeremy's daughter to sleep beside his son, Justin, Rodge walked in.

"What up Daddy?" Rodge greeted.

"Shhh, I just got the babies to sleep, if you wake them up it's your ass," Tamir jokingly replied.

"What's good though? Where everybody at?" Rodge inquired.

"Well, you know Jeremy is on base and the girls are out. They should be back soon, they been gone all day," Tamir responded.

"Oh alright, well look...we need to talk," Rodge replied.

In their entire relationship, there had never been an uneasy feeling between Tamir and Rodge, until now. Something was in the air. Rodge felt uneasy because he was going to ask Tamir to do some- thing that would put pressure on their bond. He was going to ask him to leave the comfort and sanctity of his family in the sake of capitalism.

"What up man?" Tamir asked.

"Well, me and Unc been talking and it's time to expand. And well it's a good thing, more money for all of us," Rodge said.

"This seems loaded, what aren't you telling me?" Tamir asked.

"Well we going to expand to VA, and we want you to set that up," Rodge said.

"Me? Set that up how?" Tamir asked.

He asked but he knew what he meant.

"Well, you're going to have to head down there for a while get set up to like we got it up here," Rodge answered.

"So you want me to move down there for a while?" Tamir asked.

"Not really move but you know vacate down there for a while," Rodge responded.

Uneasy, Tamir looked at his son and sat down.

"Man I ain't sign up for this, I was just trying to..." Tamir said as Rodge interrupted.

"Make a couple dollars? Well look around you, you made a couple dollars and expenses too. Come on businessman, you already know you're in, you have a lifestyle to uphold for your family," Rodge explained.

Tamir sat and looked on at the house and furnishings from the ten-thousand-dollar sofa to the large screen TV. He looked at his watch and thought of the matching Rolex he bought for Isabella. That thought expanded to him thinking of his wife-to-be going to school and the support that provided his family living comfortably in luxury. With that, he shook Rodge's hand in agreement.

"Look man, it's just like anything else, it's just business, if we had any other business we would have to expand too, which would mean we have to spend a lot of time out of town," Rodge explained.

About an hour later, Rasheeda and Isabella came in armed with bags.

"Hey Tamir, thanks again, did Jeremy call?" Rasheeda asked.

"Yeah, he said he'll call you tonight," Tamir replied.

"Hey babe, how was your day?" Tamir asked Isabella as he grabbed her by the waist and kissed her neck.

"It was good, just what I needed, to relax. How were the babies?" Isabella replied with a smile.

"They were good, we had fun," Tamir replied

"Did y'all get something for dinner? Damn!" Rodge said jokingly as he walked out of the bathroom.

"Yeah we left it at your house, go home big head," Rasheeda Joked.

A few weeks later back on the block, Tamir, Jeremy, and Rodge sat out front of the store, joked and talked. They were into their conversation and did not notice the car across the street watching them. This was not a cop or any legal issue, that situation was under control, at least in this neighborhood. In fact, it was much worse, in the car sat the local drug dealer robber, Stucky and two of his henchmen.

The streets knew everything and everyone. One of Stucky's henchmen, Teddy, told him that there was a new guy getting a lot of money fast, the new guy was Tamir.

"There he is right there Stuck, right there with Rodge," Teddy pointed out.

Now Rodge's family and Stucky had a silent agreement not to bother get involved in each other's affair. An agreement set in place by Rodge's uncle. Stucky did some work for the family a few years back that increased the family's territory and forced Stucky to leave town and keep a low profile. The story is, there was a rival crew that had more real estate and business than Rodge's family. Most of this came after Rodge's **father** was arrested. Rodge's uncle, Ty, hired Stuck to take care of them while Rodge's family moved in. The story was that Stucky just about singlehandedly took out all the captains. He left town with over two million dollars, or so the story says.

"Who the white boy?" Stucky asked.

"No, the other dude right next to Rodge," Stucky continued.

Now Stucky knew he had a pact with the family and he would normally oblige to that, but he had a particular interest in this young man. For some reason, Tamir became a target of interest. Stucky leered from the tinted windows of the Ford Taurus at Tamir. Tamir, sensing a weird feeling turned and stared at the car from behind his lightly tinted Cartier sunglasses. Through the tinted veil of the window and the sunglasses, Stucky and Tamir stared into each other's eyes. After a few moments, the car pulled off.

"Mir, Tamir, you good man?" Jeremy asked, shaking his friend out of his daze.

"Oh I'm good, yo, who was that in that car?" Tamir asked.

"What car, man you trippin' it's probably this sun," Rodge responded.

The trio headed off to get something to eat.

After that day, Stucky sent Teddy to watch that area every day. Watching every move that was made, how many times Tamir appeared and whom he was with.

Towards the end of July, Jeremy was back on base on his way to his CO's office. He heard rumors that he was going to be deployed to the Middle East. The meeting was the confirmation. He knew it was only a matter of time before he was deployed. He was not upset. Truth is, he was excited. He was however going to miss his fiancé and daughter, yet he was fortunate that he was able to spend the time he had with them. The marines were very understanding about his new family. They stationed him in New Jersey, and delayed his deployment to allow him to witness the birth of his child. His CO told him that he likely be used for his special sniper training. This excited Jeremy even more. Orders in hand, he headed home to tell his family. Jeremy was leaving in the second week of August. This meant he would be in time for the first anniversary of September 11, and the whole ordeal with Tamir being missing.

Back in Philadelphia, Isabella and Tamir were in the middle of an intense argument. Tamir had just told Isabella he would be going to Virginia for a while. Aside from the few weekends he spent there with Rodge, he had never been away from Isabella or his son for longer than a day or two. Isabella was also upset because she felt that he was submerging deeper into a life that she did not like. She noticed his demeanor changing, his overall personality was different. He was the same loving man she fell in love with, even more so now since the birth of their child. The problem was that he was focused, the more focused he was the deeper he would fall into the world that borrowed him. She was not at all insecure of losing him to another woman. She was worried of losing him to the life or losing him period.

"Babe it's ok. Like, I'm only going for a month or so, I'll be back every weekend. We'll talk every day," Tamir offered to console Isabella.

"No, Tamir, No!" Isabella yelled as she stormed away.

Tamir sat back and watched his fiancé walk away with his son in her arms. He smiled, he thought to himself how cute she was when she was mad and watched how hard she switched when she walked away. These moments that made him fall in love with her repeatedly.

"We're going out for a while," Isabella called out.

"Love you!" Tamir called out.

"Love you too," Jeremy yelled in a female voice as he walked in.

Jeremy gave Isabella a hug and kissed the baby as they passed each other in the doorway.

"Talk some sense into him, I swear I can't. I gotta get out here before I scream!" Isabella explained and raced out of the house.

"What the hell did I miss?" Jeremy asked as he greeted Tamir.

"She is mad because I told her I'll be going to VA for a couple weeks," Tamir explained.

"Wow, I gotta go tell Rasheeda I have to go to Afghanistan for a year," Jeremy said.

With perfect timing, Rasheeda walked in with their baby.

"You might as well go ahead and tell her," Tamir said.

Rasheeda looked at Jeremy as she handed him the baby.

"Baby, we talked about this day. Well, it's here I got my orders I've been deployed," Jeremy nervously explained.

"OK babe," Rasheeda said as she kissed Jeremy.

"Hold up, what the hell?" Tamir said.

"What?" Jeremy asked.

"You're going around the world for a year and its ok. I'm going to VA for a few weeks and I get damn near cursed out," Tamir explained.

"Well, first off my baby has no choice and he's going to protect our country. You have a choice and you're going to sell drugs. Big difference Tamir, come on you know that," Rasheeda explained.

"Yeah ok," Tamir said as he walked out the door.

A little while later Tamir drove over to his **mother**'s house. As he pulled up to park, he noticed Isabella heading into his **mother**'s house with their baby in her arms. She looked at him as he looked at her and he pulled off in anger. Gladys walked out just as her son was speeding down the street.

"Come on baby, he'll be ok. Y'all both need to just let off some steam and relax," Gladys said as she guided Isabella and the baby into the house.

After about twenty minutes of speeding through the city, Tamir appeared at Rodge's building.

"Hey Charles, is he up there?" Tamir asked the doorman.

"Yes, he's up there, go right up Sir," the doorman replied.

Tamir made his way to the penthouse where the double doors were open and Rodge was awaiting his friend at his bar.

"Come on in bro," Rodge called out.

"What's up man I already knew you were coming, I'm making you a drink, what you sippin' bro?" Rodge asked.

"Well I…." Tamir said as Rodge interrupted.

"It don't even matter, I got just the thing," Rodge said as he began to fix his friend a Remy Martin and Coke.

Tamir sat at the bar slowly drinking his drink as he thought about his life and the fight he was having with Isabella. It was not the argument that bothered him, it was the notion that she was actually right. This was the point virtually of no return for Tamir. He felt that he was crossing the line by taking this criminal venture interstate. He sat and began to drown his feelings of guilt and confusion in cocktails, back to back until he fell asleep at Rodge's bar.

After a few weeks of tension and anxiety before the guys took their leaves, that time had arrived again. The night before they took their ladies to New York City for a night of shopping and dinner. Late that night upon arriving back home the change was evident. Conversations were short, yet no one was tired. Even in bed, the couples did not make love they had sex. This was a first for both couples even when there was little time to be intimate, they always made love. Isabella was truly in her feelings. She did not smile the whole day, and displayed no emotion while the couple had sex. Rasheeda, while she understood, as the day became closer, the realization set in that it was a possibility that her love, her fiancé, her life would not return. She began to cry as she and Jeremy had sex. The only words spoken were the ladies telling the men that the babies would be home early in the morning to say goodbye.

Later in the morning, Gladys and Christine arrived with the babies, Tamira and Justin. Tamir and Jeremy were suiting up and packing their bags. Jeremy packed his standard issue marine bag, while down the hall Tamir packed his Gucci luggage. Both of them grabbed pictures of their families and stared at them for a few moments understanding what they were embarking on was for their beautiful families. Downstairs, Rasheeda and Isabella were in the kitchen cooking and talking to their **mother** in-laws.

"I just don't get it!" Isabella stated in anger.

"He is so smart and so full of potential. Why this route?" Isabella questioned.

"He just has to find his way sweetie," Gladys responded.

"Yeah but I fear he is going to learn a painful lesson that is going to hurt us all," Isabella interjected.

"Look at our beautiful babies," Rasheeda said attempting to change the subject.

A few minutes later, Tamir and Jeremy entered the kitchen giving kisses and hugs to the women and the babies.

Tamir noticed the look on his **mother**'s face and said, "What **Mom**?"

"You already know. I'm not saying a thing, but I can't say don't be stupid cause you're already doing that, but be careful," she replied.

"I love you too Mom," Tamir replied.

Tamir sensed the disappointment in the room; he quickly ate his breakfast and made his way to the door as Rodge sounded his horn.

For Jeremy it was a little different, however, the room had a mixed feeling of pride and fear as he stood holding his baby in his uniform. He too quickly finished his breakfast and walked toward the door. He again kissed his daughter and the women.

Rasheeda pulled him in close and said, "You better come back to us safely."

Jeremy interrupted her with a long passionate kiss. Watching this, Isabella with her baby in arms and tears in her eyes, ran after Tamir.

"Come here!" she yelled from the porch.

Tamir ran to his fiancé and son.

"What's wrong ?" he asked.

"I love you Tamir, you are my everything. Please come back to me," she said as she kissed him passionately.

"I love you too, I am doing this for our family, and I will be home soon and call you every day. I promise," Tamir replied.

With these emotional goodbyes, the men headed off in two separate directions and two separate paths, both for the same goal and motive, both involved serious risks. They said their goodbyes to each other and hugged as they left. Jeremy headed to McGuire Air Force Base, while Rodge and Tamir headed to one of their warehouses.

The plan was set for the trip to Virginia. Everyone was at the warehouse waiting for their assignment. Rodge's uncle was also there. This plan took weeks with Tamir spearheading the operation like a corporate takeover. They had the product, the staff and the risks calculated. In a few prior visits, Tamir and Rodge had meetings with several of the larger drug lords or competition. Some welcomed them some did not; no one welcomed the team without compensation. Some as simple as a Rolex or a car, others wanted product cheap with delivery. All calculated by Tamir and approved by Rodge and his uncle. He created a profit model that included all expenses, even toll and gas for the runs. The caravan was an elaborate one. There were two UPS trucks, one filled with product, the other filled with guns and ammunition. Everything was packaged in various shaped and sized boxes with address labels of different names and addresses. There was also a transport truck with Mercedes Benz, Range Rovers, and other luxury cars. The cars were completely wrapped. All the staff traveled in standard late model cars, Buicks, Chevys, etc. Altogether, there were maybe ten cars, two SUVs, two UPS trucks, and one transport truck.

The route was planned. The UPS truck, a SUV and two cars were headed to Richmond. In Richmond, there was a warehouse the team had as a midway point for product between Philly and Danville. The bulk of the product would stay there, and new deliveries received there. The other trucks and cars headed straight to Danville.

Rodge and Tamir rode in a Chevy Tahoe driven by Buck and Akeem. Buck and Akeem served as Rodge and Tamir's security. The Tahoe had TV's in the headrest; Rodge watched episodes of Martin while Tamir paid attention to the navigation system. This was a vacation for Rodge, yet for Tamir this was work. He was not nervous, but he was on point, watching everyone's speed, construction, traffic, and random police stops. He was not worried about the UPS

Trucks, which would give anyone a life sentence, if caught. He was more worried about the workers. This was a vacation for them as well.

One of the Buicks was out of formation with the other cars; this car had Shanell, Trina, Will, and Leem. Tamir noticed the car was full and driving erratically. Tamir leaned over to Rodge and told him to look.

"Man, I'm chillin', you the capo of all of this handle it," Rodge responded.

Tamir shook his head and grabbed his Nextel, "Yo what are y'all doing, this is not a game fall back in formation," he said.

Leem responded, "My bad Mir, we chillin' man, enjoying the ride."

Trina interrupted, "Mir calm down baby, we got you, and I got just what you need to make you relax when we get to the spot"

"If it isn't money, I don't want no parts. Just get back in formation and stop hot boxing!" Tamir responded in frustration.

The caravan was barely through Delaware and already showing signs of weaknesses. About two hours later, maybe an hour or so outside of Richmond, the team stopped at a rest stop. Before everyone got out of the cars, Tamir sent a group message via text.

"The trucks stay in the truck sections, handle your business, get your food and keep moving, everyone else stick with the people in your cars, do not congregate, handle your business and let's go."

Rodge looked on in pride. Rodge was not nonchalant, he knew what was at stake, in fact, he was testing his prodigy to see how he handled the team, and the entire operation without him. He knew if things got out of control, he would jump in. Rodge periodically updated his uncle.

Back on the road almost two hours later, the teams arrived in Richmond, VA. The selected teams and vehicles headed to the warehouse. The other UPS truck, transport truck, and eight cars headed to Danville. Rodge and Tamir rode past the warehouse in Richmond. Tamir wanted to ensure everyone knew what to do and everything was ok. A week prior, Tamir sent a team to visit the warehouse and secure it with surveillance and scentless stash places in the event of a raid. They spent over one hundred fifty thousand dollars for this renovation. The notion was better to spend the money proactively then spend it reactively on lawyers. As everything looked ok, Tamir, Rodge, Buck and Leem headed back on the road, headed to Danville about three hours away.

Rodge said, "Man you did pretty good you should relax now check on your wifey or something."

"That's a good idea," Tamir replied.

He then called his angry wife-to-be, Isabella did not say much; she allowed him to speak with his son, said she loved him and hung up.

Back at Maguire Air Force Base, the troops loaded up ready to head to Afghanistan. Jeremy had a nervous, excited feeling he was going to war. He looked on as the tanks and helicopters were loaded on to the humongous C4 Airplanes. Jeremy was amazed at the thousands of men like him, ready to fight, ready to kill for a living and support of their families, and fight for their country. He caught up with his spotter or partner for his sniper missions. His name was Tyler McReady, from Spartanburg, South Carolina. They often talked and worked together in training. Both of them were perfect shooters. Their lives depended on each other, so it was crucial for their bond. Essentially, Tyler was Jeremy's Tamir, in the military.

"You ready man?" Tyler asked in his southern accent.

"Ready as I'm going to be," Jeremy replied.

While on break Tyler's wife had their son, he showed Jeremy the pictures. Being the proud **father** he was, Jeremy showed Tyler his daughter. The two shared stories and experiences with the babies, until they were called on to their plane.

On the plane, the CO approached the two, he stated the basics of the mission, and they would be fully briefed upon arrival in Afghanistan.

Jeremy said to Tyler, "Basically we will be on the front line clearing the way for the other troops to push through."

"Yes, picking them sons of bitches off one by one!" Tyler replied excitedly.

Tyler was from the south, so his whole life he was fascinated with guns and shooting. While most fathers and sons spent time playing catch and playing sports, Tyler's father, Big Tyler, taught his son to shoot and kill. He was an army ranger. Every man in their family was in the military, going all the way back to the civil war, as records would indicate. So this was what Tyler lived for, the opportunity of a lifetime to show his patriotism, provide for his family, make his father proud, and kill.

The bond that he developed with Jeremy was that of the killing and providing for their families. Jeremy did not show his enthusiasm nearly as much as Tyler, but he felt it. It ran deep in his soul. In the weeks and months prior, as they trained and prepared, he fantasized about the moment of his first kill. His thoughts were justified by the actions in remembering the pain he felt when his father was taken from him, watching his mother cry for weeks, then again years later with the threat that his friend was lost in the tragedy of September 11, 2011.

Several hours later as the plane made its way over the Atlantic Ocean, most of the occupants slept, Jeremy, however, sat in a daze, thinking of his life, his past, his present, and most importantly his future. That is his family and the life that he wanted for them, his wife-to-be and his daughter, his best friends, their families and their **mothers**. All of these people prevalent on his mind, multiplied by millions. This stomped out the nervous feelings in his stomach, creating the patriotism and pride. He was fighting for his country in retaliation and for the ability for millions of families to live freely. This notion comforted him and put a subtle smile on his face as he finally drifted off to sleep. After a few hours of flight, sleep, and excited conversation, the troops arrived at their destination.

Upon their arrival, they met up with soldiers from all over the world with the same objective. To seek out and conquer Taliban and Al-Qaeda forces.

"Did you know there would be so many different countries fighting with us?" Tyler asked Jeremy.

"Not at all, but you know this is a crucial situation, they attacked our country and if that went unanswered, imagine what would go on in other countries that are not as powerful," Jeremy replied.

The two walked fully equipped with their gear to meet up with the rest of their special unit made up of all snipers from all over the globe. This was it; ahead of them was a helicopter with a destination. The outcome of this string of missions was not known. Jeremy paused in his steps and looked back as if he heard something a voice perhaps. In that split second everything was as silent as a pin drop, the talk of the military soldiers and roar of the plane engines were muted.

"Let's go marine!" a commanding officer yelled from the helicopter.

"It's too late for that," Jeremy said.

"You alright man?" Tyler asked, as he grabbed his partner.

"Yeah, yeah I'm fine, let's go, I thought I heard something is all," Jeremy responded, as they stepped on to the helicopter.

Chapter : 9

Back in Danville, Virginia, Tamir and Rodge's teams were settling into their homes. They had several modest rental homes in the same neighborhood, but not all on the same street. There were no more than three homes on the same streets but no more than one street away from each other. This way they were close to each other, but they were never all in the same home. All the houses had garages and none of the houses kept drugs in them. Rodge of course made sure he and Tamir's home was elaborate with the amenities of a five-star suite. Their bathtub was not a regular tub, of course it was a whirlpool tub, with plasma TV's throughout.

That night, Rodge sat in his room and caught up on the March madness scores on ESPN and bets via his two-way pager. Tamir looked over all of the operations books on the computer and watched the news. The reporter began to talk about the fighting in Afghanistan. He instantly reached for his phone to call Jeremy then he remembered he could not get through to him, so instead he called Isabella.

"Hey babe, what you doing?" he greeted.

"Nothing, feeding your son," Isabella responded in a noticeably busy tone.

Normally the conversation between the two was non-stop with no silence, but today it was different. There was dead air.

Tamir stated, "Well umm...we here, I was watching the news and I saw they are fighting hard over there in the Middle East, has Sheeda talked to Jeremy?"

"No not yet, but we prayed and imagine he's fine, we hope to hear from him soon. She keeps busy with the baby and around the house," Isabella responded.

That was basically the conversation and a basis of their communication over the next couple of days. Tamir was fighting a battle of good and bad inside himself. He knew what he was doing was wrong and he missed his family. He also knew he wanted the best for his family; this seemed to be the quickest and best route. This intricate organization allowed him to use his intelligence and creativity. Isabella was frustrated, she missed her man and was angry with him, and she did not care about the material possessions. She loved him eternally for rich or poor. She feared losing him to his bad decisions, and their child would lose his **father** to an early death or even jail.

Days and nights for Tamir were routine. He stayed in the house, watched the numbers and the news. At times, he would relieve stress by joking with Rodge, Akeem, and Buck and playing the PlayStation. On Friday and Saturday nights, the team would go out to the local strip clubs and nightclubs to recruit and establish clientele. Again, Tamir would stay in, not going out.

"Come on man, at least this one night, you have to come out with us, all of this work and no play is gonna make you crazy. You gotta get your shit off at least one night," Rodge pleaded.

"I'm good man, I'm not down here for that. I'm here to work so I can get back you know that," Tamir responded.

"Aww, you acting like a lame right now! I can't believe you my brother!" Rodge angrily responded as he walked out the door.

Now Buck was assigned to be Tamir's personal security, which meant anywhere Tamir went or did not go, Buck went or didn't go. Buck heard all the stories from the others about the women and the strippers, but he had yet to partake in what the locals called, "hospitality," of the south. He became noticeably upset.

"Mir, I'm saying you sure you don't want to just take a ride through and see what up though? Maybe make sure everything on the up and up?" Buck asked.

"Naw I'm straight, but look, you go ahead take the night off. I'm good here. I'm just going to call home and I'm going to bed," Tamir responded.

Seven thousand miles and ten and a half hours away in Afghanistan, Jeremy and Tyler were already on mission, making their way to hunt their first targets. Only a few hours in the country and were on their first mission. The welcome had been less luxurious to say the least. No houses with whirlpool tubs, just tents with cots, no plasma TVs, just wide-open terrain with different scenery from mountains to deserts. Of course, the team have not had a chance to enjoy this, they been hunting enemy targets they received on intel, that they were a few miles to the north, of where their base camp was stationed.

"This is exciting, I'm amped I'm going to get me a kill today, I feel it!" Tyler said in excitement to Jeremy.

"Don't be so sure, you might miss, or freeze up, maybe get nervous," Jeremy joked and laughed.

"You are crazy man! I am a better shooter than you any day even on my worst, you can bet the money on that," Tyler said jokingly.

After a few hours of back and forth rhetoric, jokes and challenges they were at their destination, a cool desert, hilly area, remote location in Afghanistan. There were ten pairs of two, spread out across the land camouflaged in the tan desert under the brush. Their .50 caliber Barrett rifles were aimed at a camp of Taliban soldiers. There were about fifty Taliban soldiers in all in of the three buildings.

As the teams lay flush in position, the CO approached each with orders.

"Ok marines, listen closely! We are to eliminate all targets, and the communication building after recovering any intel that may be in the building. Recon does not know what type of guarding rotations or shifts they are on, so we are on our own recon for now. So dig in we will be observing until further notice to eliminate the target. Stay frosty!" the CO commanded.

"We are the first ones in, I can't believe it. I have a lock on the target," Jeremy said nervously as he peered in the scope of his powerful rifle.

"Where?" Tyler excitedly asked.

"My twelve, I'm on my target's heart, I can see his heartbeat," Jeremy responded.

"I also have a lock on the target, I am on his head," Tyler said.

The CO then angrily came across the radio and commanded, "marines you are not to engage until ordered to do so."

This was how the course of the day went on, the teams just watched and waited. Every movement was documented and analyzed, not the excitement that

Jeremy and Tyler anticipated in the months of training and preparation. As night began to fall, the tension was still constant. The impatience grew. A frustrated Jeremy lay on the cold foreign ground with his finger tightly wrapped around the trigger. Awaiting that one single word that would allow him to release his rage, his anger, his pain, and his demons.

"FIRE! FIRE!" the CO commanded.

"Jeremy, what the hell are you waiting for? Take that sonoma bitch out!" Tyler demanded.

Locked in his thoughts of impatience, Jeremy missed his initial command. However, he did not need to be told again, a sinister grin entered his face as he pulled the trigger on the rifle that had been an extension of his body for the past eight hours.

Jeremy and Tyler watched through their night-vision scopes as the .50 caliber bullet entered and exited their target's head.

With excitement of their first kill, Tyler excitedly reported, "Kill confirmed, target down!"

Not knowing how exactly to feel Jeremy sat and watched over his recently deceased target through the scope. The rest of the teams were engaging the rest of the soldiers. This had become a firefight. The snipers hid in the hills above the Taliban bunker and took their targets out one by one as the victims fired aimlessly into the night, not knowing where the shots were coming from, or more importantly, who they were coming from. Jeremy back out of his daze, returned to the action and assisted his team with eliminating the targets.

"At least they can fire back, our people got attacked and blown up just going to work and living life!" Tyler said in anger as he eliminated his targets.

Although this action-packed ordeal seemed to last for a long time, it took only fifteen to twenty minutes at the most. While these were already men, they made a violent transition from boys to men. A lot of them had never been in actual fistfights and now they were professional killers, and with not one, but several bodies to prove this. Namely, Jeremy on his first mission had unleashed a battle of emotions inside of him. Frankly, he did not know how to feel. In addition, to make it worst he was thousands of miles away from anything or anyone that he was used to. His wife-to-be to listen to him, rub his back, and calm his mind, his baby girl to make him smile, to stare into her eyes, and calm his soul. As cliché as it may sound, even his **mother**, she was thousands of miles away and could not give him that loving but sometime rough voice of objectivity and reasoning, his best friends to make light of the entire thing by joking but even to feel the support that he had from them. All he had were people who either felt confused just like him or those who embraced the confusion, who are often called crazy. Tyler was of the latter, the whole hike back to base, all he talked about was the kills as if they were trophies or games. He was completely desensitized. This was the first of many missions, the beginning of a long war and battle of good and evil, and this was all inside of Jeremy.

Back in Danville, Buck had finally made his way to the club where all the stories originated. He was ready; the whole team was there in a sinful daze like a vice-filled amusement park for adults. There were strippers and drinks everywhere.

"What the hell are you doing here?" Rodge asked.

"Aww it's straight, Mir told me I could come. He good. He said he was checking in with wifey then going to bed." Buck replied.

"Naw, I don't like that! You need to be over there with him!" Rodge demanded angrily.

This was a first for everyone, Rodge showed care and concern noticeably for someone other than himself. Rodge, plagued with the feeling inside that nothing could happen to Tamir. He was a man, his own man in fact, who made his own decisions, but Rodge could not help but to feel responsible for Tamir. Rodge was secretly living the calm life that he always wanted through Tamir and Jeremy, hence, why he was so close. They were the extension of him and the piece of life that he felt he could not have on his own.

"Rodge, calm down. He's fine. We're fine. No one knows he's here, furthermore, who he is, ya dig? So relax, if anything Mir will help us blend in easier, by playing low-key, no noise, lights off, and all that," Leem said as he calmed Rodge down.

Rodge agreed and continued to drink and laugh and watch the dancers.

Trina, one of the female members of the team, listening in to the conversation, sobered up a little bit and decided to make her way to Rodge and Tamir's house. Trina was not the average woman, while she was tough and very street, she was beautiful. She had a very deceiving beauty and mystique about her. While in one moment she could be hanging out with the toughest of the guys and have them begging for her mercy. She has them begging for her love also with her beauty. While most of her time was spent standing on corners and hanging with the thugs in Philly, she just as easily could be modelling in New York. The guys on the team never came on to her though. She was one of them, like a sister. Trina had a secret though; she had a major crush on Tamir. She knew Rodge was not having that; therefore, no one else would either. Her biggest challenge this entire trip was to get Tamir alone. The planets must have aligned for her because now was her chance.

"Trin, where you going?" Rodge asked, as he noticed her make her way to the door.

"I'm out, my head rocking. These niggas is lame in here plus y'all drawling with that Tamir stuff like he's the chosen one," she replied.

"Alright, be safe and chirp me when you in the crib so I know you good," Rodge replied.

Trina smirked and nodded as she walked out the door. She managed to allude the general.

Her plan was almost complete. She hopped in her car and drove home. Her house was a block away from Tamir and Rodge's. She knew better than to park outside of his house, but her excitement almost got the best of her. She rode pass the house once, slowed down and looked into the window. The light was on and Tamir was awake walking around, it looked as if he was preparing to take a shower.

"There you are with your fine ass; I got something for you tonight," she said to herself.

She drove home and parked, fixed herself up in the mirror, hiked her skirt up and took off her heels as she made her way through the backyards to reach her conquest. She was there, only one last feat stood in her way before she would be skin to skin with her crush.

Then, "bleep...bleep...Trin you there, Trin answer me, you should be home by now," Rodge radioed on her Nextel.

"Damnit! Yes, I'm home. I'm good. Now leave me alone let me get some rest and stop drunk chirping me," she responded startled.

"Alright Trin, love you girl get some rest," Rodge replied in a drunken slur.

She put her phone on vibrate. No more distractions, the only thing between her was the storm door and some dead bolts. As she looked at the window and looked at the door, she put her three-inch stilettos back on.

"Oh hell no!" she thought to herself as she looked at the window and reached in her hair for a bobby pin.

As if planned her hair fell down to her shoulders when she removed the pin, and she went for the lock.

Trina was an expert at many things but locks, was not her thing. She struggled and struggled until something dawned on her, just try the knob. The door opened, it seems in his haste of getting to the club, Buck left the door unlocked, not good for Tamir but a great victory for Trina. She was finally in, she tiptoed around the house, as Tamir showered oblivious of the sexy intruder that was prowling around his home.

"We can make love in the shower!" Tamir sang out from the shower.

"What baby?" Trina responded as she though he was talking to her, until she realized he was singing, "Anywhere," by 112.

Luckily, he could not hear her. She decided to wait for him in his bed, dimmed the lights, locked the front door and draped herself across the bed. After a few moments and several songs by 112, the water in the shower stopped running. Trina was excited, she actually had never been this excited in her life. She had never been through so much for a guy, a guy who did not know she even liked him. As Tamir walked into the room drying off he noticed the lights were low. Unaware of him being seduced, his first thought was something was wrong, so with the water barely out of his eyes he reached for his .45. Trina reached in her purse and grabbed hers.

"Babe calm down," she said.

"Who the hell? What the hell? Trina?" Tamir responded.

"Yes, it's me, mmm...mmm... mmm and I can see that all you," she said as she stared at a towel-less Tamir.

Tamir quickly dropped his gun and reached for his towel that he dropped in the commotion.

Time seemed to speed up while Jeremy and Tamir were away, days turned into weeks, weeks turned into months. More evident of the time was the age of their children. Tamir and Jeremy's son and daughter were growing so fast. Their mothers, Rasheeda and Isabella have evolved from the most envied girls in high school and, "Round-the-way girls," to sophisticated mothers by day, college students by night. It was hard, mainly because of the noticeable void that was left by the fathers of the kids. Nevertheless, the women motivated and comforted each other. Money was never an issue. Jeremy's compensation from the marines was very good, and always on time. Tamir, well, the money he brought in was so much, that, it was becoming in issue in itself. The proud Grandparents of the babies always took turns watching them during the week while the girls were in school at night. Therefore, it would seem that everything was working out, the guys were off providing and fighting for their families and the ladies were keeping their home and caring for their children. This was how it appeared on the outside, a layer or two below there were definitely some changes, things were different, and the relationships have suffered. Tamir spent more time in Virginia than in Philly, and even when in Philly, he spent more time in the streets than at home. Jeremy continued to send letters and called as much as possible. However, he only talked about war stories rather than his family and his daughter.

In Virginia, Tamir and Trina's friendship was growing. On the nights when the team would go out to the club Tamir would stay in. He would give Buck the night off. Trina would still go to the club but leave early to sneak over to Rodge and Tamir's house. Everyone thought she had a boyfriend or, "friend," in Virginia. Tamir and Trina began to enjoy each other's company. Trina was cute, sexy, and intelligent, but she was rough. They spent time together watching TV and teaching each other things from their different worlds. For instance, Trina taught Tamir how to play tonk, while Tamir taught Trina how to play chess. Tamir, still loyal and faithful to the love of his life, he still made time to call home to Isabella. This made Trina boil with jealousy; she would usually make a face and leave the room or house while he talked to her. In her mind, that should be her, the budding friendship was great but she wanted more.

"OK babe, love you more, kiss my son for me," Tamir said to Isabella as he hung up the phone.

"Trin, Trin!" he called, as he searched the house looking for Trina.

"You finish talking to your side jawn?" Trina asked angrily from the back step as she smoked her cigarette.

"Hold up shorty, why you trippin?" Tamir asked.

"I'm saying, I'm down here with you putting in all the time, riding with you and I gotta hear all the love you this and that, F outta here with that!" Trina said as she stormed past Tamir.

He grabbed her by the arm, "Calm down Trin, we don't do this arguing and carrying on, we peoples like, what's this, what's this tone and look on your face?"

He gently stroked her cheek stopping at her lip and held her chin in between his thumb and index finger, looked her in her eyes and said, "If this is too much for you or you can't handle this you don't have to come around you know."

Now, Trina as tough as she was melted instantly inside, she was at Tamir's command. However, Tamir also knew inside he did not want her to leave either. What type of situation have they embarked on? A dangerous one, a secret one, not even his best friend knew of. Rodge was oblivious to the situation; this would have been something he would not approve of mainly because it would interfere with the operation. Trina was too close to the money and the operation. In addition, Isabella was like his sister and Tamir was his brother, to him they were perfection. While there was not anything going on, people on the outside would not understand. In fact, Trina and Tamir barely understood they had something that was sweet and savory, innocent but guilty and wrong at the same time. They had one weekend a week, over a series of weeks, but exchanged looks and empty insults in front of others. However, underneath the deep cover, they had a profound friendship.

Every night that Rodge would come in drunk, it would always be the same,

"Damn, that Trina wear too much damn perfume, I still smell her!" he exclaimed on his way to sleep, unbeknownst to him she just left, or was in the other room.

The operation was moving along as good as one could imagine, but with foreign success in a local area, comes the occasional problem. This was not anything a large sum of money or large team with large guns could not rectify. This was all calculated and planned for when the team arrived a few months prior. The team had been very careful to date with every move and for the most part, low key with every advance, but at some point, eventually, even the most quietist lion made a noise when claiming his pride.

At one of the team's warehouses outside of town, the team's captains, Rodge and Tamir were meeting about one of the rival organizations that were causing problems. These problems were not more than an occasional fight here and there and a robbery, but they were escalating, and the potential was there to turn in to a full-on war. This was what the team did not want. These wars stop money and cost money.

"I hear what y'all saying and all that, but we need to just go in and body a couple of em, na mean, show em what it's hittin for, fuck the bullshit, I'm from West Philly!" Looty, one of the captains said with anger.

"I mean seriously, I got bread coming in light, packs being lifted every week, and I'm just sitting here taking it, like, they looking at us like what kind of sweet ass niggas are we?" he continued.

"Naw, they like first off these dudes got crazy money coming in and crazy product coming in that we ain't fazing them and they out partying every weekend, we can't tell who king pinning the situation," Rodge said.

"We got them confused," Tamir, added.

"We made an opportunity for those who wanted to get down to make some money and rock with us to do so, and for those to show dat ass and they did so, now we handle it, that's all it is," Tamir continued.

"So, how do we handle it? We can't continue to let them bitch us around," Looty said.

"I got an idea," Rodge said with a smirk on his face and pulled out his phone.

"Unc, listen, I need you to send the care package, not the bread but the toys and send the gingerbread men. Ok thanks peace," Rodge said and quickly hung up.

The entire room sat in a confused daze not understanding the code that Rodge just spoke in.

"What the hell was that?" Tamir asked.

"Boss talk, you'll learn one day, we'll be good in a day or two, now let's go get a drink, y'all stressing me out," Rodge replied.

In the car on the way home, Rodge being himself, didn't let the imminent war, or seeming problem bother him. He had his grin that he was known for and nodded to the music, "Rubberband Man Remix," by TI.

"This is my Jawn!" Rodge exclaimed with excitement.

Tamir looked at Rodge almost in disbelief, how could he be oblivious to what was unfolding in front of his eyes, he thought. Tamir being a smart, prized pupil was learning fast, but his intelligence still did not compensate for his inexperience. He had never been through a turf war or a battle. He had never experienced a gunfight. In fact, Tamir had never even fired a gun. While he held a top position in the organization clearly because of who he was and how his strategies helped the organization profit, he had never been through the blood, sweat, and tears. This reality was beginning to set in. He felt that knot in his stomach, but as he looked at his best friend and brother, Rodge, he could not understand his nonchalant demeanor.

Noticing Tamir peering at him and sensing his discomfort, Rodge pulled the Black tinted 745 to the side of the road and parked. On the dark country road somewhere between North Carolina and Virginia, the sleek black German luxury car blended into the darkness with its black rims matching the black metallic paint, once Rodge turned the bright blue high intensity headlights off, they were virtually invisible against the backdrop of the night.

"What up bro what's wrong? Tell me?" Rodge asked as he turned the music down.

"Man what is this? I mean we about to go to war and you straight chillin, smiling, and partying! Word, I'm stressed!" Tamir responded angrily.

"That's because I told you, you are not built for this. I told you that from the rip. This is my life, I'm not worried about some little nickel and dime haters mad we stopping they money. They do not really want war, and FYI, this is not war, it's a quick scrimmage. If this was war, you wouldn't be here, believe me," Rodge explained.

This was one of the first times the two had a tense conversation since they started. Rodge knew it was coming but Tamir did not; blame it on Tamir's inexperience in this industry.

"So, you thought you was good just back in the cut, calling shots, planning distribution, organizing, and investing the money! And your hands wouldn't get dirty, right?" Rodge continued angrily.

"Naw Fam, this is a dirty business. We all the fuck dirty, you, me, all of us, you see, I protect you from most of the bullshit, you don't touch the shit, you ain't on no corners, you're never in the same place as it, because you my brother and I love you. However, once again you ain't built for it, but you ain't gonna sit here and act naïve, and think that the reality of battle or the consequence of your part of what you do is not here, that is what makes a snitch. You are not a snitch, are you? You understand what you are doing and what can happen, right Mir?" Rodge calmly asked as he stared deeply into Tamir's eyes, as if his eyes were lasers reading his soul to find the true answer.

It did not matter at that point what words came out of Tamir's mouth, Rodge knew the true answer by the look in Tamir's eyes, his movements and mannerisms.

This training attributed to Rodge's training by his uncle, he was trained to find and identify the weakness immediately in the character of a man, not just any man but the man closest to you. So many crime lords and bosses have fallen at the hands of their number two or best friend because of being unable to identify these weaknesses.

"I dig, I mean...I'm riding. I'm good. I'm no snitch. I'll do what I gotta do. I just don't understand how you seem to take shit so lightly. I know what I'm doing, I know it's wrong and for the most part I know the consequence of my actions, that's why I'm serious about it. At the end of the day all I have is my family, my word, and my honor," Tamir responded.

"Then that's all it is," Rodge said as he shook Tamir's hand and started the car and proceeded to play, Freeway, "What We Do is Wrong."

"Right though," Tamir said as he smiled and nodded his head to the beat.

"One more question though bro, who the hell are the gingerbread men?" Tamir asked.

"You'll find out soon enough," Rodge said with a straight face and said nothing more about it.

The next day everyone sat around the house with anxiety and impatience in the air waiting for what was coming in this care package, from home, in Philly. Tamir spent the day talking with Rasheeda, Isabella, and the babies. He even spoke with Jeremy who would be coming home on leave for a few days during the Memorial Day holiday. The main team members were at Rodge and Tamir's house waiting for the plan. Trina and Tamir have been texting each other from across the room all day, she was being really supportive about everything that was going on. Unlike Tamir, she had been through these types of situations with beef and wars. Trina even joked that she would take him out and teach him how to shoot. That led to them both breaking the silence of the room with them laughing at the same time, almost blowing their cover.

Chapter : 10

At about 7:30 PM that night Rodge got a text to meet at an abandoned warehouse fifteen minutes outside of town, in approximately a half hour.

"I got the word from Unc, let's roll," Rodge said as he got up and grabbed his keys.

"Trin, take Mir, Buck I'm gonna ride with you, everybody two to a car," Rodge commanded.

Confused at the order, everyone looked at each other based on Rodge's rare serious tone; no one questioned and just did what was told. The caravan with cars twisted and turned out of the town with everyone in the cars confused but at the same time confident in their leader. Trina and Tamir, one car behind Rodge and Buck.

"Why do you think he told you to drive me?" Tamir asked nervously,

"Cause I told him we fucking," Trina said as she grabbed Tamir's leg.

"You told him what? Why would you tell him something like that you tripping?" Tamir said pushing her hand off his leg.

"Relax! Damn, I'm playing. I don't know, was I not in there with you the whole time? I don't know what he thinking," Trina responded.

"We had an argument the other night though," Tamir explained.

"About what?" Trina asked.

"Just everything, kind of where I stand with what's going on, do I know consequences, what makes a snitch, blah, blah..." Tamir continued.

" Oh yeah that's serious, Babe I don't have to tell you about what snitches do to this business or what happens to snitches in this business," Trina said.

"Yeah, I know but it ain't even on that type time, dig me. Like we on this shit now with having to body people and all that like I don't know what I thought," Tamir responded.

"What you thought it was just about the money boo boo?" Trina interrupted

"Naw, you gotta remember with no risk there is no reward, ain't that what you told me about those stocks you been teaching me?" Trina continued.

"Yeah, listen to you, you actually listen to me?" Tamir laughed.

"I'm saying though Mir, you know there is a couple of things you have to remember; number one, Rodge love you like a blood brother, before you was even involved he talked about you like you was the damn chosen one. He doesn't want anything to happen to you and this business will change you. But he tries and he will shield you as much as he can within reason, feel me. The other thing is this is the most dangerous business in the world, even if you said I never want to be violent and hurt anyone, that's not realistic because when you doing good, people are going to try you and try to take it from you. So what will you do? You can't go to the police. We police ourselves. We are our own justice system. Sorry honey, but its kill or be killed. It's the life you chose, my sexy naive friend," Trina explained.

After about twenty minutes the cars arrived at the warehouse and train yard that was fenced in, Buck sounded his horn three times and two men in all black with hoods ran out and opened the gates. The cars drove into the warehouse and were greeted by the six black GMC Yukons and two large auto transport tractor-trailers. Rodge jumped out of the car as the rear door of the Yukons opened.

Watching everything in amazement, Tamir said, "What the..."

"The gingerbread men," Trina interrupted."

A tall dark figure exited the Yukon dressed also in all black. He had the build of a military elite or special force. He greeted Rodge with a firm handshake and hug, Rodge signaled for Tamir. Tamir walked towards them as two other men exited the SUVs and stopped Tamir to pat him down. Rodge called out that he was ok, and explained he was his brother. Tamir wondered what type of organization he was a part of. He was truly leaps and bounds away from the corners he thought this organization was confined to. This was surreal, like something out of a movie, something larger than he was.

Now it was beginning to make sense the demeanor of which Rodge possessed and why he was very confident, and so powerful. He was heir to something huge, crime family with ties and connections that seemed to span as far as the mind could not comprehend.

"Your uncle sends his regards," the man said.

"He also said you have a minor assignment for us," he continued.

"Yeah, we got a little situation down here, nothing major, but we just need to eliminate a situation before it becomes a situation," Rodge responded.

"We have your fee," Rodge continued as he signaled for Buck to open the trunk of the car.

Buck walked up with two large duffle bags full of money and a set of door keys.

"We got a house for you also with all that you need stay as long as you need, if there's anything you need just let Buck know," Rodge explained.

"Thank you. Your problem shall be eliminated by the weeks end, in addition, your Uncle sent your toys," the man explained as he pointed to the carriers, as the ramps on the trucks opened.

The men began to remove cars from the carriers. There was a red Ferrari 360, a red Lamborghini Murcielago, and a silver Aston Martin Vanquish in one of the carriers. In the other carrier there was a blue Bentley Continental GT, silver Rolls Royce Phantom, and a yellow Lamborghini Gallardo.

While the team lined up the cars, Rodge and Tamir talked with the two lead members of the gingerbread men. They were referred to as Chuck and Dave, which obviously weren't their names. They didn't have names, other than that they were known as the gingerbread men, they didn't exist.

"So we came down and made offers to all rivals to attempt to make this transition as sweet as possible for everyone, but you know sometimes pride gets in the way and clouds judgment, so there is one team we have a problem with," Rodge explained.

"Of course, so we get to come and have a little fun," Chuck joked.

"My thing is not to let anything come back to us," Tamir interjected.

They all looked at Tamir and laughed.

"Of course not and clearly you don't understand the concept of us, the gingerbread men. We make problems disappear with no trace and no clue. We are the reason there is such a thing as the 'First 48'," Dave explained.

"There is no homicides no noises nothing like that, we again just make problems disappear," Chuck continued.

"Y'all gotta excuse my brother this is all new to him, he's the money man. This part of the operations is not his forte," Rodge joked.

"Ok, so you pretty much know what to do Rodge, 'imitation bacon bits,' right?" Chuck asked.

"Yup I got you, not a problem that's definitely the move, 'imitation bacon bits,' Buck will give you all the details in a day," Rodge confirmed as they shook hands and walked away.

"Rodge come on you already know I'm going to ask," Tamir asked.

"Bro, I got you, relax, just watch and learn, take it all in," Rodge said as he laughed.

"I'm learning but come on I dig gingerbread men and all that but you gotta give me something, 'imitation bacon bits,'" Tamir pleaded.

"Ok, here you go I'm a give you this one bro only cause you my bro and you becoming a pain in my ass. Ok, so what is an imitation bacon bit?" Rodge asked.

"I don't know nigga, something you put on salad," Tamir answered.

"You not thinking. You gotta be quicker than that, and you was going run some bank with that mind? Is it real bacon?" Rodge asked.

"No!" Tamir answered.

"Right, but it has the flavor and it's in a lot of little pieces. So, now what we do is get out there and make these little niggas out here think they the real bacon with the flavor, or the 'Kingpin,' so when homeboy across the way start his beef up, he'll be beefing locally, that means when he disappears, who will the law be looking at?" Rodge explained.

"The local dudes and competition, not us, that's crazy," Tamir answered in amazement.

"Exactly, 'imitation bacon bits,' you see beef wars and bullshit cost money and stop money; it's a waste of time. If it is a problem, we just eliminate it. So what we do is get the shit in motion, they get to beefing, the gingerbread men move in, make people disappear with no trace, meanwhile it's Memorial Day weekend, we in Virginia Beach with our family chillin. Dig me?" Rodge explained.

Rodge and Tamir walked toward their new cars, Rodge's Murcielago and Tamir's Aston Martin. The other captains followed suit in the super luxury and exotic cars. They all proceeded towards the exit of the factory following Rodge's, three hundred fifty thousand, Italian, sports car.

Rodge stopped, poked his head out of the window and said, "Ok listen, be easy, go straight to y'all cribs and put these up in the garages. Don't attract any attention."

"Yeah, Yeah, Yeah, Whatever, just get out of my way, I would eat you up anyway, can't nobody see me in this Vanquish!" Tamir interrupted as he yelled out of his window.

"Trin, I'm a park in your garage," he continued.

The twenty-minute ride was bittersweet for the captains; they were indulged in a world of luxury, they were not used to that, they never dreamed of this. It was a bit of a tease because they could not drive the cars the way they imagined as kids, or as they fantasized. They could not afford the risk of attracting unwanted attention. Surely, young black men driving cars the price of houses, that were on two to four year waiting lists, would attract the attention of anyone including cops. Nevertheless, this was the life they were in, the life they chose.

In the light of the full moon on that clear night, the team made it safely, back to their homes in their modest neighborhood. The cars were easily worth two to three times the value of the houses they were staying in. As Tamir pulled his car into Trina's garage, he stood and stared at his car for what seemed to be at least five minutes.

"You coming in or what boy!" Trina said breaking his concentration.

This was Tamir's dream car, not the way that he imagined getting it, but it was there with the keys in his hand. He could still smell the hand-stitched leather and hear the roar of the engine.

"I'm coming in a second," he replied.

"Matter of fact I'm going home," he said as he looked at his phone.

Rodge sent a text for him to come home, as everyone was waiting to go over the plan. Time really did get away from him and he was holding the team up.

"Alright well go ahead then, can I get hug though?" Trina asked.

"Sure," Tamir replied.

Tamir hugged Trina, laced up his timberland boots, adjusted his fitted Phillies hat so it was just above his eyes. He looked at his diamond Rolex Daytona watch and adjusted it on his wrist and ran off back to his house. Trina watched and thought how he was just the right amount of sophistication and the right amount of thug for her. Regardless of what was going on or whom he was with, that was her heart. He was her boo.

About five minutes later, Tamir walked into his house with a room full, everyone was sitting around, Sports Center on the TV in the background.

"About time nigga, damn!" Will, one of the captains said.

"We don't have time for that," Rodge interrupted.

"Alright, so dig the move, we found a dude named Ruckus, little small-time dude, buys a little weight. He trying to come up, got a couple dudes that hustle for him or whatever, but he does not move with nobody. So we gonna give him a little offer, a car. Front him a couple packages and make him somebody overnight. Show him some things the cars, the money, the power, put him in position, let him stunt. He will be the ghost that the other dude is beefing with. So when the gingerbread men come in and get rid of that other dude, Killa or whatever his name, all eyes will be on him," Rodge explained.

"So what are the cars for? I mean I'm feeling that Rolls," Looty asked.

"Good question. We gonna step out on Thursday and Friday, and show out, stunt hard, ball out, know what I mean. Show them real money. Friday night, me, Mir, Leem and Buck going away, but y'all still hold it down out here, everything legal and clean but don't do nothing dumb, if anything go down, call my lawyer John, but be cool don't ride dirty," Rodge explained.

"Alright cool, so I figure we have a week to get everything together," Tamir explained.

Everyone agreed.

That night the team continued to iron out the details of their plan until the sun came up.

When everyone left, Tamir and Rodge began to plan their vacation. They found houses near Virginia Beach on the bay and some boats they decided to rent. Tamir sent a message to Jeremy telling him to meet them in Virginia Beach. The next day, Tamir told Isabella and Rasheeda to meet them in Cape Charles. He gave them the address of the houses they rented. Trina and her best friend, Shanell have been planning to go to Virginia Beach with the guys also, but the problem was, the guys didn't know. Trina was adamant in her attempts to go, Shanell did not know why. Trina and Shanell talked about everything they were like sisters since they were younger. This quite possibly was the one secret that Trina kept from Shanell. The crazy thing was, there was no real reason for Trina to keep it from Shanell, if anything Shanell would have helped her if she could. In the city it was common to find these friendships like Shanell and Trina's, Tamir, Rodge, and Jeremy's, even, Akeem and Buck were best friends.

These friends seemed to be able to relate with each other's situations and feel voids that were left in each other's households. Whether it was missing fathers, mothers, or even brothers and sisters. Nonetheless, these bonds were tighter than blood.

"Girl, why are you so determined to go so bad, damn, it's memorial weekend, let's go to Miami or Atlanta, why Virginia Beach?" Shanell asked.

"Cause girl Virginia Beach is going to be the look, they getting houses out there and boats," Trina explained.

"Naw, it's something else sis, I've known you too long, don't tell me you falling for Rodge," Shanell questioned as she grabbed Trina's arm.

"No, no...nothing like that," Trina replied nervously as she sipped her glass of wine.

"Katrina Wilson! Look at me!" Shanell demanded.

"What girl?" Trina asked with a nervous grin.

"Who are you crushing on?" Shanell asked.

"Ok, look I'm going to tell you something, but you better not say nothing, and you better not judge me," Trina said.

"Ok, scouts honor, pinky swear and that entire BS," Shanell said.

"Ok, so me and Tamir been chilling real tough the last couple months on the low," Trina explained.

Shanell, shocked, stared at Trina without saying anything.

"Say something girl!" Trina said.

Shanell without reply reached for the glass of wine and began to drink.

After quickly drinking a full glass of white zinfandel she said, "Girl! You know you tripping, where do I even start. OK, I'll start here, well he is cute, but Mama he's like married or something and you asking for all kinds of trouble. And you and him not even..." Shanell explained

"Not even what? The same type? Girl I know that's the crazy thing about it, and I think that's why I'm so drawn to him, he's so smart and cool, nothing like these dudes I'm used to," Trina explained.

"So wait a minute that's where you be Friday and Saturday nights? I thought you was laid up with one of these lames down here," Shanell said.

"Yeah we been chilling together real cool, like just watching TV playing games and he been teaching me stuff," Trina said.

"Girl, you know I got to ask," Shanell said as Trina interrupted.

"No, we haven't, I mean I want to, lord knows I want to but he ain't with it, he remains faithful and loyal to his girl," Trina explained.

"So why do you want to go be around that this weekend? Why go torture yourself?" Shanell asked.

"I just have to see what I'm up against you know?" Trina responded.

"I feel you girl. Well you know I'm a ride or die with you, so if you say that's what you want to do, then we in Virginia Beach," Shanell said.

Therefore, with that, Shanell and Trina's plan was set to be in tow to Virginia Beach. Rodge and Tamir were out preparing for their trip also, going from mall to mall, store to store, trying to find clothes and things they would need for their vacation and long drive across state. Everything was set, in a few days Tamir would be with his fiancé and son, his best friends, and could finally relax after months of working. He was extremely excited. He envisioned Isabella's face and his son's smile. Every store they stopped in he bought things for his family. The jewelry store is where he seemed to have lost his mind; he bought Isabella a three-carat tennis bracelet and matching diamond earrings. Of course Rodge joked with him the entire time but he was proud of the father his best friend was. Tamir was happy, this is what it was all for, the ability to spoil his son and wife to be. Rodge and Tamir bought things for everyone, clothes and sneakers for Jeremy's daughter and Tamir's son.

They completely filled the trunk and backseat of Rodge's BMW.

After a day of planning and shopping, it was time to get back to work, time to scout out the pawn they had chosen for their plan, the want-to-be drug lord whose life was going to change forever. After a few rounds in town, Buck and Leem spotted Ruckus, he hung out and seemed to handle all his business in a hole in the wall bar simply called, "The Lounge." Will and Looty rode over to the bar in a blue Lexus LS 460 and a black Range Rover, with Buck and Leem not far behind in case things got out of control.

Will and Looty walked into the bar as if they owned it. Looty walked as if he owned the sidewalk everywhere he walked. He was from West Philadelphia and did not care who knew. In fact, he wanted everyone to know. Will was more laid back and subtle, together they had the perfect balance.

They approached Ruckus and greeted him, "What's going on Ruck, how you?"

"Do I know you?" he responded.

"You should," Will responded.

"You definitely need to," Looty added.

"We see you doing your thing, but it's time to step it up and make that real money," Will explained.

"Yeah, I don't know what y'all talking about with this rah rah, but y'all might want to step out with that," Ruckus said angrily as he patted his waist focusing the attention to the gun he had on his waist.

"Come on young boy, we ain't here for all that, we are your friend, let's just say we are friends from above. We are the men who supply, who supply, who supply you. In the chain of how things work, we are here to give you a little promotion," Will explained.

"Besides you really don't have a chance with that pea shooter you holding," Looty explained as he flashed his chrome Desert Eagle that was tucked in his waist.

"Now, make things a little calmer and show you how serious we are about being friends here take this," Will said as he handed him the keys to the Lexus.

"That's yours, it's clean, all yours, no strings attached, like I said we been watching you and we see how you move and we want to help you progress, when you win, we win," Will continued.

"Walk with us," Will said as he guided Ruckus towards the door.

Reluctantly, Ruckus walked with Will and Looty with the Lexus keys tightly in one hand and the other hand securely on the gun on his waist. As they got to the door, Ruckus saw the Lexus sitting outside shining in the sunlight freshly cleaned and detailed looking fresh off the showroom floor.

"If we wanted you dead you wouldn't have seen us or heard anything, you'd be gone, so relax," Looty whispered in Ruckus's ear.

"Now, look down the street," Loots continued as he signaled Leem and Buck.

They flashed the lights on the Range Rover they were sitting in.

"That's part of the muscle," Looty explained.

"You see this is part of the team, your new team, you can either be a friend or an employee. Do you know the difference?" Will asked.

"I can either choose to work with y'all or y'all can force me to work with y'all," Ruckus answered.

"We got a smart one here," Looty joked.

"Exactly, so you have an operation now, this is your car; you get a package to move each week and twenty grand a week for moving the package. Not bad right?" Will explained.

"Especially since you was only doing like five stacks a week, yeah we know everything," Looty said.

"Damn y'all thorough," Ruckus said as he smiled.

Will and Looty looked at him with a straight face.

"Now everything will be good, ball out, have fun, live life, but you better move that package. If you don't, well we won't talk about what happens if you don't cause you will right?" Will asked.

"I got you," Ruckus confirmed.

"One other thing this conversation never happened, you work for yourself, this is all your operation, you already know what happens to snitches right?" Looty asked.

"I'm a real G with mine man, straight up and down," Ruckus said firmly as he got in the Lexus.

Looty and Will looked on as Ruckus got comfortable in his new car, Looty reached in his pocket and tossed a cell phone into the car.

"That's yours too, when this number calls you, answer. When you get directions, you follow them," as Will quickly called the phone and hung up.

This phase of the plan was set. The team's pawn took the bait, hours in, he was already making his way around town showing off in his new car, spreading the word that he was the big man in town. For months, everyone had been trying to figure out who was atop the organization that was noticeably taking over. Especially Killa Kev, whose team was rivaling with Rodge and Tamir's team. Word got back to him quickly; the team had created the perfect smoke screen. Ruckus had the same car, the same product, and the same workers. Maybe it was the design of the car, but he even drove the car the same way Looty drove the car.

On Thursday, everything was set, Tamir, Rodge, Buck, and Leem were all packed up and ready to go on their vacation. The caravan was set as follows; Rodge in his Murciealago, Tamir in his Aston Martin, Leem in the Range Rover and Buck in the Yukon. The Yukon and Range Rover full of gifts, luggage, supplies and things they would need for their trip. The only thing left to do was to hit the club that night and set off the rest of the plan. Immediately after the club they would be on the highway driving five hours and two hundred seventy-two miles to their rented vacation houses. Rasheeda and Isabella were driving down Friday, and Jeremy's flight was coming in later that day.

As the men were loading up their cars that morning, Trina pulled up with Shanell.

"What's up y'all?" Trina excitedly greeted as she quickly jumped out of her car grabbing her luggage out of her car.

Shanell quickly followed her friend's lead.

"I know y'all didn't think y'all were leaving us. That's that bullshit I be talking about," Shanell said with a sinister grin.

"What y'all think y'all doing? Y'all seriously drawing now," Rodge said surprised.

"Y'all ain't coming!" Tamir said nervously.

"Oh, my baby's coming too?" Buck said with excitement as he stumbled down the porch steps.

"Get your biscuit head on man, no they ain't coming," Rodge responded.

Buck had a crush on Shanell, so he was motivated to say the least for the extra passenger.

"Here let me help you with those, sexy Mama," Buck said as he dropped his bags and rushed over to grab Shanell's bag.

Shanell gave her flirty smile as she handed Buck her bags.

"I mean why not they might as well roll, ain't nothing here. We chilling over the way anyway, nothing major," Leem attempted to justify.

Rodge stood and thought for a while, looking at Tamir. Tamir was having an inner conflict, thinking on one side he wanted Trina's company for the ride, but then he knew that he would be on vacation with Isabella and his son.

"But she's just my friend," he thought and rationalized to himself.

"Mir, Mir!" Rodge called.

"Yeah?" Tamir answered.

"What you think?" Rodge asked.

"Oh man, I don't care, I'm just trying to get to my family and relax," Tamir responded nonchalantly.

"So it's settled then, we coming," Trina said excitedly.

The cars were loaded up ready for the trip. The final step was to go out that night to finish the plan for the rivals. Everyone was going out to attract the hate and attention, and essentially start the war between Ruckus and Killa Kev. At about 10:00 PM that night after everyone who was headed on vacation got their rest, they met around the corner from the club, "Ladies Night at the Safari Lounge." All of the money typically came out to show off, so of course, Ruckus was out showing off his new car and wealth. Like clockwork he was posted out front of the club like he owned it. With his Lexus, hadn't owned it an entire week and he already put the, "hood rich," touch on it, twenty-four-inch rims, tinted windows and of course a loud system. A sign that he was not used to having money, real money, a clear difference between him and Rodge, and his team. They had money and spent money ridiculously, but their flashy and frivolous purchases were classy. They kept it luxurious enough and did not lessen the value of cars by adding things and making them gaudy. If you spend a couple hundred thousand on a car people would definitely take notice. There was nothing you needed to add to bring more attention.

As Ruckus posted out front at the club in his Lexus attracting the attention of the ladies with his new clothes and jewelry, Killa Kev and a few members of his team pulled up in their Escalade. They also had the same type of, "hood rich," appearance, large rims, system, etc. This seemed to be the fad in this area amongst the hustlers, get money, and flaunt it in the most, gaudy way possible. Kev had been hearing all about Ruckus. In fact, this was the main reason he stepped out this evening to see the man behind the machine who was taking all his money and clientele.

As he stepped out of his money green Cadillac Escalade, and peered on to his competition, he thought, *"This little nigga? That's it? Can't be."*

Something didn't add up, he was missing something. He was definitely from the area, but sizing him up, he couldn't be built to handle enough business to take the pressure he was putting on him. He looked a little harder. He had money obviously, but he couldn't possibly have enough to be able to supply the work that had been flooding the area or withstand the robberies without retaliation. Kev walked a little closer. He became angrier and angrier, with each step.

"I should just kill this muthafucka right here, right now. He sitting here by himself flossing and stunting hard, it would just be a robbery," he thought.

Then he thought he could not be alone, he had to be attached to something larger. Ruckus was oblivious to the notion that there was someone in an earshot of taking his life. Ironically, he was enjoying his life. He was finally successful, but he could not really explain it or rationalize it. He was finally on top, really without rhyme or reason. He glances to his right and noticed Kev and his team approaching. Ruckus was too high on his own vanity to notice the hate in his eyes or the potential danger that was approaching. In just that instant as the tension and chill in the air begin to thicken, it was broken by a sound in the distance that the crowd seemingly had never heard before. This was obvious by the blank stares and silence that fell on them. It was the roar of foreign engines approaching from a distance.

The blue high intensity discharge headlight lit up the dark street and in perfect order one by one, Rodge's team pulled up. Will pulled up alongside Ruckus's Lexus in the red Ferrari 360, followed by Davey in the yellow Lamborghini Gallardo, followed by L in the blue Bentley Continental GT, then Tamir in the Aston Martin Vanquish, Rodge in the Lamborghini Murciealago and Looty in the Rolls Royce Phantom. Buck in the Range Rover with Shanell, Trina and Leem in the Yukon closed out the team caravan.

There were over a hundred people standing outside of the club staring in amazement at the exotic fleet of cars. They had taken the phrase, "parking lot pimping," to a completely new level. After a few moments of silence in the crowd the whispering started. People were trying to figure out what rapper was in town, what famous person the entourage belonged to. Will called out to Ruckus and signaled for him to come to the car. The connection was made to Kev and the crowd this was Ruckus's team. Kev took a step back. The women outside of the club looked at Ruckus a completely new way now, they were virtually lining up at his car waiting for him to come back.

"Alright Ruck when you go back to your car drive in front of me drive around the block and follow me the pancake house," Will directed.

"Alright cool, but why?" Ruckus asked.

"Stop asking questions, but dig homie in the Escalade, well he's trying to make a move on you," Will explained.

Still high on his inflated vanity, Ruckus yelled, "I'll kill that bitch right now, I'm a real G."

Everyone including Kev overheard this.

"Calm the fuck down, didn't I explain to you, you have a team now. This is what we do, just do what I say," Will explained.

Kev was now confused. He didn't know what was happening, only getting a glimpse of the shadow he'd been boxing for months, and now was everything coming to a head? After months of not knowing whom his adversary was how could he be so easily revealed and make such blatant threat right in front of him? How could they show so much money in front of him with so much ease after being hidden for so long?

"Alright look, when you walk back to your car ignore everyone but look dead in that dude eyes, keep that look on your face like you ready to rip his head off but don't say anything," Will directed.

"OK cool," Ruckus agreed.

As Ruckus headed back to the car, he locked right on Kev, looked him dead in his eyes as directed as if he wanted to kill him. His demeanor was so tense and angry, the girls who had lined up to talk to him backed completely away, without a word. Of course, Rodge being Rodge could not leave the spot without a little company of his own for his five-hour ride. He jumped out of the car, looking like a million bucks with his two-carat diamond stud earrings, and five-carat princess cut invisible set diamond chain sitting on his Gucci polo shirt.

He said, "Hey ladies, look uh I have a bit of a problem, you see I have to take a ride alone and I don't like to be alone. So, I'm wondering if someone wouldn't mind sliding outta town with me for a minute."

The girls rushed the car, but before they could reach the car Leem was already at his side pushing them back.

"Ok, you, you look like good company," Rodge said as he pointed to clearly the prettiest girl there and the one girl who did not run toward the three hundred fifty-thousand-dollar car.

"Come on shorty, get in, what's your name?" he said as she got in the car.

"My name is Veronica what is your name?" she asked.

"Oh my name is Mark," he said as he laughed and pulled off.

"So where we going?" she asked.

"On a little vacation," he replied.

"Where to?" she asked.

"Virginia Beach," he replied.

"But that's like five or six hours away," she said confused.

"I know," he said.

"I don't have any clothes," she said.

"There's malls and stuff there I got you," he said.

"Hold up," he said as he stopped the car abruptly.

"How old are you?" he asked.

"Twenty-two, why?" she replied.

"Let me see your ID," he said.

She opened up her Louis Vuitton clutch and handed Rodge her license.

"Ok cool," he said.

"So why didn't you pull off yet?" she asked.

"Oh, I have to wait for my friends. Hold on. Go ahead and call your friends, job, boyfriend, husband or whatever. Tell them you'll be back next week, you going on vacation with your new friend, Mark," he Joked.

Back around the corner, the rest of the caravan began to pull off with Ruckus now leading. As all the cars left the block Kev and his team stared confused. Buck and Leem turned the Range Rover and Yukon as if to cut off the block. They stepped back out of the trucks, walked to the back of the trucks, and pulled out some things that look like tools. Kev turned his back just for a second as his friend tapped him on his shoulder to tell him to turn around. Buck pulled out what was commonly referred to as a street sweeper shotgun and Leem pulled out a Heckler Koch MP5 and began to fire in their direction. Kev and his team the club goers took cover. Buck and Leem have perfect aim; their goal was not to hit anyone. They just want to let them hear the sound of their extremely loud hardware. With this dramatic prelude, the war started, and that act was on, starring Ruckus and Kev, and his cronies taking center stage with over a hundred witnesses.

"What the fuck was that?" Kev asked as he got up from the ground.

"Y'all good, anybody hit?" he asked checking his team.

"We good, it's time to clip up right?" France, one of Kev's goons asked.

"Absolutely, the thing is we don't miss though, you hear me? This is my town. I don't know what these niggas think this is, or who they think I am, but I want to battle, I want war! Let's route!" Kev said angrily as he led his team back to his Escalade.

Chapter : 11

As they rode off almost two blocks down the road, everything was being monitored in an all-black surveillance van. This was the same type of van used by government officials, the FBI, DEA, etc., but it was not either. It was the, "gingerbread men." They were watching their targets, more like their prey, watching how they talked, moved, everything from the tone of their voices, to their reaction time when the guns were fired on them. As Kev pulled away the van followed them at a safe distance, as not to be noticed trailing them in the shadows of the night.

Twenty minutes later and about fifteen miles in the opposite direction, Rodge's team was outside of the pancake house.

"So what's up, that's crazy, I'm a need y'all to go ride on them for me!" Ruckus demanded as the team congregated out front of their cars in the parking lot.

Everyone stared at Ruckus briefly before laughing.

"Go home man, just go home, you did ya job," Rodge said laughing.

"Who the hell are you?" Ruckus asked.

"That's not important homie. What's important is you make it home safe, so hop your little happy ass on before I stop smiling," Rodge said.

"What? Y'all keep insisting on trying a G tonight, huh? I'm Ruck! I handle mines!" Ruckus said, as Leem and Buck swiftly picked Ruckus up and threw him into his car.

Rodge walked over and said, "I kind of like you, you got heart and I respect that, but you gotta know it's a place and a time to say certain things. I know there was a little feeling in your stomach that you felt when you saw me that said maybe I should keep my mouth shut, yeah, you probably should have listened to that. This car you in, that is me, that money in your pocket that is me too, all the money out here, that is me. Ya dig, this will probably be the only time you ever meet me, so appreciate that lesson I just taught you that's probably worth more than all the money and this car, actually, it's worth your life," Rodge explained as he patted Ruckus on his head.

"Leem bring me the Gucci," he said.

Leem proceeded to bring him a Gucci duffle bag filled with easily five hundred grand. He counted out twenty thousand dollars and tossed it in the car.

"Oh to answer your question, who the fuck am I? I think it was, I'm your boss. Now get the fuck on before I terminate you and I don't mean fire you!" Rodge explained.

"Yes sir," Ruckus stuttered.

"Yo, Ruck, go straight to the crib. Don't leave until you get a call or text on that phone," Will directed.

After that embarrassing and humbling encounter, Ruckus pulled off and went straight home. Meanwhile, the team made their plans for those who stayed back.

"Yo stay low key watch the money, shit gonna be crazy the next few days," Rodge said.

"Looty and Will, y'all in charge, remember anything go wrong hit John, then me, in that order. The re-up will be in from Richmond on Wednesday," he continued.

"Yo, I was thinking about heading back up to Philly until then anyway, take it down for a few days," L said.

"I mean if that's the look that's cool, whatever you wanna do but y'all can't leave this jawn naked we still got business down here," Rodge explained.

"Look either way do what y'all gonna do, but make sure the money right and stay safe, we out," Rodge continued.

Rodge's new friend, Veronica looked on as Rodge handled his business from the passenger seat of the Lamborghini, amazed at how he called the shots and was clearly the leader of this crew, that had all of those super exotic and luxury cars.

"What are they into?" she thought to herself.

Sitting in a car that she only saw on TV in rap videos and movies, the power, the money, she landed in some type of fairytale. She could see Rodge or Mark, as she thought his name was, was more than the money, he was intelligent, had a nice personality, funny, and cute. She became aroused and excited just watching his movements and analyzing him.

Everyone pulled off leaving Buck, Akeem, Tamir, Rodge, Shanell, Trina, and Veronica.

"Alright, y'all ready for this ride?" Tamir asked.

"Yeah bro, lets ride," Rodge responded.

"You riding with me short?" Buck asked Shanell.

"I don't know, depends on what kind of music you got," she jokingly replied.

"I'm riding with you Mir; you look tired. I don't want you crashing your precious car," Trina said as she jumped in Tamir's car.

With everyone set and ready, the caravan moved out with Buck leading in the Range Rover with the address in the navigation system. Akeem secured the back of the fleet in the Yukon. They were more like a presidential motorcade under the midnight summer sky.

The road was clear, not too much traffic on US Highway 58, they averaged seventy to eighty miles per hour, each car full of conversation with the exception of Akeem's car. He was singing to himself, everything from, The Isley Brothers', "Smooth Sailing," to P.Diddy's, "I Need a Girl." In Buck's truck, the conversation was playful but at the same time insightful after Buck finally loosened up, Shanell and Buck found that they had a lot in common. They even liked the same cereal, "Cap'n Crunch." He made sure she was comfortable the entire ride. Then it happened, the song, "Beautiful," by Snoop Dogg came on.

He turned to her and belted out of his large six-foot three-inch, two hundred thirty-five-pound athletic frame and sang, "Beautifulllll...I just want you to know you're my favorite girl."

Shanell blushed and laughed; he grabbed her hand and danced with her in the truck.

"Boy you are crazy," she said as she laughed.

"Crazy for you, sexy," he flirted as he kissed her hand.

They were having a great time at 2:00 AM cruising up the highway.

A car behind, Rodge was being Rodge, avoiding questions from his curious passenger.

"So you still haven't told me what you do," she said.

"And I still won't," he joked.

"Seriously I want to get to know you," she said.

"What's to know?" he asked.

"You know, about you, who is this prince that came and carried me away?" she said.

"Baby girl, I'm far from a prince and this is far from a fairy tale. Seriously, I mean if you looking for a happily ever after you may want to rest your expectations," he explained.

"Wow that's a little harsh," she said.

"Naw sweetie that's not harsh, that real, I mean we just out having a good time I won't disrespect you and I mean no disrespect. I'm not looking for a girl or relationship, that's not me. Like I said at the club, I am just looking for a little company. Would you prefer I lie to you and tell you I want this, promise you that, have sex you and all that, then never call you again? That not me," he explained.

"I respect that," she said.

"You are definitely nothing like I've ever met Mr. Mark, I'll give you that," she continued.

"You only live once so let's just enjoy the time we have, make some good memories and go back to our lives with some great stories to tell," he said as he smiled, and he extended his hand to shake in agreement.

Just then, "Can't Let You Go," by Fabulous, came on the radio.

Veronica turned the radio up, "I like this song," she said as she nodded her head to the beat.

"But how you gonna touch my radio though?" he said.

"Oh word, you don't like that?" she asked as she smiled.

"Naw," he replied.

"Well look here, Mr. Secretive, while you with me this is ours and I'm a do what I damn well please. We only live once right? So I'm a do everything I want to this car and to you," she said as she touched his face softly, leaned over, and kissed him.

Back in Tamir's car, Trina and Tamir were relaxed talking about how she wound up coming on the trip.

"You and your missions, I swear, word you determined," Tamir said as he shook his head.

"Boy shut up, you know you wanted me to come," Trina said.

"Yeah whatever girlie," he replied.

"Oh so you wasn't gonna miss me?" she asked.

"I mean…" he stuttered as he began to explain.

"Shhh, oooh…this is my song," Trina said as she turned up the radio.

The speakers begin to blare, Floetry's, "Say Yes," playing as Trina's background singers, as she began to serenade Tamir. Another one of Trina's hidden talents and secrets was her voice, it was magnificent. Her voice was smooth as velvet and the emotions that she felt for Tamir fueled every word in the song. Tamir tried to focus on the road, but he could not help but to fall into her trance, into her spell, every note and word gave him a chill and made each hair on his body stood up. His mind was beginning to drift to a place where it was just them two alone. It was a dark setting, with Trina in sexy lingerie on the bed with a matching satin sheet.

The bed was her stage, all he heard was the words in her beautiful voice, "All you gotta do is say yes."

The lavender satin lingerie tightly wrapped the curves of her beautifully thick caramel toned body. Her beautifully sensual brown eyes locking with his, calling him, her pouty lips coated with her MAC lip-gloss begging to be kissed.

"WHOA!" he thought. Quickly he sounded the horn and pulled over to the shoulder. He needed air. This was the first time she got to him like that. In fact, he never thought of another woman so vividly before, other than his fiancé Isabella.

Everyone pulled over in suit as Tamir broke the flow.

"You good bro?" Buck asked as he ran up to Tamir's side.

"Yeah naw, I'm good just needed to stretch a little bit and get some air," Tamir replied.

"Alright we only got like two hours left to go, you need Trina to finish driving for you?" Buck asked.

"Naw I'm straight," Tamir responded.

"You straight bro?" Rodge asked.

"Yeah I'm good," Tamir replied.

"Come on let's go, finish this ride y'all," Tamir said as he jumped back in his car.

"You good babe?" Trina asked as Tamir got back in the car.

"Yeah I'm straight I had a cramp." Tamir explained.

As Tamir began to speed back up the highway, Jahiem's, "Put That Woman First," was on the radio.

He began to feel bad and became quiet. He started to sing to himself, thinking about his fiancé, wanting to quickly be in her arms. In that instant, that moment in time, the money, the material, and the wealth he was quickly accumulating did not matter. The only thing that mattered was the love between him and Isabella. He felt that he forgot to be her man in the wake of building this massive empire. Her embrace, smile, kiss, touch, and smell, were all more precious and priceless.

At the gas stations and rest area stops, they were filled with onlookers not used to seeing the cars that Tamir and Rodge were driving. Of course Rodge and Tamir paid it no attention, but the girls loved the attention. They felt like they were on an entertainment magazine show. People were taking pictures, pointing and staring. Buck and Akeem were on point making sure no one got close to them, getting out of line. Someone even asked Rodge if he was a rapper, he laughed and ignored him and kept walking. The second time someone asked him, it was a little kid.

He said, "Yes," and gave him a hundred-dollar bill.

Two hours later they reached their destination, two massive houses sitting on the Chesapeake Bay. Rodge, Akeem, Buck, Veronica, Shanell and Trina, stayed in the five-bedroom, six-bathroom house to the left. Tamir, Jeremy, Isabella, Rasheeda and their families had the identical families to the right. It was around 7:00 AM everyone was dead tired from the long ride.

"Alright y'all, I'm a go nod out for a few before my family gets here and we can go get Jeremy, I think at like 4:00 PM," Tamir said.

"Hold up there Capt, we still got something to do or did you forget?" Rodge said.

"Come on there, dream killer, what?" Tamir replied.

"We gotta go get these boats," Rodge said.

"Now though?" Tamir asked.

"Yup, I told them we be there at like 7:30 AM," Rodge explained.

Barely out of the cars, everyone piled into the Yukon and headed to Norfolk to the marina. About forty minutes later they were at the marina, everyone was asleep except for Akeem and Rodge.

"We here, come on y'all, let's go get our boats!" Rodge yelled.

As angrily waking up everyone looking like zombies crawled out of the large SUV and walked towards the dock. The women lugged their large purses hiding behind their sunglasses and hair wrapped under silk scarfs.

Rodge was extremely excited, "Look bro there's mines and there's yours," he explained to Tamir.

As he pointed, at the matching Azimut, 55-foot Motor Yachts that towered them and the other boats at the marina.

"Damn bro, when you said y'all was getting boats, I thought you meant y'all was getting little jawns or something. These is like houses on water," Buck said.

"Naw Bro, we balling out, this our vacation. We got jet skis on them and all," Rodge explained.

"So yeah, we got satellite TVs, full kitchens, four cabins each, so we good," Rodge continued.

"Wow, you keep surprising me Mr. Mark," Veronica said.

"Who the hell is Mark?" Shanell and Trina asked.

"Long story," Rodge said.

The yacht broker came out and greeted the team, and took them on the tour of the yachts, showed them that everything had been arranged at their requests. Everything was customized from the type of sheets on the beds and pillows to the food and drinks in the refrigerators.

"Everything to your liking sir?" the man asked.

"Yes we are happy. This will do," Rodge said as he paid the man from his Gucci bag.

"Here is a little something for taking care of us and making sure we are off the radar," Rodge said as he handed the man a five-thousand-dollar tip.

"Thank you, Sir. Of course, and as you asked, we programmed the navigation systems with the address to your homes in Cape Charles as well as some attractions and restaurants that we are sure you will enjoy. Enjoy your trip and if there is anything you need call me any time here's my card with my cell phone number in the event of emergencies. Just let me know when you are ready to return them. I have you chartered for the week but of course, longer charters can be arranged," the man explained.

With that they were off, Akeem headed back to the house in the Yukon. Buck and Shanell rode in the Yacht with Trina and Tamir. Rodge and Veronica took the other yacht. It was a beautiful morning as they cruised across the bay back to their houses. The sun was shining, the breeze was strong, and Rodge and Tamir were racing the million-dollar yachts across the bay. They were truly kids at heart, brothers enjoying their lives, but they were missing one, their brother Jeremy, but he would be there shortly. After about an hour and a half of playing in the bay with the huge Italian motor yachts with 1420 horsepower they were docking at the back of their rented vacation houses.

Tamir was loading his luggage and gifts into his rental house, amazed at how beautiful the house was.

"This is life, Aston Martin out front, yacht out back," he thought.

This was what the months away from his family were for; he could not wait for his son and fiancé to be with him to share in the fruits of his labor.

Just then his phone rung, "Hello, oh hey babe," he answered.

"We on are way babe, we almost there we like an hour away," Isabella said.

"We got a surprise for you," Isabella continued.

"Oh yeah? We got a surprise for you too. I can't wait until y'all get here. We'll pick up Jeremy at like 4:00 PM," Tamir explained.

"Ok Papi, how is the house? You like it?" Isabella asked.

"Yeah Mami, it's beautiful, it's a nice vacation spot perfect for our getaway, so we can get into us. Did y'all eat?" Tamir asked.

"Naw pa, I was so excited to see my babe I couldn't, but you know your son ate, he greedy like his dad," Isabella joked.

"Ok babe, well I'll cook when you get here," Tamir said.

"Ok babe, y'all hurry up and get here safely, I miss you, I need you, I love you," Tamir continued.

"I love you more my love," Isabella said.

Tamir high off the love of his woman, smiled from ear to ear, as he looked in the refrigerator to make sure he had everything needed to make his family breakfast. In the house next door, there was not much movement; everyone fell asleep where they landed. Shanell and Trina lay draped over the sofas, Buck laid adjacent to them on the reclining lounger in front of the TV as Sports center put him to sleep. Rodge and Veronica made it to the suite upstairs. Rodge lay sprawled across the bed as Veronica lay on his stomach. Rodge's hand on her head as he stroked her hair until they fell asleep. Akeem was out on the yacht, checking out the saloon lower deck. He fell asleep at the captain's chair still listening to his music.

After about forty-five minutes of prepping his room and the house for the arrival of his family, Tamir headed to his room to lay down, finally. He was going off on no sleep, tired and dragging. He was excited and wanted to stay up, but couldn't fight it anymore. The house integrated speakers blared the Jay-Z album, "The Blueprint 2: The Gift and The Curse," as he lay across the bed in his Polo Ralph Lauren boxer briefs with matching black A-shirt and polo socks. He was the only one to muscle up the energy to get somewhat ready to sleep. As he cuddled, the pillow in his arms, he smiled and thought of his fiancé. When he opened his eyes she would be there, he thought.

About two hours later, Rasheeda and Isabella pulled up to the houses in their matching blue and red Mercedes E430s with a Dodge Caravan and Jeep Grand Cherokee behind them. They looked up at the massive neighboring house with the super luxury cars out front, they were amazed and confused. Isabella rolled down the window and took off her Cartier sunglasses; Rasheeda did the same.

"Is this the right place girl?" Isabella asked.

"My navigation system said this is it," Rasheeda said.

"Mines too," Isabella said.

Amazed at the massive five thousand square foot houses, the families climbed out of the cars. No one moved too fast in fear of possibly being in the wrong place. Isabella's surprise was in the cars behind them. She brought the whole family, Tamir's mom, Jeremy's mom, her mom and dad, Rasheeda's mom and Tamir's brother and sister. The families have not seen Tamir or Jeremy in months. She thought this would be a major surprise. The biggest surprise was the one that she received, upon seeing the world of material wealth.

"Baby, what have you done?" she thought to herself.

She looked at Rasheeda as if she was thinking the same thing at the same time.

They said in perfect harmony, "Rodge!"

"I guess we don't need to stay in the hotel now, we got two hotels sitting right here," Tamir's mom joked.

"Wow, look at that car and look at that one, that's the car I have on my game," Tamir's little brother said.

"What has your son done?" Jeremy's mother whispered to Tamir's mom.

Isabella's proud father was taking his grandson out of the car seat. Everyone feared his reaction to this world of material from this obvious criminal empire. His wife, Isabella, Rasheeda, and the mothers just watched him.

"What?" he asked.

Everyone quickly turned their attention away. Rasheeda went and grabbed her daughter from the car, and everyone else unloaded the cars.

"Y'all already know how I feel, he knows how I feel. I am just going to enjoy my vacation with my precious grandbaby. Isn't that right my little man?" Juan said as he kissed and played with his grandson.

Just as the family was trying to understand and make sense of what was going on, Shanell and Trina stepped out on the top balcony of their house smoking their cigarettes. They were dressed in Burberry bikini tops and cut off shorts and polo flip flops, their hair was still wrapped in silk Gucci scarves and wearing Louis Vuitton sunglasses.

"Look girl that must be Tamir's family," Trina whispered to Shanell.

"Which one is Isabella?" Shanell asked.

"Must be the little Colombian one down there," Trina said.

They definitely caught the attention of Rasheeda and Isabella as they looked up and over at the neighboring house.

"Hi, is Tamir in there?" Isabella asked.

"Hey, no he in that house right there," Trina responded.

"He better not be in there with them whores," Rasheeda whispered.

"Stop it girl," Rasheeda's mom said as she walked up and pinched her daughter.

Awakened by the commotion, a shirtless Rodge walked out on the balcony with Trina and Shanell yelling, "We on vacation, where the weed at?"

"Roger where the what boy!" Tamir's mom yelled.

"Oh Mom, hey what you doing here, I was um saying we on vacation cut those weeds down. Cause um the grass should be perfect," he jokingly explained.

"Yeah ok don't make me cut you boy. Get down here and help us with these bags and give your moms our sugar," she replied.

As Rodge rushed back into the house he said, "Damn, y'all could have warned a nigga!"

He called Tamir, after three call attempts, Tamir answered the phone with a groggy voice.

"Hello?" he said.

"Nigga get ya dumb ass up and get outside. You got a whole family reunion out there," Rodge explained

"What?" Tamir asked.

Rodge quickly hung up.

Still half asleep, Tamir struggled down the stairs to open the double doors to the house. He completely forgot he had barely any clothes on. His entire extended family stood on his steps and stared at him in just his underwear, socks, and A-shirt.

"Boy put some damn clothes on!" a woman's voice yelled from the background.

"Mom!" he exclaimed.

"Surprise babe!" Isabella said.

Just then, Tamir was attacked by kisses and hugs by everyone, his mom, Jeremy's mom, Rasheeda, her mom, Isabella's mom, and even Isabella's dad gave him a hug and handshake. Finally, his fiancé Isabella gave him a long, passionate kiss and hug. Rodge came in and slapped him in the back of his head.

"You could have told me?" he said.

"Like I knew, did you not see the surprise on my face?" Tamir responded.

"It's all good bro, this is what we need, our family, we got plenty of space, let's live it up," Rodge said.

"What the hell are those?" Jeremy's mom yelled, interrupting the conversation as she looked out of the patio doors at the two yachts docked at the back of the houses.

"Um...surprise!" Rodge said.

"Rodge, you just don't know what to do with your foolish self. Never a dull moment with you, what are we gonna do with our son Gladys?" Jeremy's mom said.

"Come here boy," she said.

"Listen, I love you, you hear, I want y'all to be careful out here," she said as she hugged Rodge.

"I know Mom I am, but we won't worry about that now. This is our vacation, all of us, my whole family, so everyone enjoy. This is what's important, our time together," Rodge said to the room.

Tamir began to take the food out of the refrigerator, as his mom walked up to him, and gave him a big kiss.

"What are you doing son?" she asked.

"I'm about to cook Mom, why?" he asked

"No, you about to go put some damn clothes on like I told you to," she laughed.

"Oh shoot," he said as he laughed and rushed upstairs.

Isabella followed him upstairs with their son.

"Oh babe, I got something for y'all, well, I have many things for y'all but here's something special for you," Tamir said as he went into the walk- in closet and returned with shopping bags.

He reached in the bag from the jewelry store and gave Isabella, the diamond tennis bracelet and earrings. He also gave her the matching jewelry for his son.

"Babe this is beautiful, but little man can't wear this bracelet yet, he's going to try to eat it or something," she said and laughed.

"But I love it, you're so cute," she continued as she kissed Tamir.

Everyone got settled into their rooms. Everyone was happy. Rasheeda was anxious and ready to see her man. The time was approaching.

"It's time to go get my man y'all, let's go, he'll be here in an hour," she said.

"Alright we got him, let's go, plus we gotta go to the store. Akeem you feel like driving to, so Sheeda don't have to drive? I gotta take shorty to the store to get some clothes, and we need to get some stuff for the grill too," Rodge said.

"No doubt bro, it's not a problem, I'm with it," Akeem said.

"Babe lets ride too, Mom can y'all watch the baby?" Tamir asked.

"Yeah no problem we are fine," Tamir's mom said.

"Do y'all need anything?" Tamir asked.

" Y'all going to get the stuff for the grill, right?" Juan asked.

"Yeah pop," Tamir said.

"Ok, bring the ladies some sunscreen, I want to take them out on the boat and take your little brother out fishing so you and I can run and get some bait and poles later. Oh, grab some nice wine for the misses and me. Might as well make the most of this vacation, let me show how to really romance your lady," he joked.

"I got you pop," Tamir responded.

"We'll be back in few hours," Tamir said.

As they walked out to the cars, Shanell and Trina looked on from the balcony, "I told you this was going to be hard, he going to be with his wifey the whole time," Shanell said.

"I'm good Nell, Virginia Beach right down the way, its Memorial Day weekend, the bikers are down," Trina said.

The cars raced off down the highway. Tamir and Isabella laid back in the luxury of the two hundred eighty thousand, Aston Martin. The image that Tamir played in his head, the entire time, him and his lady, not a care in the world, just his dream girl, his dream car, he was acting his dream out with open eyes, on his way to meet his best friend.

"Baby this car is hot," Isabella said.

They rolled the windows down and opened the sunroof as they got on the Chesapeake Bay Bridge. Sean Paul's, "Get Busy," was blasting from the speakers. Isabella was winding and dancing in the seat, this was the first time she was able to relax in months, though she would not admit it. She was finally with her man. She rested assured he was not in danger. She was not worrying about school, and her baby was taken care of. So she was free, letting loose, her vacation had begun. Tamir looked at her and smiled.

In the car ahead, Veronica and Rodge were listening to, "Magic Stick," by Lil Kim and 50 Cent.

Veronica turned down the music down and said, "Mark, I know that's not your name."

"Ok and how do you know that?" Rodge asked.

"Cause everyone has called you Rodge," she explained.

"Beauty and brain," Rodge joked.

"So what else do I have to figure out?" Veronica asked.

"Nothing, I told you from jump what this was, so you thinking too hard ma," Rodge explained.

"I like to figure things out, that's just me," Veronica said.

Veronica liked challenges. The more Rodge resisted, the more puzzles she had to solve, the more she liked him. With her, she often got bored with the guys she dated, her beauty attracted all types, the ballers, the intellectuals, and professionals, but she never encountered anyone quite like Rodge. He did not chase her, he was direct and straightforward with her, and it was what it was.

Chapter : 12

After about an hour of driving, they made it to the Air Force base nearby Hampton, Virginia. Jeremy was already waiting outside with his bag in hand and his uniform on. There he stood, a perfect soldier, his six-foot athletic frame, in his marine blues with cap and all, awaiting the arrival of his friends and fiancé. As he stood out front of the terminal the cars pulled in front, barely coming to a stop as Rasheeda went flying out of the SUV into her man's arms. He dropped his bags and picked up his fiancé. They kissed and hugged passionately while Tamir, Isabella, Rodge, and Akeem, walked up to greet Jeremy. Akeem grabbed his bags. Veronica stood by the car and analyzed everything, still not knowing what to think of the situation, or the people she was recently introduced to.

"What up bro, I'm glad to see you made it back with no bullet holes," Rodge joked.

"Yeah I'm good," Jeremy replied as he smiled.

"My brother is finally home look at you, "Mr. Soldier," Tamir said as he shook Jeremy's hand and hugged him.

"Man look at you all cut up all crazy now; you look like something off a movie or something," Tamir joked.

"Aww man that what constant combat and MRE do to you, I tell you what though I can go for a real meal right about now," Jeremy replied.

"Look at y'all though; pull up in a Lambo and an Aston though?" Jeremy said walking towards the cars with Rasheeda by hand.

"Aww man just a few toys for our vacation, that's nothing, much more at the spot for us all to play, relax and chill," Rodge explained.

"We just gonna stop at few stores, get a few things and head right back over," Rodge continued.

They all decided to drive up to the premium outlets in Williamsburg, to do some shopping. Rodge and Veronica got a little closer as it seemed, he took her from store to store shopping and joking to have a great time. It was like old times again for Tamir, Isabella, Rasheeda, and Jeremy. They walked and talked about the things they experienced, over the time, they had been away from each other. The guys bought their ladies ice cream cones on this hot day. Jeremy, still in uniform was saluted almost everywhere they went. He was thanked for his service. They stopped at the wine and spirits store and bought some nice champagne, wine, and beer for the house. When they got back out to the parking lot, Rodge threw Jeremy the keys to the Lamborghini.

"Here you go soldier boy have some fun with your lady, I'm a have some fun with mine," he said as he and Veronica, jumped in the back of the Range Rover.

As they were at that light, Tamir and Isabella pulled up in their Aston Martin Vanquish, alongside Jeremy and Rasheeda in the Lamborghini.

"You ain't ready for this, you been away too long," Tamir joked as he revved up the powerful, 460 horsepower V-12 engine.

"Shit, I'm always ready bro," Jeremy replied as he revved the 580 horsepower V-12 engine in return.

The other drivers cheered and stared as the light turned green. The ladies struggled to put their seatbelts on as the cars quickly reached one hundred miles per hour, weaving in and out of traffic. Akeem struggled to catch them both while Rodge was oblivious to everything. He was busy maneuvering the curves on Veronica with his hands and lips. Finally, they reached Interstate 64.

"This is where I'm about to lose him babe, so hold on, and I hope you know how to get the house babe," Jeremy said as he laughed and grabbed Rasheeda's leg.

"Babe, Oh my god!" Rasheeda screamed.

As the car reached an excess of one hundred seventy miles per hour, Jeremy smiled and turned the radio up, listening to, Jay-Z's, "What They Gonna Do."

Right on his tail, Tamir was fighting to keep up, "My brother nice in the wheel," he said as he laughed.

Isabella was relaxed with her hand on her man's thigh, laid back in the seat with a subtle smile. Her brown eyes were hidden behind her Prada sunglasses. Listening to and fueled by, "U Don't Know (Remix)," by Jay-Z. Tamir hit the clutch shift to sixth gear and breezed past Jeremy at one hundred ninety miles per hour. Isabella still relaxed without too much motion raised her hand and waved. The racing stopped as they got to the Chesapeake tunnel and bridge. They all laughed and smiled at each other waiting to go through tolls, of course there was more trash talk. The sun began to set as they cruised over the bridges and made their way back to the house. As if they we in sync, they cruised over bridges. The song that scored this scene for both cars was, "'03 Bonnie and Clyde," by Jay-Z and Beyoncé. They said great minds think alike, it must be the case for the two couples because word for word the guys sung Jay-Z's part to the ladies, and the ladies sung Beyoncé's part to their men.

As they finally arrived from their exciting adventure, it was easy to notice which house was theirs, the smoke was billowing from the backyard and the music was already playing. The parents were out on the deck talking and drinking while, Juan was already working the grill. On perfect cue, the anthem to every bar-b-que blared through all the speakers in the house and on the patio, the drums, horns, and guitar intro and the words, "You make me happy," from, "Before I Let Go," by Maze featuring Frankie Beverly. Tamir and Jeremy's mothers got up and started dancing. Tamir and Jeremy just watched from the doorway for a moment. Then Jeremy walked up and started dancing with his mother.

She screamed, "My baby is home!"

She kissed and hugged him.

"Hey Mom," he said.

He was a spitting image of his father. They continued to dance, for that moment he took his mother away. It was as if she was dancing with her deceased husband, like they used to at the parties, to the same song years ago.

Rasheeda brought Jeremy his daughter, he held her, danced with her, played with her, fed her, and changed her all night. Rasheeda just watched him play daddy, in fact her and Isabella watched both of the daddies, as the mothers were on vacation. The fathers stood by each other's side all night joking and giving each other tips on everything, from how to burb the babies to changing them. All the mothers thought it was the cutest thing to see. Juan just laughed and shook his head. Rodge finally reappeared with

Veronica after the babies and Tamir's brother and sister were finally asleep. The party was still going.

"Where everybody at bro?" Tamir asked.

"Buck and all them went to party in Virginia Beach, it's supposed to be jumping down there tonight," Rodge explained.

"And you ain't go?" Jeremy asked.

"Naw, I'm chilling, my brother home, all my mothers are here, my family is here, and this is where I need to be tonight," Rodge replied.

"Naw, I wore him out," Veronica said.

Everyone just looked at her without reply or expression.

"See that's the problem y'all young punks don't know about romance," Juan said as he got up with his drink and the remote control.

He went over to the music control room and turned on what seemed to be a playlist that he programmed.

As he reappeared on the patio, he said, "I told you I would teach you something son. Come here baby," as he grabbed his wife's arm and put his drink down.

All the couples sat around on the patio holding each other watching as, "Can't Get Over You," came on the speakers, Juan held his wife close and dance with her to the rhythm of the song.

Rasheeda's mom said, "What are y'all sitting there for? He is trying to teach y'all young men something. Get out there and handle your business."

Following Juan's lead and Rasheeda's mother's orders, Tamir and Jeremy grabbed their women and danced to the beat closely and slowly.

Something electric was in the air because to everyone's surprise when the next song came on, "Kissing You," by Keith Washington, Rodge leaned in with Veronica's back on the patio to the bay, kissed her deeply, grabbed her hand, led her to the floor and danced with her as if he were serenading her with his movement. The couples stopped dancing in shock and looked at Rodge; they had never seen him like this before. Moreover, who was this girl?

"Babe do you see this?" Tamir asked Isabella.

"I know pa, what happened to him?" she replied.

"Yo, is he singing to her, what y'all do to my brother?" Jeremy asked.

They all laughed and continued dancing.

"Go head Papi, that's what I'm talking about, 'ganar la mujer'!" Juan said.

This was an amazing night and it was the first night of vacation, no stress or worries. Finally, they were all back together. As the music continued to play, the couples walked off to the boats. Juan and his wife sat by the dock, Rasheeda's mom, Jeremy's mom, and Tamir's mom, began to clean. Tamir, Isabella, Rasheeda, Jeremy, Rodge, and Veronica, took the yacht out into the bay to sit under the moonlight. They talked for once not about money not about fighting, stress or the ills of life, they just talked about little things like memories from high school and how the waves moved the boat. Everyone's minds were free and at ease, all except for Jeremy, his mind was in Afghanistan. He kept thinking about his next target and his hunger for the next target. What happened to him, something just clicked in his mind, he tasted something, he was ready to kill again. He thought every minute he idled they were planning to do something to him, his unit, his country, and his family.

"Jeremy, Jeremy, Jeremy!" Rodge called.

"Sir yes sir!" Jeremy responded.

"What the fuck?" Rodge said.

"You good?" Rodge asked.

"I'm just tired man, I been flying all night. I was just in a little daze that's all," Jeremy explained.

Rasheeda rubbed his back and said, "Ok babe lets go to bed."

"Yo what's so crazy is we could sleep out here, the jawn got four rooms on it," Tamir said.

"Man ain't nobody trying to sleep on no damn water when we are looking dead at two big ass houses," Rodge said.

"Man live a little. It's vacation, do something different, why did we rent two yachts if we ain't gonna use them?" Tamir asked.

"Yeah whatever, me and shorty got plans," Rodge said.

"Y'all some party poopers, I'm with you babe, lets drop them off and come back out," Isabella said.

"I hate to be a party pooper too, but I know my babe wanna sleep in a house since he been sleeping outside for months," Rasheeda said.

"Yeah maybe another night," Jeremy said.

Tamir took the boat back to the dock at the house and let the Rasheeda, Jeremy, Veronica, and Rodge off. He and Isabella went back out and spent the night in the bay. As they got back into the bay, they went into the master cabin and Tamir turned on the TV.

"Oh no, none of that, I've been waiting for this, turn that TV off and come turn me on," Isabella said as she took her clothes off.

"You can scream as loud as you want no one can hear you out here," she joked.

Tamir smiled and quickly obliged his fiancé's request. He stopped her from undressing and said, "No baby, I'm the captain of this ship, I'll handle that."

He slowly undressed her as he kissed every part of her body that he uncovered. It was like the first time all over again. He sat at the end of the bed. She stood in between his legs with her back to him; he kissed the back of her neck and shoulders and began to unfasten her bra. He paused.

"What's wrong babe?" she asked.

"Nothing my angel I just want to admire you for a moment," he replied.

"I love you," she said.

He reached around to unbutton her shorts and stopped again and said, "Wait a minute, we got all night, we on our own private yacht. This is like a dream so let make the dream complete."

He ran upstairs and grabbed a bottle of wine, two wine glasses, and turned on the radio. Isabella waited for him on the bed topless, smiling with her hair down, resting on her shoulders. The dimmed lights illuminated her beauty. She truly was angelic. She was not posing but she could have been a model waiting for her man.

Tamir, such the old soul in the young body, that was what his mom and others called him, knew what he was doing when he turned on the Isley Brothers. The perfect song for the moment, "Smooth Sailing Tonight," they were out on the open bay, the waves calmly rocking the boat, not too intruding, just enough to remind that they were guests, in the aquatic wonderland. He strolled into the room to the beat of the song with the glasses and wine. As Isabella held the glasses, he popped the cork and poured the nicely chilled wine.

"Now this is perfect, the perfect drink, the perfect song, my dream girl, on a dream boat," Tamir said as he smiled and kissed Isabella.

They drank their wine with intermissions of passionate kisses. Tamir sat his glass down and leaned in and kissed her forehead, then her nose, and then her lips, still wet from the sweet wine.

She bit his bottom lip gently, and whispered, "I missed you so much, my love. You are my king."

Tamir replied, "And you are my queen, I am building your kingdom for you and my prince."

He continued to kiss her body sensually as she lay back onto the satin sheets. He licked and kissed her uncovered breast, exciting and erecting her nipples. Her body shivered in excitement. He continued down to her navel as he could feel the heat from her unfastened shorts and the top of her panty line. He gently removed her shorts as she pointed her toes in the air to assist him in removing her shorts and pink lacey bikini cut panties. He kissed her pelvic area as her waist trembled and she gasped deeply, her body was calling for its lover. She wrapped her smooth hairless legs around his waist and pulled him close.

"Make love to me my king," she begged.

He obliged his beautiful queen as the midnight tide and currents began to move the boat, and the waves crashed against the side of the yacht. The music blared and everything was in perfect rhythm, the gentle swaying of the yacht, to the baseline of, "If Only for One Night," by Luther Vandross. The title of the song could not be more descriptive of the mood or the feeling of this moment for the young couple. This one night they were literally miles away from everything. They escaped inside of each other's love and passion. Their bodies sung to each other, talked to each other, healed each other from the pain of the distance they suffered over the previous months.

They made love over and over again and all over the yacht. They had fun. One could say they, "christened," the yacht. The made love in the shower, in the galley, they saloon, Tamir even convinced Isabella to make love under the stars, and the moonlight atop the top deck. The passion and love were definitely in the air. Rodge and Veronica were back at his rental house making love under the stars on the balcony off his bedroom. Rasheeda and Jeremy were trying to quietly make love in their room, trying not to wake the babies or the parents, for that matter in the other rooms.

"I see now why Bella wanted to sleep out on the boat babe," Rasheeda said.

It did not matter they were away from each other for so long and the passion could not be contained any longer. After they finished Jeremy held her tightly in his strong masculine arms and whispered, "I will protect you with my life, I will die for you, and I will kill for you," as he drifted off to sleep.

After watching the sunrise over the horizon from the top deck, Tamir taught Isabella how to drive the boat back to the dock, as she sat on his lap. She wore just his shirt and he was just in his shorts, as they pulled to the dock, and he dropped anchor. She ran down below and grabbed their clothes. As they were getting off the yacht, her father and Tamir's brother were walking towards the yacht.

"Come on son, let's go, gotta get out there and catch them fish," Juan said as he tugged on Tamir's shoulder.

"Go ahead babe, I'm gonna check on the baby and we'll have breakfast ready when you come back," Isabella said.

Jeremy was making his way down from the patio on his way out to the yacht also.

"Bro you up too?" Tamir asked.

"Of course, I'm always up this early," Jeremy explained.

"Where's Rodge?" Tamir asked.

Tamir's little brother pointed to the balcony on the neighboring house where Rodge's leg was hanging from the balcony. He and Veronica never made it back in the house. They were asleep, barely dressed, and knocked out to the world.

Juan, Jeremy, Tamir, and his brother headed back out into the bay on the yacht. They spent hours on the water. Juan taught them all how to fish. This was the first time any of them had this type of father, type of activity, or fished for that matter. Even Juan, though he would not admit it was pleased, feeling a bond with Tamir, as the son he never had.

Fishing was one of the things that his father taught him back in Colombia, but he did not get to pass on or share with his son, as he had a beautiful daughter. They had fun. They laughed and joked all morning. Once the boys got the hang of fishing, they had a competition to see who caught the biggest fish and the most fish. Tamir's little brother caught the biggest fish with help from Jeremy, and Juan of course caught the most.

Later that day after they got back, the vacation went on with more barbeques and good times with the family. Next door, Trina had met some friends at Virginia Beach. She brought home a man named Russell. He was from outside of Baltimore and dealt drugs in between Baltimore and Washington DC. His friend Rick accompanied him; they were bikers. Their bikes parked outside the house, a black Honda CBR 954 RR and a red Honda CBR 954 RR. They were amazed by Trina's beauty and the way she talked, but when they pulled up to the house and saw the cars, they were truly astonished.

Tamir walked over to the house to get Rodge when he noticed the bikes out front. When he walked in the house, he noticed Rick who was half-asleep with some girl he never seen before. No one else was downstairs. Tamir was a little suspicious but this was a Rodge affair and there was part of a team here, so anything was possible.

He called upstairs, "Yo, where y'all at?"

After a lot of movement upstairs, first Akeem came to the banister overlooking the foyer, followed by some girl in just a bra and panties. Then Buck and Shanell popped out, Shanell wearing Bucks shirt. Finally, Trina came out draped in a bed sheet.

"Sup, Mir?" she said with a sinister grin.

"Wow!" Tamir said shaking his head.

"What? What's the problem?" she asked.

"Not a problem in the world," he said as Russell walked out of Trina's room in his boxers.

Russell asked, "What's up sexy, you ready for some more or what? Oh...who that?"

"Nobody babe, I'm coming," she said as she pushed him back in the room.

"Yo, just tell Rodge come holla at me when he get up or whatever," Tamir said as he began to walk out.

"Mir, hold up let me talk to you," Trina said.

"We don't have anything to talk about, let me get back to my family, you get back to your one-night stand or one-night love or whatever you got poppin'. Y'all have fun!" he replied as he stormed out.

Trina rushed down the steps to chase him out the door. As he walked out, he was walking across the lawn back to his house and Isabella was walking out to the driveway. Trina came out the door wrapped just in her sheet calling Tamir's name. Isabella noticed and looked over as Tamir ignored her.

"Babe, what she want? Why is she naked and calling your name and chasing you?" Isabella said becoming angry.

"Baby it's nothing, come on let's go, I was just looking for Rodge, I don't know what's going on over there," Tamir said as he grabbed Isabella's hand and walked back in the house.

"That's alright. Go 'head with wifey, we'll talk later!" Trina yelled.

Isabella had been very understanding and trusting this entire time with this distance, but with changes in her man, this would alert even the most naïve of people. She stopped the questions vocally to Tamir, but her mind continued to process and analyze. Call it women's intuition, but something was not right, even the first time she saw her on that balcony, she had a funny feeling about her. Of course, she went right to Rasheeda and told her what was going on.

"See girl that's what I mean about those dudes and those whores in that life, they have no shame, they all the way down there, doing god knows what and you up here looking dumb. I ain't like the way that rusty looking bitch looked when I first saw her!" Rasheeda said angrily.

"But seriously, girl you think he would cheat on me?" Isabella asked.

"I want to say no, he's loyal to his family, he love you. Y'all been through so much, but temptation is a bitch and he been in that world, that life so long, Mama. You never know," Rasheeda explained.

"But don't stress girl what happens in the dark comes out in the light," she continued.

Isabella sat at the dining room table quietly thinking.

Later that evening Rodge appeared with Veronica, he immediately noticed the looks on Rasheeda and Isabella's faces and Jeremy and Tamir was across the room with their babies. There was definitely tension in the room.

"What did I miss, who did what?" he asked jokingly.

Isabella and Rasheeda quickly grabbed Rodge and took him into the foyer.

"What kinda smuts you got my baby down there fooling around with?" Isabella asked grabbing Rodge's arm.

"What the hell are you talking about sis?" Rodge asked confused.

"You got orgies popping off over there and naked women running after my man calling his name," Isabella said.

Rodge laughed.

"It ain't the hell funny boy!" Rasheeda said as she punched Rodge in his chest.

"Oh y'all serious? I think Akeem found some jawn last night," he explained.

"Ain't nobody talking about Akeem. We talking about that smut y'all running around with, Trina, Tina or whatever her name is," Rasheeda said.

"What?" Rodge said shocked.

"Trina is part of the team, she like one of the niggas, in fact she got a dude over there now, don't nobody fool with her," Rodge explained.

"You sure?" Isabella asked.

"Yes!" Rodge said.

"Then why the hell is she running out of your house naked, chasing my man, yelling his name talking about she'll talk to him later?" Isabella asked.

"Wait, today this happened, word?" Rodge asked.

"Yes, I saw it with my own eyes," Isabella explained.

"But, why ain't you ask him? Why you asking me? I'm sure it's nothing, he don't even talk to her or nothing, like when we all out, he be in the house talking to you or emailing Jeremy or sleeping. He don't come out that house, word on everything. I wouldn't even let anything go down," Rodge said.

"He said it wasn't nothing," Isabella said.

"It probably wasn't, they was probably joking with him or he saw strangers in the house. You know he don't play that bullshit, he be serious all the time especially with them. And it is a freak show over there, word, it smell like straight sex and Hennessey in there," Rodge said and laughed.

"But seriously I think the distance is getting to you sis, I'm a have your hubby back to you soon," he continued.

"Ok Rodge, I trust you with my baby down there, thank you," Isabella said and hugged him.

Rodge confused by what he just heard walked over to Tamir and took him out back.

"What the fuck is going on with you and Trina?" he asked.

"What are you talking about?" Tamir asked.

"Don't get cute with me bro; seriously your wife is cornering me about her chasing you outside naked and all that. What is going on?" Rodge asked.

"Naw it ain't anything you know she got a smart mouth she play too damn much. That's all, I don't know what they doing over there, I came to get you and everybody was in that thing naked, all crazy," Tamir said shaking his head and laughing.

"I know I said the same thing, I'm saying I peeped you and Trina getting closer, you know messing with her is definitely not a good look," Rodge explained.

"Plus, you got a bad wife that is loyal and loves you, why risk losing filet mignon for steak um, ya dig?" he continued.

"Yeah I know bro. We just cool sometimes when I can tolerate her," Tamir explained.

The two walked around the front of the house in time to see Russell, Rick and his girlfriend getting on their bikes. They began to rev their bikes up.

"Yeah that's nice but mines sound better," Tamir said as he jumped in his Aston Martin and revved up the engine.

"Damn, that's nice, y'all really are getting money," Russell said.

"Naw, who told you that?" Rodge asked.

The way Russell said getting money was code not just for being rich, but rich from selling drugs.

"Trina," Russell said.

Rodge and Tamir looked at Trina.

"I don't know why she would have said that. We don't get money. We work for a family real estate business," Tamir explained.

"Naw it's cool, we good. We looking for some work anyway, a nice connect on a large amount," Russell explained.

"Naw homie you got the wrong dudes, unless you looking for some construction or real estate. We don't get down like that," Rodge said.

"Alright, well if y'all know of anything Trina got my math," Russell explained as he and Rick raced off.

"So have you completely lost your mind, Trina? I mean why would you tell some random ass dude we getting money?" Rodge asked angrily.

"I was taking some initiative, the boy was telling me about his operation and I thought that might be another come up for us," Trina explained.

"See that's why you shouldn't just think or do stuff like that, holla at somebody let them know what you thinking, then you got people all in the crib, we all vulnerable," Tamir explained.

"What? Who the hell are you talking to ain't nobody talking to, you don't run shit Tamir!" Trina yelled at Tamir.

"That's another thing, what is this crazed tension you got with him, you chasing him out the house naked? What is that?" Rodge said.

"That was…" Trina began to explain as Rodge cut her off.

"You are tripping, this is why you shouldn't have come. And he does run shit, he runs the shit that pays you, so think about that the next time you part your lips to disrespect him, as you disrespect him, you disrespecting me!" Rodge said firmly.

"Ok, Tamir I'm sorry," she said as Tamir turned around and walked in the house.

"Buck and Akeem, y'all just gonna let some random dudes come all up in our shit, we don't know them, damn we really on vacation, cause y'all lunching right now," Rodge said as he walked into the house behind Tamir.

"He swear they the fuck royalty and they know everything," Trina said.

"They are right though, we slept all the way around. Too comfortable, they could've robbed us; they could've been cops or worse, DEA," Buck explained.

The next day after talking to Tamir, Rodge decided it was too risky to have Trina there. She was becoming a liability and too careless with her actions and emotions. He directed Buck to take her back to Danville. Of course, Shanell went with them. Tamir and Trina did not talk or even exchange looks as she loaded her things in the truck and headed off.

Chapter : 13

The rest of vacation was salvaged and very nice. Everyone had a good time yachting, barbequing, and partying. They went to the beach on the yachts and took out the jet skis that were on the yachts. They went to King's Dominion and Busch Gardens.

Meanwhile, back in Philadelphia, Rodge's dad was finally released from prison. His brother, Rodge's uncle, Charles, picked him up and drove him to the house he had waiting for him.

"A lot has changed since I been down," Derrick said.

"Yeah but you'll get used to it, more importantly, you're retired, sit back and enjoy life," Charles said.

"I know what that means; I'm not slow, sit on my ass and stay out of you and my ungrateful son's way. Y'all forget who started this," Derrick replied.

"You are still a hot head, fifteen years ain't do nothing for you. You recently paroled, it's a young man's game now. This thing ain't the same no more D, understand that. I don't even do much. I more so, focus on the business. Our investments, real estate, our legal life, let the young dudes have that run and gun it life," Charles explained.

"Yeah whatever, I'm a hustler. You still soft, that life ain't been you," Derrick said smugly,

"Yeah that's why you just sat down for fifteen years and I built a multimillion-dollar empire and made your son prince of the city, giving him any and everything though?" Charles replied.

"Yeah whatever, well for right now you my chauffeur, so boy less talk and more driving home James now," Derrick joked in an English accent.

"Yeah it's good to have you back home too bro," Charles said.

After about forty minutes of driving, Charles pulled up to a two-story single family house in the suburbs of Philadelphia, the house had a two car garage with a Mercedes s430 in the drive way.

"Here you are bro, your new home," Charles said.

"Ok this is nice," Derrick replied.

"I told you you'll have everything you want and need, all the toys in the house, furniture big screen TVs, food, money, and you even got a new Benz, now get your whiny ass out of my car," Charles joked.

"Ok, I want to go take a shower alone and relax in my own bed and watch some TV for a while, I'll call you later," Derrick said.

"Alright that cool here's your phone. My number is in there already. Call me if you need me. The navigation system in the car is programmed if you need to go anywhere," Charles explained.

As Charles began to pull off, he called Rodge, "Neph, I gotta tell you something."

"What up Unc?" Rodge replied.

"It's your dad," Charles said.

"What about Derrick?" Rodge said.

"He's home," Charles said.

"What you mean he's home?" Rodge asked.

"I just picked him up from prison and dropped him off," Charles said.

"Well, he better not call me and stay out of our way," Rodge said.

"Well I tried to tell him to relax, but if I know my brother, he is going to try to find his way in," Charles said.

"He don't know anything about our operation though, I don't want him to mess anything up. I had to clean it up when he got locked up last time," Charles continued.

"I know Unc," Rodge replied.

"Well go ahead and finish enjoying your vacation, I just wanted to give you a heads up," Charles said.

Rodge a little taken by the phone call that he received just stared out at the bay. His emotions began to race inside of him. He had always dismissed his father and said he would not care when he came out. That day had come, and honestly, he did not know how to feel. He didn't know him, but should he have?

"That's not my place or my job to build the relationship, I'm the son," he thought to himself.

Noticing Rodge, distracted and away from the family, Veronica walked over to him and rubbed his back.

"You good babe?" she asked.

"I'm good, short," he responded.

She turned his cheek with her hand and noticed a tear. She did not know Rodge too well, but from what she did know, this was not right, this was not Rodge. She was right; he had never showed this type of emotion. No one had ever seen a tear fall from the eye of Rodge, including Rodge himself.

"I'm good," he said as he walked away.

Veronica, thinking something had to be wrong, walked up to Tamir and Jeremy and told them to go check on their friend.

This got everyone's attention. Rodge never had problems, what could be wrong? Jeremy and Tamir handed their women their babies and ran off to Rodge's side.

"Bro what's wrong, you good?" Tamir asked.

"Why the fuck didn't he just stay in there? Why didn't he just die?" Rodge asked angrily.

"What, Rodge, who?" Jeremy asked.

"My punk ass pop, I mean your pop died defending your family like a real man. And Mir, your pop, just left, he ain't no man but he knew to stay the hell away if he couldn't man the fuck up!" Rodge explained.

This was a shock to Jeremy and Tamir to hear their best friend talk like this. In all the years, they have known each other they shared so much and been through so much together, yet Rodge had never opened up.

As the tears continued to flow, Rodge continued, "He's a fuck up! He can't do anything right, he got my mom stuck on that shit and took her away from me. I never had a mom or family because of that coward!"

"But he's back now, after fifteen years in the joint, maybe it's different, maybe he's different," Tamir offered.

"Naw, he ain't different, he's still a half ass hustler and fuck up. All he wants is this money and to fuck up my life. I should do us all a favor and go kill him myself as a man. He left me to live and learn on my own as a boy, and let him see the man that made me to take his life!" Rodge said.

Rodge walked down to the dock with tears racing down to his cheek. All of his emotions were a wreck, he felt years of pain, years of anger, sadness, yearning and rage.

"I'm not you, I'm not a coward, I am good dude, and I'm smart!" Rodge yelled out to the bay.

Tamir and Jeremy's mothers heard Rodge's yelling and ran to Jeremy and Tamir.

"What is going on?" Gladys asked.

"Rodge's father is home from jail," Jeremy explained.

"Oh my god, we talked about this day Gladys," Jeremy's mom said.

"What day Mom?" Tamir asked.

"The day that all Rodge's feeling would finally come out," Gladys explained.

"You see Rodge carries around pains and feeling that he won't allow anyone to see. He hides them behind his material possessions, wealth, and personality," Gladys explained.

"That's why if you notice, he never had a serious girlfriend or relationship, that would mean opening feelings. And the fact that he didn't have a mother, he may fear that if he depends on a woman, as even someone to talk to and confide in, she will be taken from him," Jeremy's mom explained.

"That makes sense Mom," Jeremy said.

"You guys are his family. He sees that you'll never leave. You fill a void in his life, big voids of his father and mother. He's really going to need you guys," Gladys explained.

"And Mir, you need to really watch him and don't let him do anything crazy, we don't want to lose our Rodge, he is our family, that's our son now and both of your brother, we have to make sure he knows he's loved and we're here," Jeremy's mom explained.

The two caring mothers walked out to Rodge on the dock and embraced him; he broke down and cried in their arms. Still in shock and at a loss, Jeremy and Tamir stared at each other, wondering what they were in for. The seemingly strongest member of their team was breaking down. Tamir was already thinking the team could not see this. They would be taken as a sign of weakness. Jeremy was thinking how killing Rodge's father was not such a bad idea. His thirst for killing was beginning to come back. Rasheeda, Isabella, and Veronica approaching them interrupted their thoughts. Veronica had entered into a world no love conquest of Rodge's had ever been. She was close to him at a very vulnerable state. She did not think about how she could benefit materially from this. She was opportunistic in that she thought this was a way to tame and conquer the untamable. A way to get her an amazing man, by being with him through a very hard time.

"OK y'all what can we do what's going on?" Rasheeda asked.

"We heard him yelling about his dad, did something happen?" Isabella asked.

"Yeah he's home, and this seemed to trigger something deep in Rodge," Tamir explained.

"What does that mean his dad is home?" Veronica asked.

"No disrespect, but you already know too much, and we don't know you like that," Tamir said.

"Baby, stop it, she was there when he started to open up, and we wouldn't know what's going on if she didn't say anything," Isabella said.

"Thank you," Veronica said.

"Oh don't feel privileged yet, Ms. Thing, you still aren't all the way in and we watching you. Understand, that is our brother and we love him, so if you got little money motives or whatever you think is going on, you can check that shit right here," Rasheeda turned and said to Veronica.

"Oh no, I understand, trust me. If I didn't care for real, I wouldn't have said anything and let him go through his motions," Veronica explained.

"I do care, it is something about him that I really like, and I will keep it one hundred right now and tell you my motive, to be with him. Not because he got money or any of this shit. He is amazing. He is smart, funny, and the shit he does physically, umm girl..." Veronica continued.

"Ok we get it," Jeremy said interrupting her.

"Well I think we gonna make the move back to Philly soon, he needs to be around the family," Tamir said.

"Yeah babe, I think that will be good, but keep him away from his pop," Isabella said.

"V, can you come to Philly? See that's the thing we don't know anything about you, or who you are," Rasheeda said.

"I just graduated from college with my degree in Psychology of all things, I was working for a doctor's office as an assistant for the summer and I'm looking to go back to school to get my masters. So that's me, I'm an only child, some friends, no boyfriend, no kids, and to answer your original question, yes, I can come to Philly," Veronica explained.

"Well I don't know how Rodge gonna take him now having a girlfriend, especially by our choice. But we can put you up in Philly when we go back," Tamir explained.

"Put her up where? Not in our house," Isabella said smugly.

"No babe, I know, I'm saying we can get her a spot in Philly if Rodge isn't accepting of his new girlfriend living with him. And y'all can show her around, help her find school or something," Tamir said.

"This is something, you just happened to be in the right place at the right time and you got a whole new life, man, house, and everything. Isn't this some shit?" Rasheeda said.

"Look I don't want to cause any problems. I want to help. I don't want anybody's money. I can stay right where I'm at, I'm good," Veronica said.

"No girl, you alright. I'm sorry you new to this whole thing. Rodge is our heart, you have to understand. We been through so much. So, of course, we protective of him," Isabella explained.

"Alright, look, let's just make sure he straight. He would and has done the same for all of us. He is the main concern right now," Jeremy interrupted.

"So look Veronica, you have to put that on him, I mean love affection, go hard. He has never been close with girls, like opening up and with all this, I do not know how he's gonna react, but we got your back. But understand if you slip up and you have any false motive or anything, crazy pop off, you dealing with a serious situation. You saw what happened back down the way, the team we run with," Tamir explained.

"I got it, I'm up for the challenge, but I'm telling you I'm just looking for a good man to build with, kind of like what y'all got, not to sound corny," Veronica explained.

That night the plan was formulated. The girls quickly jumped into action to understand and learn, who this woman was who they were allowing into the inner sanctum of Rodge. The three of them went to the supermarket to get food for Veronica to jump right into wife mode, preparing his dinner that night and breakfast in the morning. Isabella and Rasheeda figured the best way to get her into position was to teach her all of the things that Rodge sees Tamir and Jeremy get from them. While the girls went to work on dinner at Rodge's vacation house, the guys were out with Juan on the yacht talking, letting Rodge vent and express all of his feelings. Juan talked about being a man and explained that a parent does not define whom the child would be. They bonded and related. Rodge was distant at times but he still listened and tried to take in what his true family was trying to get him to understand.

Rodge was beginning to come back around and was his normal self. Veronica was working her charm, and it was working. Rodge was noticeably close to Veronica and allowing her to be affectionate with him. Tamir was working the business, making the plans and arrangements for he and Rodge to return to Philly immediately. He explained the plan to Akeem and called the team back in Danville. He laid out clear and concise directions to keep the operations running seamlessly without him being there.

The next day Rodge and Tamir went out on the Bay in one of the yachts to discuss the plan. Rodge was against it at first but he finally came around. The only thing left was to head back to Philly and restore life that they were somewhat detached from.

"Man you right though, why leave the city to that piece of shit, that my city," Rodge said referring to his dad.

"Exactly, so let's get back up the way and we'll make sure everything is cool. It's better to keep an eye on home up close than from a distance, especially if your dad is anything like you say," Tamir said.

"Yeah, I don't care what my uncle said, he definitely going to try us. I saw it in his eyes. I heard it in his voice, it's crazy, my father is my biggest enemy, I feel it," Rodge said.

While no child wants to feel that way, Rodge could not have been more right. At the same time Rodge and Tamir were having their conversation, back in a Philadelphia suburb, Derrick was having his with an old friend, Stucky. Charles and Rodge were not the only visitors. People were sending letters, and accepting collect calls from Derrick. In fact, Derrick was the reason Stucky never strayed too far away from Philly. He had been monitoring the entire operation from the time Derrick was sentenced to the day he was released.

"So you been telling me there's some new cat in our operation getting money?" Derrick asked.

"Yeah D, some hot-shot young dude, he definitely ain't fam, and he be bringing some white boy around who look like a cop or something. It just doesn't look right," Stucky said.

"See this that shit I been talking about, they careless with it out here. They have no idea what they doing, letting others in, getting our money, and bringing narcs around," Derrick said.

This was a crucial moment and piece of misinformation. Derrick had a special distaste, disregard, and paranoia for cops, especially undercover narcotics officers. This was why he just spent fifteen years in jail, for a shootout in South

Philadelphia involving the death of an undercover narcotics officer. He managed to escape life in jail and death by a maze of technicalities. When he fled the scene that day the cops approached and killed the wrong man. That man, unbeknownst to everyone, was Jeremy's father. Ironically, when he broke Derrick's arm that day. His lawyers argued that the officers did it. It was the same arm that they claimed was used to kill the undercover officer. The city being under fire from the killing of the wrong person did not want to fight publicly which Derrick's lawyers were planning to do. The result was fifteen years in trafficking and other related charges.

Clearly, no one knows the relation to each other or the responsibility Derrick had in the death of Jeremy's father. However, ironically, Stucky and Derrick believe Jeremy maybe some kind of narc based upon Derrick's paranoia.

"But it's something about the other young dude that's up there playing your son real close too though D," Stucky said.

Stucky was right, referring to the connection they made when they spent a few moments staring at each other behind the tinted windows and sunglasses. Tamir had a weird familiarity to him but Stucky had been away so long and was so consumed with the life that took him away. The missions, the money, the murders, the drugs, and the vices to ease the pains and guilt, the problem was it erased too much. It made him forget too much. If he had not been so deep in, he would have noticed why he was so familiar, he would have noticed the young man he had been stalking had his stance, his smile, his demeanor, his walk. He would have realized he was a young Stucky standing on that corner, not in a metaphoric way. Tamir was Stucky's son.

Stucky ran away to build for his family also, or so that's what he told himself. He connected with Derrick and his organization years ago for an opportunity when he lost his job. It was ok for a while, but he became caught up in the life quickly and it consumed him. The cars, money, women, and power took control of him. He would still check in every now and then until he could not. That was when Derrick got into the shootout in South Philly. The decision was made he would go clear out the rivals and disappear, making way for Charles and the organization to emerge stronger. With the police officer, being killed, there would surely be a war on dealers and a drought was surely coming. Therefore, they would capitalize by destroying all rivals at the same time and let the cops handle all loose ends. When they finished, they were virtually the only organization standing.

A connection existed that none of them understood, that lied beneath the fellowship of Jeremy, Rodge, and Tamir. Their fathers connected them all, that connection was about to come to the forefront, but they had no idea.

"I'm back now, we gonna figure all this out and I'm taking my operation back, fuck what Charles and Rodge talking about," Derrick said.

Back in Virginia, everyone was preparing to leave, saying their goodbyes to Jeremy as he was heading back to work, back to duty in Afghanistan, to fight for his family and his country. Jeremy felt reinvigorated holding his daughter and fiancé.

"You know what you have to do boo," Rasheeda said.

"I know babe, come back alive," Jeremy responded.

His mom as well as all the mothers hugged him and kissed him.

"We are proud of you," Christine, his mother said.

"It's been a pleasure, next time we get together we will go hunting," Juan said.

"Be good make us proud son," he continued as he saluted and shook Jeremy's hand.

Jeremy turned to Rodge and Tamir, "Y'all already know, handle your business, but be safe. We all we got, take care of my babies," he said.

"That's all it is, we'll be right back at it sooner than you know. Your family is our family, we take care of them as ours," Rodge replied.

"And look after our brother Rodge, he needs us too, although he's Mr. Tough guy," Jeremy said.

"Oh don't worry, I got him," Veronica interjected.

"Oh you do?" Rodge said as he grabbed her by the waist and kissed her playfully.

After a powerful vacation the family was back in Philly, the three couples were at Rodge's penthouse in Center City. The women looked around, and Veronica looked in part amazement. The other part was the work that had to be done. Rodge was the definition of a bachelor, and the penthouse was a true, "bachelor pad".

"Girl, you have your work cut out for you," Rasheeda said as she smiled at Veronica.

There was still evidence of the wild trysts that Rodge had before he went to Virginia, expensive bras on his bar near boxes of condoms.

"So what kind of work did y'all do in Virginia?" Isabella asked Tamir smugly,

"Bay, don't start," Tamir replied grabbing his fiancé by the waist and kissing her.

"Forget the business down there, I know the business I want to start up here with my baby," Tamir continued.

"We need to clean first, and then we need to shop. Babe, I need some bleach and lighter fluid," Veronica said.

"Lighter fluid though?" Rodge questioned.

"Yes, I'm burning all this stuff from your whores," she said as she picked up a thong with a remote control.

The whole room laughed except for Veronica.

"And the first bitch that show up here on some movie shit with nothing on but a coat getting cut. There's a new queen of the city," she continued.

"I knew I liked her, she gonna fit right in," Rasheeda said as she gave Veronica a high-five.

Over the next few weeks, Veronica spent time getting her new home in order and bonding with Rasheeda and Isabella. Shockingly Rodge became extremely close and comfortable with her. The group dates and activities definitely helped. Tamir, Isabella, Rasheeda, and their babies spent a lot of time at Rodge and Veronica's. Veronica spent her days without Rodge, hanging out with Rasheeda and Isabella shopping and playing with the babies. The women also helped her find a school to attend, to pursue her master's degree.

Rodge and Tamir continued to handle their business around the city still managing to avoid Derrick, Rodge's father. However, Stucky was keeping a close eye on them, per Derrick. He was planning something; he managed to keep it away from Charles. This was not good; historically, when Derrick had a bad idea, Charles could be the voice of reason, but without him knowing, he could not stop him. In this situation, Charles could have told him who Tamir was, who Jeremy was, and that it was not a good idea to have Stucky back in town.

Saturday before Father's Day, the women were out with the babies shopping for their men. They decided to surprise Tamir with a visit from his son and goddaughter. He was up on the block by one of their stores. This seemed harmless enough, but Tamir never wanted to expose his family to this dark side of his life. As he sat in front of the store with Rodge and Charles, he saw his fiancé's Mercedes pull up. Shaking his head, he greeted the women and babies as they exited the car.

"Yours is no better nephew, she's here to look," Charles pointed out to Rodge.

The women clearly stood out. They looked like they stepped out of a magazine or off a TV screen, with handbags that cost more than cars. Their clothes and handbags combined could have purchased any one of the houses on the street they were parked on.

"Bay what are you doing here?" Tamir asked as he kissed Isabella.

"What you don't want your whores to see what you got at home?" Rasheeda joked.

"You always got something to say, shut up sis," Tamir replied.

"We just wanted to stop by while we out shopping, plus Justin wanted to see da-da," Isabella explained.

"This is not a place for y'all, seriously though, y'all know that," Rodge explained as he signaled for Saul.

They were getting attention from across the street, in a black Chevy Lumina with tinted windows.

Stucky sat watching, *"Jackpot, so there's the family, that's where the money is going,"* he thought to himself.

Back across the street, "We appreciate the visit and the love but y'all gotta go, seriously, this isn't safe," Tamir said as he rushed the women back in the car.

"Saul, follow them out of here make sure they good," Rodge directed.

"Where y'all going from here?" Tamir asked.

"Where we damn well please, damn!" Rasheeda said angrily.

"Babe don't mind her you know how she get," Isabella said as she kissed Tamir.

"You need to mind me with y'all ungrateful assess, try to come and make sure y'all cool and get rushed off. We were going to make dinner for y'all, but now starve!" Rasheeda said.

"We love you too sis," Rodge said.

The women pulled off with Saul following them, watching for anything suspicious, but he didn't see Stucky following behind him. Once the women made it to their home, Saul left and headed back to the block. Stucky sat outside of the women's house and watched.

"Oh yeah definitely found the honeycomb hideout," he said as he picked up his phone and called Derrick to update him on his latest findings.

Back across town Tamir's phone rung, it was Jeremy calling in from Afghanistan.

"What up bro, I just wanted to make sure I called to say Happy Father's Day, well it's Father's Day here already," he explained.

Tamir put the phone on speaker.

"Thanks bro, this is perfect, Rodge here too and he just found out he's a father," Tamir joked.

"Yeah, ok keep on messing with me, you won't be able to be a father again, I'll shoot yours off," Rodge joked.

"Uncle Charles here too," Tamir said,

"What up Unc, Happy Father's Day," Jeremy said.

"Thanks, but you know I'm not a father you know that," Charles explained.

"Yeah but you been a father to us, Me, Tamir, and surely Rodge and we appreciate you," Jeremy explained.

"Well it's been a pleasure, y'all are good kids, and I appreciate y'all too," Charles said.

"Yo, I was thinking about this all day and this is another reason why I had to call, you know we were destined to be brothers. At the same time the cops killed my dad, by mistake, or so they said, Rodge your pop got locked up, and Tamir your pop ran off. Ain't that crazy, then my mom moved us out there. That's fate or destiny. The lord knew we needed each other to be strong and make it through. I saw that on vacation last month when we were there for each other. Anyway, I gotta go, love y'all, peace," Jeremy said as he rushed off the phone.

Charles sat for a moment analyzing what he just heard. He was the only one who knows everyone. He just did not know Jeremy's father's story. He knew he was killed by police but did not know the circumstances. He heard the line Jeremy just said, "by mistake."

He then thought about his brother's case and he made the connection.

Then he remembered the next thing he said about Tamir's father, *"At the same time he ran out,"* he knew Stucky ran out on his family.

In fact, he remembered having conversations with Stucky, talking him into leaving. Saying that this would be good for the family. Think of all the money his family would have and they would never have to worry about money again.

It just clicked in his mind, Stucky said, "I'll be leaving little Mir without a father in this cold world."

"Oh shit, y'all are connected," he blurted out.

"What Unc?" Rodge asked.

"Oh nothing just thinking about what Jeremy was saying. That was deep, everything happens for a reason," Charles said.

"What the fuck did you do Derrick?" Charles thought to himself.

But he was still puzzled, he knew for a fact Stucky had two million, what happened to it? Why didn't the family get any of it?

"So Mir, did your pop ever like try to come back, or even like drop money off or anything?" Charles asked.

"Naw, he just disappeared, left a cowardly note saying how he wasn't strong enough to support us and my mom can do better without him and left us," Tamir responded.

"Jeremy said his dad was killed by mistake, did his mom sue the city for that?" Charles asked.

"Of course she did that, how they got the house around the way. Why so many questions Unc?" Rodge responded.

"Naw I just find this interesting. I finally understand the background of my nephews. I'm sorry," Charles explained.

"Sorry for what Unc?" Tamir questioned with a puzzled look on his face.

"Just sorry that you all had to go through any of this," Charles explained.

"Everything happens for a reason. We've made peace with it all. We're in a good place. We have a good life, all of us. If none of this happened, we would not have the families we have now. I would not be sitting here now. I would not be the man I am today," Tamir said.

Charles accepted that and in the pit of his stomach he had a horrible set of secrets that he does not quite know how to process or what to do with. He knew two things, what happens in the dark would surely come to light and that his brother' would eventually do something that would bring this all to a head.

"I can't tell him, and I can't kill him," he thought of his brother.

Meanwhile, Tamir being as calculating as he was, thought about the questions he was asked, the reasons why, as well as everything Jeremy said. There was a deeper connection, but he couldn't quite figure it out. Rodge also analyzed this, causing an awkward silence at the table.

Rodge and Tamir decided to leave and head back to Tamir's house to meet with their women. Back at the house, they explained that they spoke with Jeremy.

"We know, we talked to him, he called us first," Rasheeda said.

Tamir and Isabella went to their room. He explained what happened as well as the questions Charles asked. Isabella was his best friend. She saw what he could not; therefore, he thought maybe she could make sense of what was not making sense to him.

"Baby that does seem a little strange but maybe it's all coincidental," she offered.

"But babe Charles seemed spooked, for the first time he seemed shaken up, I've never seen that man shaken up like that," he explained.

"So let's go back to the beginning, I'll go to the court and look at the case of Jeremy's dad where his mom sued the city and look at Rodge's dad's case on Monday," Isabella offered.

Isabella was in school to become a lawyer so this was her passion, she was learning her way around the court system.

"Ok babe thanks, just don't go to our moms with this, I don't want to upset anyone," Tamir said.

"Of course not boo," Isabella said.

Chapter : 14

Outside of the house, Stucky had all the Intel he needed for now. He knew this was a house of importance, with people of importance. He saw Rodge, Tamir, and their women, so he left. As he left, his ex-wife Gladys and his two other forgotten children arrived. If he did not remember Tamir, he surely would not remember his other two kids, but surely, he would have remembered his old love. Nonetheless, he just missed her as she pulled up right after him.

Father's Day was a day of love and fun in the house with men grilling out back after the women made a horrible attempt, or so the men said. Much like every other holiday, music and laughter filled the air. Rodge and Tamir bought Juan a, "Man kit," from them and Jeremy. It was equipped with fishing rods, tackle box and top of the line hunting rifles. It was something to show their appreciation for their adventure and time on the Memorial Day vacation.

"Thanks fellas, this is great, this rifle is for hunting. This one is for you Tamir, hurt my daughter," Juan joked and laughed.

"I thought we were passed that," Tamir asked.

"We are but I have to keep you on your toes," Juan said.

Monday morning, the women headed down to the court as Isabella said she would.

"Why we here Bella?" Rasheeda asked.

"I just want to do a little research, keep my skills sharp plus I just curious about some stuff," Isabella explained.

"Ok well lets hurry, it's toxic down here," Rasheeda said.

Isabella got all of the documents she needed for both cases and began to read them. The times of both incidents coincided with each other. Jeremy's father was killed where Rodge's father was arrested.

"Oh my god!" she said.

"What girl?" Rasheeda asked.

Isabella stormed out of the courthouse with Rasheeda tugging at her arm.

"Tell me, what it is?" Rasheeda pleaded.

Isabella fought within herself. Should she tell Rasheeda? How will she process this? How does she tell Tamir? All of their worlds would be rocked with this information.

"I have to get to the car, when we get to the car, I'll tell you," Isabella explained.

Upon arriving to the car, Isabella sat down started the car turned the air on and turned off the radio.

"Ok girl, I have no idea how to say this," Isabella said.

"Just say it, please," Rasheeda pleaded worried, beginning to shake.

"Rodge's dad is responsible for Jeremy's dad being killed," Isabella explained.

"What!" Rasheeda exclaimed.

"That makes no damn sense Bella," Rasheeda said.

"Girl, I know look at these court papers, they show Rodge's dad was arrested exactly where Jeremy's dad was killed, that's why his dad was killed by mistake," Isabella explained.

"Oh my god," Rasheeda said as she read over the court papers.

The women drove home confused not knowing how to handle the situation. Every relationship would be affected by this revelation.

When they pulled up at their house, they look at each other and said, "We have to tell them."

"If he is out, he is dangerous, they can control him and have an idea of what they are dealing with. Also, if I tell Jeremy he can finally have some closure. Maybe my baby can have some peace in his heart," Rasheeda said.

That night Rodge, Tamir, and Veronica were at the house preparing dinner.

"Listen, we need to talk, have a serious conversation," Isabella said.

"We been through a lot together and we are family. It's better if we are honest so we can continue to get through anything that comes our way together," Rasheeda said.

"Y'all scaring me," Rodge said.

Tamir, noticeably silent, had a feeling in his stomach that he knew what was about to be said.

"We discovered today a few things, some of why y'all are connected and how Jeremy's dad died," Isabella said.

"What?" Rodge said surprised.

His surprised tone was masking what he already began to figure out in his heart.

"Yes, Rodge your father is responsible for Jeremy's dad being killed," Rasheeda said.

Rodge stunned, sat on the sofa with Veronica by his side rubbing his back.

"So what do we do with this information?" Tamir asked.

"I don't think we should tell Jeremy," Rodge said.

"Why? He needs to know," Rasheeda said.

"He's across the world with no family, powerless, he would go crazy. Think about it, you're not there to console him Sheeda," Rodge explained.

"Yeah Sheeda, this is heavy," Tamir said.

"Damn, too late, I already told him," Rasheeda said.

"What!" they exclaimed.

"When?" Tamir asked.

"Well I mailed it in a letter today," Rasheeda explained.

"So he's going to get a letter expecting something nice and instead it's going to be, surprise we found out why your father was killed and who was responsible and he's here amongst us in the same city as your fiancé and daughter!" Tamir said angrily.

"We need to go kill him!" Rodge said.

"Babe that's your dad," Veronica said.

"No he's not, he is nothing to me. This is my family and he hurt my family," Rodge replied.

"What about Christine, Jeremy's mom?" Isabella said.

"I have no idea, I don't want to upset her. She is in a great place. We shouldn't disturb that and make her relive that pain," Tamir said.

"She's going to hate me," Rodge said.

"She couldn't possibly," Rasheeda said.

"That man took her husband away, the father of her son," Rodge replied.

"Ok I think we need to call her over and our moms too and just tell them. We have not had any secrets and this shouldn't be one. We need to be a tight unit. Plus, with him out what other damage can he do? What if she finds out another way? We need to tell her, if for nothing else, to protect her," Isabella offered.

Everyone called his or her mother's; Rodge called Charles and arranged for everyone to meet at the house. Within the hour, all of the parents were there. With the news, understandably Christine was shaken up and in tears. She relived those events.

"That man is a monster, he harassed us weeks before. I remember it like it was yesterday. I can never forget him, he told Phillip he owned me, our house, the street and everything on it," Christine explained.

"I'm so sorry for my brother's actions," Charles offered in condolences.

"Thank you," Christine replied.

"I can assure you my nephew and I are nothing like my brother," Charles continued.

"We see that, you raised a great young man and we love Rodge as one of our own," Gladys said.

"So what do we do?" Rasheeda asked.

"Are we in danger?" Isabella asked.

"Rodge let me talk to you for a minute," Christine said as she excused herself and Rodge.

"You know I love you like a son, and I would never hold you accountable for your father's actions," Christine said.

"Thanks Mom," Rodge said.

"Don't thank me yet, I do have a request," Christine interrupted.

"I have a request, I know what you do, and I have lived my life in a positive light not judging others but now I ask for something," Christine explained.

"What you need Mom, anything ,name it," Rodge said.

"I want him gone, that man has to go, get rid of him Rodge please, he needs to pay, suffer for what he did to us, he is a monster!" Christine pleaded with tears in her eyes.

"Say no more Mom, I got you," Rodge said as he hugged her.

Rodge now had the authorization he needed from someone he had held in high regard, as a mother, to eliminate someone who had caused nothing but pain and problems. Vindication was on the way. He now just had to figure out a way to do this without bringing suspicion to himself, from his uncle, best friend, or team. However, he wanted to be the one to make the kill, he wanted to kill his father. He wanted to end the life of the man who helped give him his.

A few weeks later in Afghanistan, what Tamir and Rodge feared was coming to fruition. Jeremy received the letter that would change his life forever. The smile that he always had quickly disappeared as he read the letter written by his fiancé. He could sense his uneasiness in the ink and the pen strokes in each line. As he read each line he visualized, and his heart became colder and darker occupied with rage and anger just as his fellow marines had occupied territories in the foreign lands they were in. As he finished the letter, he knew he had to get home, not to see his family but to eliminate his new target. Rodge's dad, Derrick, this was the new mission, nothing mattered but the mission. Tyler approached.

"Jeremy are you ok?" he asked.

"I'm ok, we have a new mission stateside are you in?" Jeremy replied.

"What the hell are you talking about?" Tyler asked.

Jeremy took his time and calmly explained everything to Tyler. Tyler being his partner and loving the thrill of the hunt and kill was in. They crafted their plan and started working on their leave and how to become AWOL. Jeremy explained that he had resources at home and Tyler's family would be well taken care of if anything happened. Luckily, they were able to get leave to return home for a few days, so off to Philadelphia they were headed.

Back home, Rasheeda felt it was odd that she had not heard from Jeremy in weeks. She had no idea that her man was making his way back to Philadelphia. She also had no clue what type of monster she unleashed. She released a trained killer whose only focus was to kill his target and not stop until the mission was complete.

Everything was tense in the family. Tamir was paranoid of Derrick. Charles still had one more secret and he wondered if that was going to come out. He attempted to determine if his brother had contact with Stucky since his release, but Derrick kept acting as if he did not remember whom Stucky was. Rodge was creating his own mission of how to kill his father.

Stucky continued his reconnaissance on the entire family and organization, waiting for word from Derrick to make his move. It was going to be one of two things, either he was taking hostages or killing someone important, either way it was going to end bad. As time went on Derricks impatience grew, as did his anger and rage, which meant more than likely, he was going to order someone to die.

There was a storm brewing in Philadelphia, and this was the proverbial calm before it. Jeremy and Tyler had arrived; they set up shop in an abandoned house in West Philadelphia armed with sniper rifles and side arms. They had no idea what their target looked like. Jeremy had a vague memory from when he was a little boy so the first part of their mission was recon. They have to find the target to confirm what he looks like and where he was without anyone knowing he was in town. In order to do this they planned to watch Charles closely and see when he encounters Derrick.

This was especially hard for Jeremy to be so close to his family but not to contact them. This was a mission however; it was a conflicting battle inside of him constantly. His mind had shifted to marine mode, although he was about a week or so away from being AWOL. He was a marine on a mission. If Jeremy was on a mission in Afghanistan, he would have no contact, and this was the same for him now. Tyler was fine he was happy to help his friend and to do something he loves. They spent the day settling in their temporary quarters, as they were trained to do, securing their perimeter and getting the clothes and supplies they needed for their mission. They accessed the roof of the building and watched the store that Charles was at most of the day. They waited to see if Derrick would show up. They saw Tamir and Rodge come and go, like ghost cloaked in the shadows, they watched every move.

Back at his home across the city, Rasheeda worried more that something was wrong and that she caused it. Surely, by now Jeremy had received the letter, but no call or return letter. This was very strange; she could feel in her heart that something was wrong.

"Sheeda, don't worry, he's just processing this in his own way. This was a lot for him to take in," Isabella offered.

"Yeah girl, no news is good news," Veronica said.

Back across town, Tamir was watching Rodge as if he was waiting for him to snap, he knew his brother. He knew all of this wasn't just going to pass. Rodge did everything as normal as possible but he was calculating everything, trying to figure out the best way to accomplish his directive commissioned by Christine one of the mother figures in his life.

"You know, I think I want to see the bastard," he said.

"What, Who?" Tamir asked.

"I want to see my dad," Rodge said.

"You sure?" Charles asked.

"Yeah," Rodge responded.

Charles called Derrick and told him to come down to the store. At first, Derrick made a few excuses, but he then agreed to come down. About two hours later, Derrick pulled up in his Mercedes S430. Tyler and Jeremy watched from half a block away from the roof. Jeremy knew it was him he felt it in the pit of his stomach. He had instant flashes of the fight between him and his father, and when his father was killed.

"That's him!" Jeremy exclaimed to Tyler.

"That's the sonoma bitch?" Tyler asked.

"Yup, now we need a car to follow him," Jeremy said.

"That's no problem J, let's just say in another life I was a Repo agent for fun," Tyler explained.

Tyler went down and secured a vehicle.

Meanwhile up the street, the tension was thick outside the store between Tamir, Rodge, and Derrick.

"Son, what's up? Who the fuck is this?" Derrick asked.

"Don't even worry about it, he's with me, he's family," Rodge replied.

"Yeah OK, speaking of family, missed you on Father's Day, nothing for your old Dad?" Derrick asked.

Derrick had a way of getting under Rodge's skin.

"Hmm...ok so anyway, why am I here?" Derrick asked.

"What are you planning? You out now what can we expect?" Rodge asked.

"I'm minding my business, like you should. You forget I'm the parent? You don't question me!" Derrick replied.

"This is beginning to get out of hand," Charles said.

"Beginning to get out of hand? It's already out of hand. My son speaks to me with no respect, in front of strangers. Nonetheless, y'all got all kinds of people all up and through here getting our money!" Derrick argued.

While this argument ensued, Tyler and Jeremy were getting tightly in position to follow Derrick when he drives away.

"Once again Derrick you have no idea what you are talking about, you make no sense, and this young man is the reason you have as much as you do now, he is one of us," Charles explained.

"Shit, here you go, you know what, I'm the reason any of y'all have anything thing. Son, you forget who owns what? This is my block, my operation, and my city. I don't need this, I'm out, next time you call me out make sure you got at least a hundred grand for me, make it worth my time!" Derrick said as he walked back to his car.

"Wow! See, he's a piece of shit, and he'll never change. We gotta do something about this Unc," Rodge said.

In the car, Derrick called Stucky.

"Ok it's on, you ready?" he asked.

He set the plan in motion. He told Stuck to take whomever he could out of the house, babies preferably to take for ransom.

"It's time to take my operation back. Shoot anyone in your way!" Derrick said.

In Derrick's vanity and arrogance, he did not notice someone with more hate in his heart than he does, was trailing him. Jeremy and Tyler followed

Derrick right to his house. They watched for a minute to make sure this was his house, and they went and dumped the car. They scouted the area for another location to set up camp until the perfect time to strike, and eliminate their target. They found an unoccupied home on the next street with a good view of Derrick's home. They were able to snipe him, if that's how they were going to assassinate him.

Back at the store, Charles, Tamir, and Rodge were still talking about their encounter with Derrick.

"And what the hell does he mean next time you call me out make sure you got at least a hundred grand?" Tamir asked.

"It means we are at war with my brother," Charles said.

"So what's his play Unc?" Rodge asked.

At the house, Rasheeda received a call from Jeremy's CO; he advised her that he must check in before he returns from leave because he had new orders. This was a surprise to Rasheeda, as she did not know he was on leave.

"Girls, guess what? So I get a call from Jeremy's CO, apparently, he's on leave," Rasheeda explained.

"What? So where is he?" Isabella asked.

"Call Rodge and Tamir," Veronica said.

"Babe, Jeremy is off on leave somewhere, have you talked to him?" Isabella asked Tamir on the phone.

"What? No, I told Sheeda that wasn't a good Idea," Tamir said.

"I'll call you back," Tamir said as he hung up.

"Yo, Sheeda just found out Jeremy is on leave, he must've got that letter and dipped," Tamir told Rodge.

"I told her, so he's probably here somewhere and if he ain't telling none of us, that's not good," Rodge said.

Rodge was right. He was off the radar. He disappeared in plain sight, and he didn't want to be found. That only meant he was on a ledge he didn't want to be talked down from.

"We have to find him before he finds your dad," Tamir said.

"Or do we really want to?" Charles said.

"Think about it, he's a trained assassin. He is trained to kill in silence. He is in marine mode right now. This could be a good thing," Charles continued.

"I don't know about that Unc, he could get into a lot of trouble," Tamir said.

"Yeah, it's either that or Derrick is taking us out, understand, my brother is looking at us as enemies, especially you for some particular reason," Charles said.

"This man doesn't care about anything but money and power, no family no blood, nothing, just money and power, and we in the way," Charles explained.

Back at the house, the mothers just arrived, Jeremy's mom, Tamir's mom, Rasheeda's mom, and Isabella's mom.

"So let me understand this, my son is here somewhere but no one has talked to him?" Christine said.

"Yes Mom," Rasheeda explained.

"Oh dear god, what is our baby up too?" Gladys said.

"Why did I tell him in that letter?" Rasheeda asked.

"It's ok you were doing what you thought was right," Veronica said.

A little later that evening, Christine and Gladys sat out back and talked, while Rasheeda's mom and Isabella's mom cooked dinner. Isabella and Rasheeda were playing with the babies when there was a knock at the door.

"See everyone's worried, this is probably Jeremy coming to surprise you," Veronica said.

She could not have been more wrong. As she went to open the door, Stucky kicked the door open causing her to hit her head. She was knocked out instantly. Rasheeda and Isabella got up holding their babies.

"No, no sit down!" he said.

Two of Stucky's goons came rushing behind him as he waived his guns.

"They'll take them off your hands, and put all of your money and jewelry in this bag," he said as he threw a bag on the floor.

Isabella and Rasheeda fought. Stucky fired a shot.

"Bitch don't make me," he said as he pointed the gun in their direction.

With all the commotion, the other **mother**s came rushing in.

"Ah welcome to the party, slow down, put those hands up and put your money and jewelry in the bag too," Stucky said.

Gladys came walking in last and she noticed him, "Terrance?" she yelled.

"Naw bitch you got me fucked up!" he replied as he fired a shot in her direction.

But the truth is, she really didn't have it mistaken. She was looking at her ex-husband as he fired a shot in her direction. The man who walked out on her years ago and abandoned his family, was back.

"The next one won't miss! Call me another name and watch my aim improve. Just give us the babies, the money and jewelry and we will be on our way!" he demanded.

Gladys stood frozen and shaken, her mind and emotions could not process what was happening. So many questions began to flow through her mind.

"Why do you want the babies?" Rasheeda asked.

"Cause I love kids, ask your man. Now, I don't have to say what's going to happen if you decide to follow us or call the cops. These cute little babies won't make it to see another day," he replied.

Stucky and his goons fled with the babies. The girls called Rodge and Tamir. They were there within twenty minutes with Charles.

"This is my brother, I told you he is not playing. He doesn't care. He is about money and power," Charles said.

"But how did he know where our families lived?" Tamir asked.

"He had someone following them and watching," Charles said.

"But it was…it was…" Gladys tried to say.

"What **Mom**?" Tamir asked.

"It was your **father**," Gladys said.

"My **father**?" Tamir asked.

"Wait a minute, now this is entirely fucked up. So my **dad** is the reason Jeremy's **dad** was killed and he sent Tamir's **father** to kidnap the babies and rob them?" Rodge asked.

"So it would appear that, yes, he is using Stucky, and Stucky is Tamir's **father**," Charles explained.

"They all need to die! Fuck them all! I want my son now!" Tamir exclaimed.

"The one hundred grand, that's what he was talking about," Rodge said.

Just then, Juan arrived with his hunting shotguns in hand.

"Let's go, where is my grandson? He comes in and robs my wife and daughter and takes my grandson, where is he?" he asked.

"Where the fuck is Jeremy? He needs to know his daughter has been kidnapped," Rodge said.

Chapter : 15

Back at Derrick's house, Tyler is on duty watching as a minivan pulls into the driveway. Two crying babies are taken into the house. He wakes up Jeremy. Jeremy noticed that he had his daughter and his godson. Jeremy lost control; it took everything for Tyler to calm him down. The rage in Jeremy's heart was just multiplied by ten or even a hundred times. It was like his enemy was intentionally playing with him, as if he knew he was being stalked and hunted. The truth is, Derrick had no idea, he had an adversary so close, and a few hundred yards away from taking his life.

Charles called Derrick, "Ok bro, where are the babies?" he asked.

"What are you talking about? But hey, I have a question for you? You got something for me? Maybe a hundred grand? You know what? Maybe a cool million actually?" Derrick replied.

Tamir grabbed the phone, "Look you piece of shit if you don't give me my child I will..."

"You will what? Boy sit down, respect is what you will learn right now. You see, I have the power and control. You have nothing. I have what matters most to you. I can destroy it with the pull of a trigger, so again you will give me my respect and return my power, and I will think about returning whatever it is you think I have," Derrick said as he hung up.

The house was a wreck, the women were hysterically crying. The men were cursing with anger and rage. When suddenly Rasheeda's phone rang, her mother answered, the southern accented voice gave her an address and hung up. The voice was Tyler; he took the number from Jeremy's phone, seeing how the situation escalated.

Charles looked at the address and said it was Derrick's, "But, who was the voice and how did he get the address?" Charles questioned.

The families quickly organized and set off to Derrick's address. They had a team of their security, or muscle in a black Yukon ahead of them. They rode in a black Yukon to not attract any attention. They parked down the street from Derrick's house. Rodge, Tamir, Charles, Juan, and the members of the security team ahead of them loaded up their weapons and just waited and watched, as they knew that they could not storm the house. The babies were in there and they knew between Stucky and Derrick, the babies would be used as human collateral.

In the distance Tyler and Jeremy were watching.

"Your friends are here," Tyler said.

"You did that?" Jeremy asked.

"Yup, figure we could use reinforcements," Tyler explained.

"Ok, well let's get my baby back," Jeremy said.

As Jeremy began to lock on his target, Tyler signaled to Tamir and his crew with his flashlight. After a few moments, he finally got their attention.

"What's that?" Tamir asked.

"Appears to be someone signaling us from that roof," Rodge said.

"I bet that's who called Sheeda. I bet it has something to do with Jeremy," Tamir said.

"Unc call him now," Rodge said.

As Charles called Derrick, he began to talk with him. Rodge, Tamir, and the others moved closer to the house. Jeremy had his sights locked on Derrick and Tyler was locked on one of the goons.

"So, lets knock on the door. They don't expect us to be here. Just clear the house out and trust someone is supporting us from the roof," Rodge said.

"OK, let's get our babies back," Tamir said.

Tamir cocked his .45, steadied his hand, counted to three, and knocked on the door. Stucky answered the door, shocked.

"Hello Dad," Tamir said.

In that quick instant, his life with his father or what he knew of him quickly flashed before his eyes. He saw the pain that this man caused his mother, his brother, his sister, and himself. What was even scarier to him, he saw an older grungier version of him. Tamir cringed at the thought as a tear came to his eye.

He angrily whispered, "I'm not and will never be you."

At the same time, Stucky or Terrance, Tamir's father, shocked that the man he's been stalking was his blood, his son. He froze. Maybe, if he spent a little more time with him as a child, the events would not have reached this extreme climax. Maybe, if he would have reached out to check on his son and family from time to time, he would have at least recognized that the person he was stalking, was his first-born child, the fruit of his loins. Maybe, if he would have taken the time to play catch, he would have caught the.... With that thought, Tamir shot him in the head. There was no reasoning left, no time to think or react, this man was the monster who attempted to destroy his childhood, and had the audacity to steal his child.

That shot signaled Jeremy to fire. He shot Derrick in the heart with his .50 caliber rifle. Tyler quickly shot his target in the head as he reached for his gun. Rodge ran in and shot the other goon twice, once in the head and the other in the chest. The entire ordeal was surgical and took no more than ten seconds. They quickly grabbed the babies and fled the scene. They drove around the block to scoop up Jeremy and Tyler, who jumped in, as they pulled off.

Everyone was quiet in both trucks except for Tyler who was on the phone with his wife. The shock had set in. Their connections were magnified by the bigger shock that Tamir just killed his father, and Jeremy killed Rodge's father.

"It had to be done," Charles rationalized in a somber tone.

Rasheeda held her daughter in one arm and held Jeremy in the other. He smelled like battle, sweat and the outdoors. He had not showered in days. Rasheeda didn't care because her man was safe. He had been through an ordeal and needed her love.

Tamir held his son close and tight, he promised never to leave him. Not because he was just kidnapped, but because of what just happened with his father. He wanted to be sure that he killed that part of him. He was not his father.

"You are not a killer babe, you are a protector, you are our protector, and we love you and we are proud of you," Isabella whispered to him as she held him.

The Yukons moved quickly back into the city, like a diplomatic convoy. Charles, now on the phone with his connections to clean up the mess at Derrick's house. Appreciative of Tyler and his help, they offered to charter a plane to send him to see his family, before he is due back in the Middle East.

"I think it is a good idea, that we call get away for a few days to escape this madness," Charles said.

Back at the house, they went to pack and get their parents. Charles arranged for a plane to await them at Philadelphia Executive Airport. He chartered a Bombardier Challenger 604 private jet, so they all could comfortably fly to South Carolina. With everyone still on edge, Charles did not feel it would be a good idea to have to deal with airport traffic or a commercial airline.

On the plane, the mood was very tense, everyone was trying to grasp or make sense of what was going on. Gladys silently looked out the window, as if the answers to her questions were in the clouds. She felt closer to God at thirty thousand feet in the air.

"Where was he all of this time, was he really still around? He had to be to know about the babies. Would he really have killed me? Did he really hate me? Did he blame me? I'm the one he abandoned," she thought as she stared off into the clouds.

She then focused her attention on her son.

"He just killed his father, he killed my husband," she thought as she struggled with a myriad of emotions and feelings.

A few seats up, Rodge was quiet for once, struggling with a similar internal battle.

"He had to go, it was him or us, but I should have been the one to do it," he thought as he watched Jeremy.

Within a few hours, they were in South Carolina awaiting the arrival of Tyler's wife and baby on the tarmac. As she arrived on the plane, there was a noticeable difference in her mood and the others. She was a sweet country girl with seemingly apple red hair.

"Hey y'all," Candace said as she greeted the group with a big southern smile.

Tyler grabbed and kissed his wife and baby as he introduced her proudly to his newfound friends and family.

Just as quickly as they touched down, they were taking off again for a quick flight across the state to the coast. They were headed to Myrtle Beach. Candace seemed to get the women to open up and talk about the babies, motherhood, and tips she found helpful. The plane was divided. The men sat towards the back talking about what happened and the women were in the front talking about the babies, and how the engines and cruising through the air seemed to keep them calm.

Finally, they arrived at their hotel. It seemed as if they rented the entire top floor of the hotel overlooking the Atlantic Ocean. Charles put everyone in suites. He felt that was the least he could do, shouldering the responsibility of his brother's actions. After a quick dinner in the hotel's restaurant, everyone headed to bed, except for Christine and Charles. They stayed and talked at the bar. He really felt bad and apologized profusely. Maybe, it was the drinks and the music, or the extreme stress they been under over the past forty-eight hours, but they bonded. They managed to smile and laugh, and begun to dance. They found solace and comfort in each other's arms. The two retired to Charles's suite.

The next day, Charles, Jeremy, Tyler, Rodge, Juan and Tamir went out shopping, discussing the events that recently occurred.

"That chapter is finally closed. It's time to start the next. Let's do it. Let's man up," Tamir said.

"What are you talking about?" Jeremy asked.

"I know what he's talking about, don't you Charles?" Juan asked.

"Yeah he's talking about finally going to marry the women," Charles replied.

"Yeah let's do it. Everyone is here. The resort performs weddings. Life is too short," Jeremy agreed.

Juan called his wife Abigail. He told her to secretly start planning the wedding with the hotel, and get the women together, while the men went out to buy suits and rings.

Rodge fought with everything he ever knew or thought, up was down, right was left, he decided to propose to the closest woman to him, and who went through all of this with him, Veronica. If she said yes, he would be getting married also.

Quietly in the jewelry store, Rodge said, "Give me the biggest bridal set you have."

"What?" all the men said.

"Y'all heard me, it comes a time when you have to man up, plus this is umm...for tax purposes," Rodge tried to explain with a smirk on his face.

Truthfully, Rodge was madly in love. Veronica had made it into his heart; she said she was going to get her man and she did. He bought her a five-carat, D class, pear cut, diamond engagement ring with a three-carat invisible set wedding band to match in eighteen-carat gold.

All the men rented tuxedos that matched, as Charles and Juan tried to coordinate with the mothers over the phone. The women wore three different colors that matched beautifully, even Veronica who didn't know she was a bride. Isabella wore soft green, Veronica in a soft pink, and Rasheeda in white. Everything was planned. The beach was being set up beautifully, and there was a priest available. Now, they had to find a way to surprise the women.

That night everyone had dinner. The men had an idea.

"So, did you see they were setting up a wedding on the beach?" Jeremy asked.

"Yeah it looks beautiful," Isabella said.

"Yeah let's crash it," Tamir Joked.

"Seriously, let's crash it," Rodge said.

"So, we will find you all dresses and we will rent tuxedos, and just show up," Tamir said.

Rodge got up and approached Veronica and got down on one knee.

"You can't crash it without one of these," as he opened up the box revealing the beautiful engagement ring.

Veronica started to shake. The women, including the mothers gasped. They were astonished. Rodge of all people was proposing.

"So will you marry me? I mean I was wild and out of control, but you showed me a different way of life that I love. You let me know it was cool to be me and that someone can love me for being me and I don't want to lose that," he said.

"Yes! Yes! Yes!" Veronica said as she cried and hugged Rodge.

The plan was set. The men gave the women their dresses that were actually bride's dresses, picked out by their mothers. As they got dressed, the joke was on them and they were actually about to get married. They assumed it was just a, "Man," error.

"I swear, men, so you gonna buy me a wedding gown though?" Rasheeda questioned.

"But babe, that's all they had in your size," Jeremy replied.

"Really? Really Jeremy? Where the hell did you go, David's bridal? You so cute though, come here," she said as she kissed her man.

The other women were giving similar responses. Tamir said this would be part of the joke to show up as the bride. In Tyler's room, he told Candace the whole thing, she thought it was cute and funny and swore herself to secrecy.

About an hour later, as the couples arrived, they noticed there was no one there but their families. Even Veronica's mom and dad were there.

"What in the world? Mom, Dad?" she said as she began to tear up.

"I love you babe, surprise," Rodge said as he smiled at his bride-to-be.

Her father ran up to grab her arm to walk her down the aisle as the men took their place at the altar. Of course, Juan walked his daughter down the aisle and Charles walked Rasheeda down the aisle. As the men waited with giant smiles in their tuxedos, one by one, each man said vows to his new wife.

Jeremy began, "I was a boy trying to find my way when I met you. You helped make me a man. You have defined for me the meaning of unconditional love, accountability and responsibility. You have given me a gift that I can never repay, our beautiful daughter. I promise to spend my life and beyond, working to repay you and protecting our love, our child, our bond, and our union. With this ring, I promise that I will always return to you with a smile no matter how far I travel, how many battles or wars I fight for, you are my strength, my courage, my honor, my pride, my all, my life, my air, and my love."

Then Tamir took center stage and said, "You helped me to edit and complete a challenging chapter in my life. You showed me that not everything is going to be perfect, but our love is. Your faith in me keeps me alive every day, motivated and inspired. You also made me a man, a father, a best friend, a lover, and now a husband. With this ring, I will cherish my duties with pride, and I promise to continue to stand by your side each day, and write each word and each chapter with you, my best friend, and my partner for life. You are the best thing that has ever happened to me and God blessed me the day I met you. May God continue to bless us through good and bad times. I love you forever and always."

Finally, Rodge said, "Yeah what they said." Everyone laughed.

"But seriously, I never thought I would meet someone who would make me want to commit for more than one night, let alone the rest of my life, but you have done it. You have seen things in me and shown me things about myself, and with this ring I want to continue to find things in not just me, but both of us together. The Bonnie to my Clyde, you are my family, and I love you," he continued.

The pastor pronounced them all men and wives and told them to kiss their brides.

As everyone cheered, Rodge, Tamir, and Charles's phones began to ring and beep excessively. It appeared to be a problem.

They received text messages that read, "Get to Danville immediately!" As they were trying to make sense of the situation, two military officers and two military police approached Tyler and Jeremy, and told them they were to report immediately.

The End

Fallen Soldiers

The Rise